Also by Paulette B. Maggiolo

The Myth of the Earth in Colette's Novels
(Dissertation thesis published by the University of Middlebury,
Vermont)

The Guilty Teacher

Le Professeur Coupable (in France)

The Terrorist Trap

No Such Word

Paulette B. Maggiolo

iUniverse, Inc.
New York   Bloomington

No Such Word

iUniverse books may be ordered through booksellers or by contacting:

iUniverse
1663 Liberty Drive
Bloomington, IN 47403
www.iuniverse.com
1-800-Authors (1-800-288-4677)

ISBN: 978-1-4401-2599-7 (pbk)
ISBN: 978-1-4401-2600-0 (ebk)

Printed in the United States of America

iUniverse rev. date: 3/2/2009

Cover artwork: The painting of the historic Clinton Inn in Tenafly, New
Jersey, that is incorporated in the cover artwork is used with permission
by artist and Tenafly borough historian Alice Rigney. The painting
depicts the historic 1908 building as it appeared in the late 1940s and as
remembered by the author when she and her husband lived in Tenafly.

To my sister, my children, my grandchildren.

Vir spit qui pauca loquitor

(He's a wise man who says but little)

ACKNOWLEDGEMENTS

My sincere thanks to:

Annette
Denise (daughter)
Denise (sister)
Kathy
Kathleen
Kimberly
Sallie

And especially to Elizabeth H. Cottrell, owner of Riverwood Technologies—she has been both indefatigable assistant and wise advisor, whose perseverance and belief in me kept me on track....

PROLOGUE

▼

AT TIMES, THE FOURTH POKER PLAYER was so pleased with himself he couldn't stop the whirlwind of thoughts in his head. The other three credulous players had fallen in line with his elaborate plans so easily and completely, he couldn't believe his good luck.

That night, he was unable to fall asleep. He turned. He twisted. He stretched his long legs. He got up. He stood near the bed, annoyed with himself, wondering why he'd made the silly move. He was reluctant to admit he was worried about his spouse's reaction to the upcoming event, while at the same time he was exhilarated. He had done it; it was too late to change his mind. It was all downhill from now on.

He looked down at the naked woman sleeping on her stomach, a pale blue satin sheet covering her buttocks and legs, her tiny feet comically peeking out. He was tempted to tickle her foot to wake her up. It would be the greatest sin of self-indulgence. He must not go near her this evening. Whereas, for all those years she had never turned him down, and she always helped him lick his wounds, tonight the agitated state that kept him awake was of his own doing. She would certainly remember later on that he had the nerve to want her to nurture him while he had betrayed her all those past months.

She sure could sleep. When she decided it was time, she shut off all the switches. She said she simply dropped into the arms of Morpheus.

Recollecting the time he woke her up at four o'clock in the morning, a wave of delight suffused him. It was shortly after they married. He was aware she resented his weekly poker games. She didn't voice her irritation. It wouldn't have been right. The fewer words of acrimony expressed between husband and wife the better. They were the generation who'd been brought up to cope silently. Coping then meant you were able to joke about adversity–or at least you'd be quiet about it. Or as in this case, you shifted gears.

"Don't ever wake me up again after an all night poker game with your loud, drinking buddies," his sweet bride told him later that morning after his caressing hands had awakened her at dawn, "Unless you've won a lot of money that you'll give me to buy whatever I want for myself." Amused, he had agreed.

The following week they again made tender love in the wee hours of the morning. Soon after, though, he was attacked by his irate mate pummeling his chest. "You, skunk, you left your winnings on the night table. A one dollar bill! Do you think that's how cheap I come?" He grabbed her hands and held her, laughing. They made long, leisurely Saturday morning love again, both of them giggling. He chuckled at the memory.

In her sleep the woman heard him and admonished, "Go to sleep. Stop gloating over whatever you've been doing lately. Since you won't tell me what you're up to, I don't want to know, and I don't care. For God's sake, stop fidgeting and go to sleep."

"Yes, sir, general," he answered forcefully.

Once again he stretched between the smooth bed linens that smelled of lavender. He lay on his side, his back to his companion. He changed his mind. He wouldn't fall asleep away from her, he knew it. He turned around and moved closer to her–very close. He threw his long arm over her still slender hips softened by the inexorable passing of the years. Instantly, he went sound asleep.

"Par for the course," she mumbled with a grudge, "He's snoring and I'm wide awake."

And as usual, he'd ambushed her. If she tried to move away, now he'd close his powerful hand gently over her breast to trap her. He would pull her closer to him yet. He'd hold her tighter and tighter. She smiled. She didn't mind. As a matter of fact, she loved it. She admitted blissfully to herself, *I love the potent male smell of this big man. He's my whole life now that our three children are on their own. I love that he owns me. I am his woman. We can never be separated. After almost forty years, our love is stronger than ever. I'm truly blessed.*

She sighed with contentment.

The inner voice kept on, *Nevertheless, I'd like to know what he's been cooking up these last few weeks: he behaves like a kid thrilled with his own pranks and no fear of punishment. Will he ever tell me? Probably not.*

If she only knew…

CHAPTER I

▼

IT WAS ONLY SIX O'CLOCK IN the morning and already Christine was reading. Not just reading, she was studying. She didn't mind. She loved the challenge of an intellectual contest; school work and good grades were her whole life. Besides, she truly enjoyed the French philosophers on the list given to hopeful students who were preparing for the exam: from René Descartes, to Malebranche, to Rousseau, to a newcomer named Jean-Paul Sartre.

In her favorite canvas chair by the open kitchen door, her feet on the small wall surrounding the terrace, she was the only one up at that hour; she was plunged into Montaigne's *Essays*.

Mother Superior had forbidden her students from reading Montaigne, because she claimed to be horrified that he had written about accepting with gratitude what nature had done for him. In fact he was well-pleased with himself. Christine was not sure she understood what Montaigne meant. She shrugged. She had never yet met anyone satisfied with the way they looked. They were too short. Too tall. Too fat. Too skinny. Not enough this. Not enough that. If they had blue eyes, they'd like brown eyes. If a girl was a brunette, she wanted to be a blond. *Like me. I was the smallest in every class. I wanted to be tall and statuesque, well-proportioned where it matters. Not almost flat-chested.* Fleetingly it occurred to her with what part of his anatomy Montaigne might have been quite satisfied. She felt the hot blush creep on her cheeks. The man was a philosopher. He must have meant reason; judgment; mental powers; a sound mind.

Two years before, Mother Superior had told Madeleine Tourneau her younger daughter was ready to go to college. Although she was too young at that time for the University in Caen, Christine had obtained good grades in the preparatory institution and now she was getting ready for the Entrance Examination in the Department of Education in September.

Claudette, her best friend, attended the public school system. She made sure Christine read everything she herself did–to cover the notorious blanks in the restricted literary education of a girl in a private Catholic school.

Thank God, for reasons better understood by Madeleine Tourneau than by her own daughters, their mother never ever asked to see what book they were reading. A strange lapse, if you were to ask the girls.

Outwardly, Christine was deep into sixteenth century philosophy. Not so deep however, that she couldn't hear the rumbling of the guns somewhere between the Coast and Avreville. Aware the war was getting closer, she was, all the while, not missing a word of the conversation in the kitchen between her sister and her mother. They had all gotten up earlier than usual because it was better to be up than to toss in bed worrying about current events.

It should have been a desultory conversation about the weather–a beautiful, warm spring day. The sun already shone through the redolent Normandy dampness. Birds chirped on the branches of the green apple trees over Christine's head. The three women intended to go to the market square to buy fresh asparagus and a basket of juicy red cherries. They talked about the new spring outfits they wanted. Christine longed for a white linen suit–a straight skirt, a single breasted Chanel jacket. She saw it in the window of La Mode Parisienne. She would accessorize it with various scarves and jewelry pieces. She probably wasn't going to get the suit this month. Philippe Tourneau told his wife and daughters to forget about spring shopping for clothes.

The so-called "phony war" was getting nearer. When it started in Norway and Denmark last April, it was supposed to end within weeks. Instead, in no time, it spread over the Netherlands and through half of France. While at first the French believed the soldiers would soon return to their families, they knew better now. Since the Belgians had refused to expand the Maginot Line, why would Hitler hesitate to invade this very convenient neutral country?

Philippe Tourneau lamented, "How could the French government have been so stupidly blind? If only the leaders of the country had paid attention to the predictions of Charles de Gaulle years before. The young officer had foreseen that after nineteen eighteen, future wars would be highly mobile. Paul Renaud had also warned the French generals with alarming reports of German mechanization."

Hindsight did not help. It only convinced the French civilians they were doomed. Hitler's armies could not be stopped.

In this, a would-be-peaceful day in May, death was unreeling inexorably in the direction of Avreville. Brainwashed by fifth-column panic-mongers, some stubborn people still tried to believe the pitiful French army would rally at the Loire River.

In the kitchen, Nicole was whimpering, "Mom, you don't mean it."

"I wish I could make your father see it's foolish."

Angrily, the girl interrupted her mother, "I can't believe Dad wants us to leave our house this morning."

Christine closed her book. It was the first time she had heard of her father's astonishing decision.

Madeleine explained, "Your father believes you girls will be safer at his friend's farm out in the middle of nowhere in the hamlet of Orgenay."

Nicole moaned, "Mom, the Germans are soon going to be all over France. I want to stay here at home. I don't want to go!"

My sentiment exactly, thought Christine, who was frantic with worry and fear. She was certain she was going mad. She'd stop in the middle of a room wondering why she was standing there, what she was looking for, how she'd gotten there. What was it like in places where the Germans had already arrived? What will Avreville be like with the enemy all over town?

"Christine, come here," cried her sister. "Come here and tell Dad you don't want to go. It's *your* fault if we're leaving."

Perplexed, Christine entered the kitchen. For a few silent minutes she watched her mother pack some bread and cheese with pieces of cold chicken in white table napkins. Nicole turned around. She sighed. She pushed back the bolt on the bottom half of the kitchen door. She grabbed her sister's hand and pulled her outside on the patio. Christine spoke first, "Sis, why do you think it's my fault we're going to Orgenay? I didn't..."

Nicole cut her off, "But it's because of your nerves, your trembling, your crying. Mother gets mad at you, but Dad babies you, as usual"

From inside his office where he was rustling papers, their father shouted, "Go to your rooms and start packing, girls."

Nicole shrugged. The obedient daughter mumbled, "Let's see what we can take with us; come, Christine."

"That's right, dear," said Philippe with a twinge of reproach, but somewhat mollified, "Help your sister, please, Nicole."

"Yes, Father," was the meek answer.

The girls went upstairs in silence. They no sooner entered the cozy, small lounge between their respective bedrooms when Nicole exploded, "Sure, it's because of you Dad wants us to go to Orgenay."

"But why? I didn't..."

Once more her sister snapped at her, "You don't talk, all right, but we all know you're scared stiff. No doubt you believe what Sister Jane told you."

"Sister Jane?"

"What did she say to her class?"

"Nothing."

"Oh, but she did. Your favorite teacher is an idiot, Christine. I know her, remember."

"How could you?" the younger girl sobbed.

"How could I what? Say such a blasphemous thing?" Nicole laughed. She shouldn't be so cross at her own sister; the kid couldn't help being petrified of the arrival of the German soldiers in Avreville. Aloud she went on, "I still believe Sister Jane scared you girls out of your wits. She told you we're going to be raped, didn't she?"

"Don't say that word. It's a bad word."

"Rape. Rape. Little old Jane-Marie-Joséphine-Anne didn't use the word 'rape'. She couldn't let the word pass her lips. What did she say about the German soldiers?"

When she saw the silent tears running down her sister's cheeks, Nicole was instantly chastened. At times she pushed too hard to try and make Christine aware of the world around her. How could a girl almost sixteen years old still be so naive? With all the books she read! Nicole assumed she skipped over the descriptive parts of the male body and she simply ignored the literary innuendoes. Did she really not comprehend what they were referring to? Certainly she had seen Michelangelo's naked David staring her in the face when she meandered in a museum, or his brother when she opened her biology manual.

Last week, in a street in Avreville, both sisters witnessed a male dog astride a female–the six-legged, two-headed animal, the show for on-lookers with lascivious grins on their faces. Christine blushed from ear to ear. She walked faster to get away. From what? The disgusting sex act or the taunts from the boys across the street? *Granted the remarks were in very poor taste,* thought Nicole, amused. In such a case, mother would advise her daughters to simply "consider the source" and dismiss the whole thing. Later in the day, Nicole felt sorry for her sister who obviously had been crying her heart out in the secluded gazebo in the garden, where she took refuge with one of her poetry books.

CHAPTER 2

▼

NICOLE RETRIEVED HER SUITCASE FROM UNDER her own bed, "Go get yours, Sis, we have to pack. We can only take so much. Or rather so little," she amended.

She added, "There won't be very much space for luggage with the four of us in the car, and whatever Mom and Dad want to take away from this house in the city to place it safely at the Audineaus' farm."

The information brought some relief to Christine's troubled mind. Surely her father wouldn't make the perilous trip to the Loire River today if it were only because of her distress. She stammered, "Dad didn't ask me, but I'd prefer to stay here. With the walls around the property and the tall iron fence on the street side we should be safe. I don't want to go to Orgenay."

The girls had seen crowds of displaced people passing on the main highway three or four days prior. Christine knew she'd feel vulnerable in the family car. Uprooted. Homeless. Cold and trembling like a newborn baby left naked for a moment. The outside world had become a threat, a menacing evil which could not be stopped.

By eleven o'clock, the Tourneau family took to the road like millions of other frightened refugees. One member of the family was missing–the son. The eldest of the three children, Jacques, was hiding in some unknown-to-them southern village, ready to escape to England to continue the fight in De Gaulle's army.

Inside the comfortable Peugeot, Christine forced herself to relax. She saw the stubborn people who'd decided not to budge watching the caravan from their doorsteps. Some were peeking behind their shutters left ajar. They seemed puzzled by the endless crowds fleeing ahead of the enemy. Didn't they realize there was no place to go, no safe asylum anywhere?

Opposite decisions to remain or to leave were equally loathed. Both groups were queasy. If you stayed, would it be said you were ready to bow in front of the conqueror? Would you soon become a spineless bunch of defeated morons? If you cluttered the highways with miles and miles of nomadic families going nowhere in particular, were you helping the '*Boches*' win the war? It was said that one divides in order to conquer.

The Tourneau automobile was brought precariously low by the heavy suitcases Philippe tied inside the luggage rack on the roof. The girls saw him add three huge boxes to the already loaded trunk. They didn't know what he was taking to Orgenay, but they presumed it was affidavits and other legal documents from his office. Madeleine had kept their fireproof, metal safe box, depositing it by her feet inside the car. The staggering amount of records was no surprise. Philippe owned one business, his wife another. Philippe's line of tourist charter busses traveled most countries in Europe. Madeleine owned a chain of retail food stores which were scattered all over Normandy.

Inside the Peugeot, numerous packages of various shapes and sizes rested on the floor and on the seat between the girls. Christine was surprised when Nicole reached over to her with one hand. With the other hand, she was pointing to a brown parcel. The long, cylindrical carton contained their mother's precious possession–her new corset. One evening at dinner time, Madeleine complained about the extravagant cost of the indispensable item. "Yet," she explained, "I had to buy it before they're no longer available. What's a woman to do without a well-made corset?" She was taking the darn thing on the road to freedom– complete with stays, laces, whalebones and all. Her daughters exchanged an amused look. Much later that night, Nicole had declared, "I'll never wear one of those stiff hairshirts. If I'm fat one day, I'll bounce freely–and happily." Christine had reminded her how shocked Grandma Tourneau was when the girls were bra-less under their thin cotton dresses on a very hot summer afternoon. "Wantons," Blanche Tourneau had declared.

In the late afternoon, Philippe pulled off the road to park under an old oak tree in the commons of a tiny village. He lit a Gauloise and sat back. He filled the car with acrid smoke.

Madeleine, who'd been snoring faintly, woke up. The three women got out to stretch their legs. They walked to a nearby field of spring potatoes. A good place for their picnic. They spread a thick, white linen tablecloth on the grass.

Nicole joked, "If we had time, we could make a fire and really have our potatoes in their 'country dress,' as we say."

"As in the olden days," her father rejoined promptly. The man was helping with the preparation of the frugal meal. He realized Nicole was trying to keep things on an even keel. *We must make an effort to stay coherent,* he thought. *We must remain calm. We must stick together. Help one another.*

It had been a mistake to leave their home. His mistake. But there was no turning back. Going in the opposite direction against this human tidal-wave would be suicidal. They would keep on going south. They would cross the Loire River. They would make it to his friends' house. The manor was three hundred years old. A fortress. Not overly large. Not noticeable from anywhere. Well hidden inside ten acres of forest.

The right place for Nicole and Christine. The girls would enjoy the company of Catherine and Suzie, who were the same age as his daughters. When the Germans had settled all over the territory, Philippe would bring them back to Avreville.

Meanwhile, it would give him and Madeleine a chance to see what life would be like from now on. Philippe's business was at a standstill. People had no money to travel –- assuming they could get gas and new tires, which could not reasonably be expected. Besides why would one go away from the Feldgrau soldiers in his town to simply find more of them in the next place? On the other hand, Madeleine's business would go on, war or no war, German occupation or no occupation: people still had to eat.

Christine and Nicole had never picnicked with their parents before today. The meal alfresco gave the bizarre day a welcome taste of adventure. Yesterday, the maid had roasted a corn-fed chicken full of abundant yellow flavor. Naturally, there were hard-boiled eggs, bread, brie, and peaches. The feast was declared excellent.

Last night, when her chores were finished, the maid Sophie–who had known "her girls" since pre-school time–embraced Nicole and Christine. It was a tearful moment. For the time being, Sophie would go to her son's house to take care of the young nieces and nephews sent from Paris. With her three grandchildren in Avreville, she would now have eight others. She would be busy.

While Madeleine and Philippe sat with a second glass of wine, the two sisters drank their "blushing water." Neither one liked wine. They'd never acquired a taste for it. To make them feel grown up when they were very young, their father added a few drops of red wine to their well water. To this day it was their beverage at the dinner table.

Christine looked at her mother, who had started to put the remnants of their meal away silently. She wondered what the intimidating woman was thinking. As usual, Christine would never dare ask her.

Ever since they were inquisitive toddlers, both sisters felt their mother didn't have time to answer childish questions. It didn't occur to them nowadays that if they started the conversation instead of always waiting to be talked to, the woman might turn out to be less formidable. They were too much in awe of her to even try. Especially Christine, who dreaded her mother's ferocious temper outbursts.

When he didn't have his son to side with him, Philippe stayed out of the "female world," as he called it. It did not fool Christine. It was easier for him to remain neutral. Whatever he might attempt to say in defense of his younger daughter, Madeleine wouldn't hear. Not too surprisingly, he managed to score a few points when Nicole was on the carpet. Christine was jealous. She asked her brother, "Why did they have me? They had a boy and a girl. I must've been a mistake." The boy kept telling her she fretted too much about little things. He'd say, "You're the cutest mistake and I love you." That always made her feel better. She adored him—her big brother.

Christine could usually tell when her father was at a loss in front of one of his wife's sullen moods because he overplayed an exuberance of high spirits. As now. "Let's get this show on the road again," he bantered. "It's obvious we won't get to the Audineaus' house before tomorrow. We won't find rooms anywhere. Too many people ahead of us. Every inn must be filled by this time. We'll have to sleep in the car."

Philippe drove on. Madeleine remained silent. In the back seat, the girls held hands. They dozed on and off.

A loud throbbing in the sky just above their heads instantly turned into the whizzing of shells hitting the convoy of civilians. "Get out. Get into the ditch," Philippe yelled. He was already out of the car. He shoved the three women down roughly.

Christine's face was smack in a bunch of nettles. No time to argue. No time to worry about the red patches which would soon appear. No time to think about the itching and burning. Nobody had ever died scratching the welts it left. What fell from the sky was not benign.

From the corner of her eye, she saw her mother following the example of her husband. On her hands and knees, Madeleine crawled from here to there. She forced a couple of rebellious women to lie down. She instructed them to shelter their heads with their arms for protection. She told those with young children to cover up their children with their own bodies.

Philippe picked Christine up. He laid her down on the side of their car. He returned to help the wounded. Nicole and Madeleine were doing their best. They spoke to those who were hurt and needed help. They covered the faces of the dead with whatever pieces of clothing they found.

A unit of Civil Defense arrived with two civilian ambulances. The gray-haired man in charge conversed a few minutes with Philippe Tourneau. He advised him to move on immediately with his three ladies. A division of panzers had crossed the Loire River at Blois. No time to waste. The stranger pointed out a couple of secondary roads not on any map and much easier to travel. Philippe thanked him.

The big car was angled toward a narrow lane on the left. It led them away from the carnage. No one spoke. They were too stunned.

Christine knew her mother was upset by any display of weakness. She dug her nails deep into the palms of her hands. The self-inflicted pain brought on a more rational stream of thoughts. Why those people and not us, she asked silently. Why did the murderous piece of shrapnel select an innocent two-year old? Why not me?

She must have slept, because all of a sudden (or so it seemed to her), the car had stopped in front of the Audineaus' house. "What time is it?" she mumbled.

Nicole answered, "Almost three o'clock in the morning."

They dragged themselves out of the vehicle. Groggy. Still half asleep. At the front door Martin and his wife hugged them all in turn. "We're glad you made it. Needless to say, we were worried. The girls waited, but a while back they went to sleep. Your beds are ready. We'll talk at breakfast."

Christine continued her interrupted night between coarse linen sheets in a comfortable double bed. It felt good to change clothes and to be able to stretch. She was careful to remain as far as possible from Nicole. They weren't used to sleeping in the same bed. She turned to her side. She cradled her face in her folded arm to keep it from rubbing on the rough material, or else her skin would tear. She'd be quite a sight the next day.

At six o'clock in the morning, Catherine and Suzie Audineau burst into their room, "Wake up. Come and see the holes where the three barns were. We were bombed yesterday by two Italian planes with black crosses on them. Come and see."

So Philippe Tourneau decided then and there his daughters would return to Avreville with them after all. "In 1914 the Germans remained in the Ardennes. In 1940 they are in every town and every village. There's no escaping the army of occupation," he sighed. "We might as well face the 'Krauts' together."

Philippe left his crates of documents with his friend for safe keeping. Now that the car was almost empty, Madeleine occupied her rightful place next to the driver–with the new corset between them. It was returning to Avreville.

The departmental roads were almost free of refugees. Perhaps the wretched people were afraid of getting lost. Afraid if they wandered on someone's property, an irate farmer would get at them with his hunting gun. "For a landowner, any stranger on his fief is a 'gypsy,'" Philippe muttered ruefully. He paused to consider. "The Germans on one side, the cantankerous Frenchmen on the other–six of one kind, half a dozen of the other. We shouldn't be here. Let's see if we can return to Avreville."

The long column of cars returning to the homes they should never have left was inching forward at a snail's pace. A German soldier was speaking to the driver of the car ahead. "Lean out the window, Christine," Philippe ordered. "Listen to what that man is explaining."

She translated, "If we want to pass those other cars in front of us, we can go about three miles in the left lane to the next intersection and we'll be allowed to cross the river on one of their pontoon bridges."

"Let's do that." Philippe pulled out. Other drivers blew their horns. They shouted obscenities. Several vehicles left the line and followed the Tourneaus. Maybe this guy knew something they didn't. He seemed to understand what the "*Boche*" had said.

In no time the Peugeot was bumping its way on a temporary floating bridge supported by hollow cylinders.

Nicole teased in a shaky voice, "Good thing no one asked me my opinion."

Madeleine agreed. "I would much prefer to swim across." From inside the car, they could not see the floating road. It looked as if the car itself was walking on water. Madeleine's rigid back told Christine her mother didn't like the bridge any better than she did.

The crossing seemed to last for hours. When they climbed up to a firm, real country road, they realized it had been only a few minutes of biblical miracle. A serious-looking German guard saluted them. Philippe was still doing his best to make his women believe life would go on without unpleasant incidents. "The Teutons are a disciplined race. They're not like us feisty Latins. In no time we'll be used to seeing them around. We'll ignore them. We will go on."

If anyone in the car said "Amen," they did so silently. How could anyone have believed what Philippe said less than twenty-four hours after the horrible assassination of defenseless civilians on the country road yesterday?

Looking at the impassive, erect men in their Feldgrau uniforms, Christine shuddered. Were they all so thoroughly brainwashed that to any German–in or out of uniform–every French citizen from the cradle to the grave was an enemy of the Reich? In her history books, Christine had encountered countless examples of traditional enemies. It had been Prussia against Austria, until in 1870 Bismarck decided to use France to unify Germany. Four decades later, the most devastating of all–The Great War. Only twenty years after the armistice of Nineteen Eighteen, another world war: by all accounts, a new generation of Germans who had been taught to hate. Indoctrinated, fanatical Hitlerites dedicated to systematically eliminate from the world the non-Aryans. Christine was terrified. *The French people have fallen into the hands of inhuman evil-doers*, she thought.

CHAPTER 3

▼

JUST AS PHILIPPE TOURNEAU HAD PREDICTED, life in Avreville went on as before—at least on the surface it did. Everyone simply ignored the "Occupant." It could be done because there was still plenty of food; the gardens and orchards swelled with fresh vegetables and luscious fruit of all kinds. The stores were filled with goods. Philippe told *his women* they could and should buy the outfits they wanted. They did.

Christine paraded her Chanel suit, her white leather sandals and matching handbag; Nicole wore her blue one wherever they went. Madeleine bought her favorite perfume—Shalimar by Guerlain.

They had gas for their automobiles. Their restaurants served the usual excellent food. Late on Sunday afternoon, when they were not traveling or visiting relatives, the Tourneaus met their friends and business acquaintances at the popular Café des Sports. Avreville was a beautiful Normandy town. It had, as all European cities had, a fascinating historic district—fourteenth century narrow, cobbled streets leading up to a great cathedral. A magnificent example of Gothic style. It also had a bustling commercial district. On the large, pleasant Place de la République, several renowned restaurants boasted busy, outdoor terraces. Lively bands competed to entertain the habitués.

Each family always occupied the same table, unless some German officers had arrived there first. It was aggravating to have to move. But move the French civilians did. Conversations flew back and forth between people who'd known one another a long time. Nowadays, there was a strained silence if one was next to a table invaded by the despised men in uniform. Stress was caused by the forced curtailing of one's emotions. Philippe Tourneau and the other men exchanged meaningful looks. They spoke volumes with their eyes.

That afternoon, a table of German officers was the center of attraction. In serious conversation with his countrymen was a major well known by the regular clients of the Café des Sports. To them all, the man was known as

"Peanuts" because until April, he was the guy who went from table to table selling peanuts and crackers to them.

The smirk on the face of the arrogant major confirmed it–*he was Peanuts.*

Philippe Tourneau forgot to lower his voice. He sneered, "That's how well prepared those bastards were. They scattered French-speaking peanut vendors in the midst of gregarious, inebriated French army men."

"likely all the peanut vendors spoke French as fluently as this one."

"And they also knew how to report on the topography of region: roads, rivers, hills, bridges…"

"Buildings, factories, barracks, schools…"

"A new breed of spies for sure," a friend at the next table rejoined.

"If we had been smart enough to recognize a German spook in our midst," a man said bitterly.

Philippe mumbled, "We were stupid and they want us to know how clever they were, don't they?"

Fearful of repercussions, the wives quickly turned the attention to the food which was deposited in front of them. Everyone ate silently. At least the French citizens were silent. The Germans, however, continued their boisterous conversations.

CHAPTER 4

▼

CHRISTINE TOURNEAU WAS MORE THAN EVER engrossed in her studies. She was very apprehensive. The Entrance Exam was approaching much too rapidly. On the one hand she was flattered adults believed in her academic prowess; on the other hand, it was whispered she didn't have a chance because the admission office would declare her too young to live in a boarding school with girls three or four years older. Another strike against her was that she was a product of a private Catholic school. She knew that most college educators were agnostic Voltairians. Sister Jane had warned her, " The socialist professors will go out of their way to confuse you, Christine; mark my word."

First, she needed special permission from the Academy of Normandy. While many students were told they were too old if they passed their twenty-second birthday, Christine was too young. Madeleine Tourneau filled in the necessary forms. Mother Superior wrote a letter of recommendation: their best student should not be denied her right to prove she was college material. It was the first time Avreville Catholic School could present one of their precocious girls for the contest, and Mother Superior was proud.

Soon an official document granted Christine permission to attempt the unfeasible. From five o'clock in the morning until her mother forced her to go to bed around eleven, Christine studied. She was so engrossed in intellectual nourishment, if they hadn't called her at meal times, she would never remember to eat.

Claudette Cadivet had completed her freshman year at the university. Math was not Christine's strong point, but it was an easy subject for her friend who tutored her skillfully. Claudette was a persistent teacher. She wanted Christine at Caen with her in September. She promised, "If I can make you get an average grade in the written math exam, you'll be on easy street because the rest is a piece of cake for you."

Still, Christine was anxious.

Like a good teacher who knows how to boost a timid student, Claudette declared, "Remember when the university computes the grade average, math gets multiplied only by two; whereas, what you're good at–history, literature, foreign languages–all those get a coefficient of three or four. You'll have a definite advantage over us math kids."

Christine tried not to worry about what her mother would say if she made a fool of herself and failed. Better not even think about it, there would be time enough if and when it happened.

One hundred and twenty-five young women registered for the entrance exam. One hundred and twenty-five well-qualified candidates and only twenty-five would be accepted. On Sunday evening they arrived with a suitcase, ready to spend the week in seclusion. They were isolated from the rest of the world in a private school rented for the occasion. They kissed their parents good-bye. They went to the rooms assigned to them. They continued to study fretfully.

Until the results of the written tests were announced on Thursday morning, it was life in a convent. From the dining hall full of chatter and excitement, to the silent exam rooms where nervous young women on pins and needles waited to hear the subject of the next essay. It was read aloud by the proctor opening a sealed envelope in front of them. What was it going to be?

At eight o'clock on Thursday morning, sixty students were invited to remain for the oral exams which were to begin promptly.

Christine was one of them.

She and the other lucky contestants didn't look at the sixty-five, no longer hopeful girls, who went to the phone to call their parents to come and pick them up.

Christine walked up and down the halls, sizing up the new situation. She peeked in classrooms where four or five college professors sat talking to one another behind a very long table. Facing them, one single chair would hold the victim–the student who would make her presentation and answer their questions.

On each door, a cardboard indicated the subject–History of the Twentieth Century. Middle Ages. Literature of the Gold Century in Spain. Oral Fluency in English. And so on. And so on. The students needed to select eight such rooms. Once the young woman entered, she walked to the table where she was told to pick up one of the folded pieces of paper. Inside was the topic of her oral presentation.

Sixty bright young women declared themselves more frightened by the austere old professors in the flesh than by the written exams. They waited to hear what a candidate had pulled in history or in another subject. What were the teachers like? How mean? How sneaky?

Christine decided she needed sleep. She was exhausted. Might as well get it over with. She was first or second in each of the rooms she selected. She was in and out. She refused to use the twenty minutes of preparation allowed by law. She didn't need them. She took five minutes to jot down the main points and declared herself ready to speak.

By six o'clock on Thursday, she was home in bed.

On their way to hear the results of the contest Sunday morning, Nicole teased her nervous sister, "You shouldn't be jittery. You must be well rested. We've seen neither hide nor hair of you since Thursday evening."

Madeleine snarled, "You never surfaced for the last sixty hours, Christine. I'd come to believe you might not get up this morning, either."

"But I've got to know, Mom."

"Yes, you do. We all do."

"We're there," Philippe said while he was searching for a parking space. He added ruefully, "And we're late. I can hear the voice over the loudspeaker naming number five."

They tiptoed to the back of the crowd of parents and contestants. They held their breath. They didn't hear the name of Christine Tourneau. The twenty-five lucky students and the three on the waiting list had been called. The crowd was silent. Girls who were accepted shared tears of joy with their parents. Others, tears of frustration.

An exasperated woman turned around. She stared at Christine. She spat, "Well, naturally, you're number two. Wouldn't you know?"

CHAPTER 5

▼

THE YOUNG WOMEN WERE GRANTED THEIR wish. Their fathers knew it first. Captain Cadivet had called Philippe Tourneau a few days before, "I got a call from Colonel Laplace of the Gendarmerie of Caen. He wanted to know if I approved of our kids rooming together."

"And you did."

"Naturally, Philippe. Your daughter's much too young to be on her own in a town full of soldiers." He added with a touch of exasperation, "Mine is not much older. We'll be relieved to know they're together."

"Did Laplace tell you anything about their landlord?"

"Yes, as a matter of fact, a good man, he said, a history professor at the university."

"Madeleine will be happy to know. Thanks, Paul."

Philippe waited for his wife to receive the confirmation from the Dean of Students. Deep down, both Philippe and Paul would have liked their respective spouses to be more amicable toward each other. There was nothing they could do. Both Madeleine Tourneau and Diane Cadivet were strong women who kept to themselves. They managed to be civil on the few occasions they met. Neither one would ever attempt to move toward a possible friendship. Philippe vaguely suspected Madeleine felt insecure in front of Diane Cadivet, who always gave the impression she was the "*grande dame*" of the Gendarmerie–a musician who had been a concert pianist. Perhaps it was Claudette's mother who was in awe of the business woman who had usurped a position many men envied. Philippe didn't delve into his wife's feelings too deeply, it would be a waste of effort.

CHAPTER 6

▼

THE TWO COLLEGE STUDENTS WERE PLEASED with their spacious room in the stately old house of Professor Hureau and his wife–twin beds, two desks, two chairs, an armoire on both sides, their own bathroom down the hall.

The freshman year went so fast, it was soon but a blur in Christine's mind.

The second year went even faster. Later on, she had to search her memory to recall a few good moments. "Claudette, do you remember the Sundays in Caen we spent in a movie theater from noon until dark?"

"Of course I do. It was our way to forget we were hungry and there was nothing to eat at the college."

"We were bored with books and exams."

"Wasn't it clever of us to watch three or four movies in succession, all for the price of the first one. We never left our seats."

"Until just under curfew time, we returned with pounding headaches and growling stomachs."

"Which didn't prevent us from falling asleep as soon as we got to bed, if I recall."

If the first two years of college seemed to belong to another lifetime, the summer between them leaped into focus whenever Christine murmured to herself the sweet name of André.

André.

André Grassin.

The man of her dreams.

The man she would marry one day.

The Grassins––mother and son––owned a coffee torrefaction outside Avreville. The huge bins where the coffee beans roasted were hellish. The only time Christine had been there with her classmates, the stench of burnt organic plants was so overpowering, she refused to return with her parents.

The Grassins also owned a Parisian pied-à-terre, *Rue de Grenelle*, beside their big house in Avreville. The Tourneaus visited them in the capital a couple of times each summer. In Paris that year, Christine had fallen hopelessly in love with a man who was twenty-two years old. *So what, if André is grown up and I am still a kid; time would take care of that.*

For the whole week they were tourists. It seemed the young teacher of English and German had nothing better to do than chaperone his twin sisters—Jackie and Josie—and their friends—Christine and Nicole—all over Paris. He took the four girls to several museums. He rode the *Bâteau Mouche* with them at night. He taught them the art of getting around in the *métro*. He threw in several instructive hours of French history whenever the place demanded—at the *Panthéon*, the *Champ-de Mars*, the *Palais de l'Elysée*.

Christine was in love. Oh, yes, she was in love.

In the summer, Christine volunteered two months of her well-deserved vacation at a camp for deprived city boys. It was a scouting project. The boys were ten to fourteen, lively, turbulent, boisterous and lovable. Many of them had never been in the woods, never camped outdoors in tents, and never even seen a working farm. Christine loved to tease them, "Look at the white and beige cows, they give us white milk. Look at the brown ones, they give us chocolate milk."

Mademoiselle Tourneau inherited eight of the youngest ones. They kept her busy from morning to night, no sooner the hour of singing around the campfire was over, she fell asleep right there on the ground and had to be coaxed to go to bed. She groaned. She was too tired to get up and walk to her tent. A friendly soul would put her on her feet and lead her to her cot.

On such a night, she was walking groggily between two older women, whose husbands were prisoners of war in some stalag in Germany, when she believed she saw André Grassin in conversation with the camp director. *Couldn't be,* she thought. *I'm really exhausted. I have visions. I do need to rest.*

University students were to have no vacation between semesters. Too much leisure time for an elite. Instead, they were to become civic-minded. They had to accept whatever jobs were offered to them.

Christine worked at the switchboard at the post office. Often she had to translate a conversation between a German and a French civilian. She didn't tell her parents, who would have worried. She quickly forgot what she heard—even if it was a conversation of no interest between a soldier and his girlfriend—more so if some black-market transaction was taking place. She was treading on thin ice. It added to her nightmares. Between the dangerous bilingual calls, there were long moments of boredom. To alleviate it, she read. She read and kept to herself. The postal clerks liked it that way. The unwanted helper didn't get into their hair; she minded her own business.

Every so often her mind wandered back to camp last summer, and a tall, dark, handsome man who was now almost twenty-eight and still not married. He was waiting for her to grow up–she was certain of it.

She felt grown up. Where was André Grassin?

CHAPTER 7

▼

THE SIGN ON THE DOOR OF the restaurant said, "Closed because of illness in the family."

Unexpected tourists were rare. The faithful patrons had been told the place wouldn't be open today. They all knew why. Many had expressed their best wishes to the lucky birthday-girl on the preceding Sunday.

Inside, behind the front door, but with her chair pushed to the corner so she couldn't be seen through the narrow glass panels on each side, the owners' ten-year-old daughter was concentrating her attention on approaching footsteps on the street. When she heard the martial German boots, or the shrill laughter of one of their women, the girl signaled the waitress who stood by the door of the dining room in the back.

Immediately the waitress turned to the revelers. She waved her right hand–its palm toward them–in the air in front of herself. Warned, tense, edgy, they became silent instantaneously. The young children and toddlers who'd been running around the tables stopped in their tracks immediately. If some kids thought it was a game, most sensed it was not–everyone from two to ninety froze.

No one looked a relative or a friend straight in the face for fear of what they'd read in their eyes. They didn't want to inhale the detestable odor of terror. Panic was not on the agenda this afternoon.

If the footsteps stopped in front of the restaurant, one hundred people held their breath.

As soon as the Germans and their French whores decided to march on, the conversations resumed.

At first in whispers. . . Soon again in cheerful tones of voice.

Danger–for the moment–forgotten.

For everyone assembled there, today had been declared a holiday–it was Christine Tourneau's eighteenth birthday. She kept telling herself she dearly loved all those people here today. They were her world. Her life. Still, she didn't believe anyone in this room could begin to fathom the depth of her loneliness. Where was André? Would he ever return from wherever he was at the moment? *Return?* the inner voice echoed. *You're dreaming, girl. He never told you he loved you.*

She shook her head, trying to banish the negative thoughts. Firmly, she told herself, *André loves me and he knows I love him.*

Among the guests in the room was André's grandfather who said André had joined the Free French Army of De Gaulle, which was fighting along with the Americans somewhere in North Africa. André's grandfather was friendly with all the men in the room, but his mother was standoffish. She'd been heard to say she resented her son did not send his two yearly allotted postcards to her. Christine didn't bat an eyelash, but she wondered if Marcelle Grassin suspected the two cards had indeed been sent to her: *Doing fine. Thinking about you. Claude.*

During the day Christine carried the cards in her handbag. They went wherever she went. They were her well-kept secret. She never showed them to anybody. The days they arrived in the mail, she told herself she was lucky she got home before her mother. In the evening she placed them under her pillow. Before she turned her nightlight off, she whispered, "I love you, André Grassin."

Neither Jackie nor Josie attended the birthday party—the excuse given was some studying for the end of the year exams. Christine wasn't sure she'd have been brave enough to inquire about their brother's whereabouts.

Probably not.

She alone knew the name of the man she loved. It was her secret. It would remain her secret. Until André gave her permission to disclose it. That day would be their engagement day. She could wait—but, please, God, not too long.

After graduation, Claudette planned to marry Antoine's oldest son, John, who would inherit the popular restaurant. Their lives would unfold peacefully in this little French town.

Christine knew Claudette's scenario by heart. It was simple: she would be a woman with status and just enough wealth. She would bear one child. "One is enough," she says. She would live surrounded by relatives and friends. Christine tried to understand her best friend and to see the future through her eyes. She couldn't do it. "I'm afraid I'd be bored if I spent my whole life in Avreville," she admitted. To herself alone she said, *John is not André. I'll never be bored when I'm married to André. As Claude right this moment, he's living and adventure. . . No, we'll never be bored together.*

At night in Caen, the two roommates, Christine and Claudette, could not always listen to the only news they wanted to hear any more than the other college students could. The German Kommandatur forbade the French citizens to listen to the British Broadcasting Corporation—the BBC.

The girls lived in a house of strangers. They waited until their hosts were out; then they tuned in to the BBC, which kept the French informed about the war. The enemy had ears, however, and they had to be careful. The young women filled many dark, cold, hungry evening hours searching their own souls and exchanging ideas about their future.

When Christine foresaw a very dull life in a little Normandy town, Claudette laughed, "You expect the excitement of war-time to continue to entertain you: deadly planes, Gestapo, curfews, snipers, no shoes, no soap, no food, no young men. It will all change when the Germans are kicked out and we go back to a normal life."

"What's a *normal* life, Claudette?"

"That's it. You don't remember living in peacetime. Believe me, it provided enough ups and downs without the country being occupied by the Nazis. After they've been kicked out, I hope there will be no more cataclysms. You and I have had more than our share."

Christine murmured slowly, "I envy you, Claudette. I wish I could look forward to a bright future. My insides churn when I contemplate what could happen to me in the years ahead."

Claudette snickered, "You're too romantic. You're waiting for a knight in shining armor. Not me. I'm a math student. I like additions. The sound of cash registers will be music to my ears. All the novels you read, Christine, have distorted the horizon. You fantasize about men, but love is prosaic. Commonplace. Tedious. You're confused, my little friend."

At home Christine's sister sounded exactly like Claudette. Nicole had fallen in love with an attractive French lieutenant who wrote that they would get married on the very day he returned from wherever.

Both young women were in love with men of flesh and blood.

Christine was in love with love.

Champagne was poured again. Once more people tapped with their knives on the crystal glasses, "Happy birthday, Christine! Many returns."

Antoine himself paraded the cake on a tray. Everyone duly admired it. The pyramid of the *"Pièce Montée"* was made of dozens of miniature cream puffs anchored together by sticky caramel, and decorated with colorful Jordan almonds. It was the traditional European birthday cake, served also on religious holidays. Christine had seen it in the homes of her Jewish friends as well as on Easter Sunday at Grandma's house. The waitresses served everyone. Then they placed trays of tiny French pastries here and there on the tables.

It was a day to reward everyone's taste buds. A day to remind people that in the past, such things as chocolate éclairs, flaky *napoléons* and *baba au rhum* had indeed existed.

Once again, Philippe Tourneau stood up, his champagne flute raised in front of him, "Happy Birthday, darling."

Once again, they all stood up. "Many happy returns, Christine."

From the corner of her eye, Christine saw her mother wipe a furtive tear.

CHAPTER 8

▼

In her fitful sleep, Christine kept on scratching her neck where the stiff old lace itched. Half awake now, she thought about the men who should have been at the banquet. Her brother—they had not heard from Jacques in months. Her friends - more than ten of the boys had vanished from their classes at the university. Others had stopped going to their city jobs. It would be self-destructive for a man between the ages of twenty and fifty to be caught in the streets by the goose-stepping patrol after curfew. And an earlier than usual curfew was not always announced on time. It wasn't safe during the day either. A sudden order from the dreaded *Kommandatur* behind the swastikas up there on Government Square would have a dozen terrified Frenchmen shoved into a paddy-wagon—civilian on the outside. Bound for the Third Reich.

Because Philippe Tourneau was too old to be drafted by the Germans and sent to work in Nazi factories, the French puppets at City Hall made him a member of Civilian Defense. Invariably, Christine had to suppress a chuckle whenever she saw her dignified father in army fatigues and heavy black boots.

Every day of his life, Philippe had worn a three-piece suit—well-cut British worsted, a starched white shirt with a collar that seemed to be ready to strangle him, and a conservative tie. If it hadn't been for the Occupants being very real, Christine would've believed her father was playing war games in his camouflaged twill with a wide leather belt around his thick waist.

CHAPTER 9

▼

AT CAMP THAT SUMMER, HER JOB was completely different from the one last year. She was the cook. "Le chef," as the kids called her affectionately. She couldn't remember when it had been decided–prior to the opening of the place. Probably at a meeting of leaders she forgot to attend. The director told her she was right for the task.

She was bewildered, "Why me?"

"Because no one else wants it." He begged, "You'll take it, won't you?"

She giggled, "That makes sense."

"Seriously, Christine, we know you'll do the job well. Four of the older boys will be your assistants. They'll peel potatoes and onions. They'll lift the heavy bags for you. They'll cut the meat. You'll get their help. Other counselors might not."

"Right. I don't want to cut up dead chickens and rabbits. So what will I do, then?"

"You plan the meals. Remember, it is for seventy kids and ten adults. You shop in the farms. You keep a budget. You can do it."

When Christine told her father, he was amused, " I can't quite picture my ninety-five pound daughter stirring the brew in the cauldron."

She was annoyed with him, "If I'm the witch, at least I'll be the good one, the one who feeds the kids."

Philippe sobered up. He squeezed her hand affectionately. "You're a brave girl. I'm thinking how much work it's going to be for you, darling, to keep the tree trunks burning under the huge pots." He paused, "Have you told your mother yet?"

"No. And I'm not going to tell her," she answered.

"Tell her you're the dietitian, darling," he suggested, chuckling. She shrugged. She didn't care if her parents didn't believe in her. The camp director did. The kids never complained. The food at the camp was so much more plentiful than at home in town. To them, Christine was a miracle worker. She laughed a lot. The kitchen tent was the happiest place. They adored her.

Chapter 10

▼

During the summer camp one night, a visitor came who made "Christine's boys" fidgety. Who was the tall man who stood talking to the director? They were both looking in Christine's direction. A helper, who'd been present last summer, was not at all pleased to see the man. He predicted, "Christine will go walk in the woods with him. She did last year when that big guy came."

It was a balmy evening in July. The aroma of a meaty rabbit stew permeated the woods. Fresh parsley, thyme, bay leaves. The lack of salt not too obvious. Lots of red-skinned potatoes. A dish fit for a king. A king of hearts.

Christine had not seen André arrive. She was completely unaware he'd been looking at her the whole time he was talking with his friend, a few yards away from her.

When a masculine arm pushed the plate of the boy on her left across the picnic table, she was startled. A male voice ordered, "Kid, follow your dish. Go and sit on the other side. That's *my* place, you see."

Christine's fork stopped in mid-air. She was jostled by André's knee as he straddled the bench. His long fingers squeezed her shoulder. "Hi, lady, I was told you're the one responsible for the feast. It smells great. I'm famished."

Christine was speechless. Mute. Dumb. Staring at him. Unseeing.

André brought his right fist under her chin, playfully, "Shut your mouth, sweetheart, before you try to greet me."

She didn't need to look around to know all eyes were on her, the newcomer known only to a couple of male leaders. She finally managed to utter, "What are you doing here?"

He smiled, his bright eyes filled with tenderness, "I'm paying you a call."

"Just like that?"

"Just like that, sweetheart. But it took a lot of finagling, let me tell you," he laughed.

A huge, heaping plate of stew was placed in front of André. "That's exactly what I'm doing right now. I'm paying you a call," he insisted, all the while gobbling up the food as if he had not eaten in days. "They say you're a magician. They're right. This stew is very good. But then I've always known you're an enchantress," he grinned from ear to ear.

Christine became mindless. She couldn't speak. She had become aware that the clinking of forks and the boys' chattering had stopped. She was the center of attention.

André leaned over. He whispered, "Look at them all. Busybodies. Let's not talk while we're eating. I've got a couple of hours. We'll catch up with our news on a full stomach."

Fine. But she could not eat. Her throat was too tight.

If André noticed she didn't touch the rest of her food, he didn't let on. His eyes were full of mischief when he leaned toward her again. He murmured, "I've always said you're the prettiest girl in Avreville. Seeing what a great cook you are, I've decided I'll marry you some day."

Before the young woman recovered from shock, the man stood up. He put his strong hands around her waist. He pulled her up and set her down on the other side of the bench, "Let's go, Christine. We have to talk."

For the next two hours they walked hand in hand in the country lane surrounding the farm. They did very little talking. They strolled. They stopped. They looked at each other. If André controlled his impulse to touch her, she was unaware of it. His voice was casual, yet strong. Her eyes couldn't get enough of him.

When André knew he could no longer keep his hands off her, he reached for a branch. He waved it, playfully, "What's the name of it?" She knew. She told him, "Hawthorn." She inhaled the fragrant flowers. She picked up a couple of wild blossoms, "Your turn to name those," she teased. He didn't know.

"What kind of scout are you?" she asked impishly.

"The best," he replied, grabbing her hands to pull her close to him, "The best. I always manage to find you, don't I?"

When it was time for him to leave, he stammered, "I've got to go, little one. There's so much I'd like to say. There's not much I can promise you at this time. Please wait for me."

"I will."

"Please do, honey, I'll be back."

His long arms encircled her. She looked up at him, her eyes full of tears. He bent down to kiss her. Their first kiss—her first—was heavenly sweet.

André moved away. Christine staggered a little. He came back. He lifted her up on a tree stump so they could face each other evenly. "Was that your first kiss ever, darling?"

Her hands lingered on his forearms where she'd taken hold for balance. He locked her close to him again, kissing her possessively. Then he turned and ran.

He was gone. Christine was deliriously happy. God–wherever God was–had answered her prayers. She would be Mrs. André Grassin. Someday. She could wait.

CHAPTER 11

▼

THE VERY FIRST MINUTE SHE ARRIVED at her grandparents' house after closing the camp with the other counselors, Christine burst out with her exciting news, "Grandpa, Grandpa, André and I are engaged."

"Engaged?" Blanche murmured, surprised.

"Engaged?" Pascal roared, squeezing the girl's shoulder very hard.

Christine moaned, "You should be happy for me; let go of me." She pouted. Tears flooded her green eyes. The old man's fingers loosened, and the bruising grip eased up a little.

Huffily, Christine rubbed her shoulder. She explained, "All right, we're not officially engaged. André did not have a ring for me. But when the war is over, we'll get married."

She was so obviously ecstatic, her grandmother moved forward to hug her. "That's lovely, child, I hope you'll be very happy together."

Turning to her grandfather, the girl waited. The man glared at her. He was deliberately mute. After a measured silence, as if he had carefully considered his words, he uttered in a voice full of pain, "I hope you don't mean it. You can't be serious."

His bitter reply jarred her hard enough to make her retort unthinkingly, "I've never been more serious in my life. I don't care how you feel about it. It's none of your business, anyway."

She turned around. She bent down to pick up her luggage. "I'm going home right now."

"Don't do that," mumbled Pascal contrite. He went on, softly, "Let's talk calmly. You surprised me, that's all."

Blanche was relieved. She took the girl's hand and pulled her toward the living room, "What does your mother think about it?" she asked.

"She doesn't know."

"She doesn't know?" echoed Pascal in crescendo.

"Nobody knows. Neither Dad, nor Nicole, nor Claudette. I came here to tell you first."

Pascal relaxed visibly. "I see," he grunted.

The subject of André Grassin was not brought up again, each person preferring to keep their own counsel. Besides, there was so much to talk about. The big question on everyone's mind was America. After Pearl Harbor, how rapidly could the U.S.A. become prepared to fight the Germans on French soil? The campaigns in Africa and Italy were taking their toll. What was next?

Christine told her grandparents she did not want to remain in Caen by herself after Claudette's graduation at the end of the school year. What then? If she interrupted her studies when she was three-quarters of the way, what would happen?

Pascal continued his daily visits to their tenants. Although he was semi-retired, he still had a herd of milking cows. He cultivated a huge garden. Their orchard held hundreds of fruit trees. In the last couple of years, he had fed Philippe and his family as well as his other children and grandchildren.

The farmers on his land agreed to the unique barter system prevalent in France in those years: they turned over half of the profit to the proprietors, and kept the other half for themselves and their families. They did not own the land or the houses they lived in. On the other hand, they lived rent free. All expenses for repairs were paid by Pascal. Everyone seemed satisfied. Especially since the Tourneaus were not hard to get along with. If they suspected there was a little more gain on one side than the other, they shrugged; they no longer had children to raise, whereas the young farmhands did. And the beloved land was still theirs to pass on to their children—none of whom had remained after the Great War to cultivate the fertile Normandy soil.

Christine liked to accompany her grandfather. She was always greeted with affection by the older people who'd known her all her life. They lavished her with their best fruit, their tender chickens, their sweet apple cider, and a bottle of Calvados for Mister Tourneau.

Frequently a woman would put a warm pie or a quiche on the back seat of the car. "Take it to your grandmother, girl; she always takes care of our grandkids. She knits, she sews, she brings medicine—she's a blessing, your grandma is."

At the end of the week that went by much too quickly, Christine begged her grandparents not to tell her news to anyone. They promised. They too wanted to keep her engagement to André a secret. They had their own reasons. Aware they did, she knew she could trust them.

CHAPTER 12

▼

CHRISTINE NO SOONER GOT HOME THAN Claudette arrived, bursting with excitement, "How do you like that, we're not going back to Caen."

"We're not?"

"Didn't your parents tell you?"

"They're at work. I've not seen them yet. I don't know where Nicole is."

"I know where she is. She's helping your mother. They're going from store to store. Nicole says it's less boring than the post office. She doesn't care if they don't mail her a paycheck."

"How do you know we're not returning to Caen?"

"Everybody got a letter from the Academy yesterday. We're going to Coutance instead."

"Why Coutance?"

"My father believes it's because it will be somewhat safer for us should the Americans decide to invade Normandy. He says Caen could be a disaster."

"Soon?" There was excitement in her voice.

"Not that soon, my father says." She sighed resignedly.

A week later, both families, the Tourneaus and the Cadivets, had other news: they were all moving from Avreville to Le Mans.

Philippe had bought a fleet of taxi-cabs in Le Mans. Before the war, the city had sold each of the twenty-five franchises to twenty-five men who could afford to buy the license and the car. The *Kommandatur* distributed gasoline permits to the drivers because not only the civilians needed to be taken to their doctors or to the hospital, but also the Germans rode in the taxis.

Little by little, the number of cabs had dwindled to four or five, simply because the men were at war. Or they were hiding in the maquis. Or they could no longer buy new tires, nor repair their vehicles. Philippe Tourneau, on the other hand, had connections. He knew several good mechanics who had worked for him when his tourist buses were in demand. He also had funds, and informed each owner he was paying cash. Soon there were six or eight taxis stationed on Government Place, and others in the yard of the train station with a new name on their roof: "Tourneau."

Madeleine didn't object to the move. It put her closer to her most important stores. She was expanding south. Le Mans was the center of the region.

The Tourneaus bought a big house on Mariette Street. The wide avenue was parallel to the highway called Route de Paris, but that section of the city was more a high class suburban district. Unfortunately, at the moment, Philippe and Madeleine were unaware that the vast Clemenceau barrack was adjacent to the perimeter of their orchard. Or if they did, it didn't alarm them.

When Captain Cadivet was promoted Chief of Gendarmerie of Le Mans, neither Claudette nor Christine complained. Claudette mused, "What would we have done if only one of us was moving?"

"We're going to Coutance together, remember?"

"True, Christine. But I'm glad we'll be coming back to the same town. I don't ever want to be separated from you."

"We'll never be separated. You can be sure we'll still be friends when we're old, old ladies," Christine assured her half-prophetically.

CHAPTER 13

▼

THROUGHOUT THE YEAR IN COUTANCE, THE girls would have several encounters with the Occupant.

They lived much further from the university buildings than they thought at first. At a fast pace, it took them nearly a full hour morning and night. With compulsory attendance at breakfast, in order to be there by seven o'clock, they had to leave their room at six on the dot.

One pitch dark, cold morning—with the not very tantalizing pasty bread on their mind and growling empty stomachs—they were running full speed when Christine bumped into a hard, immovable force that shouldn't have been there. China went flying, falling on the pavement in a clatter of broken pieces. Hot liquid burned Christine's foot.

The talking obstacle spat a slew of German obscenities.

Christine yelled, "Run, Claudette, run. Tell them I've been delayed." She stopped to holler, "Ouch, you're hurting me."

A powerful clamp on her wrist was holding her still. The man's large hand was crushing her bones. She screamed. At first in French. Then in German, "Let go of me."

The soldier did not let go of her arm. Still holding on to her, he bent down. He deposited a tray on the ground. On it were the remains of what must have been a much more pleasing breakfast than the one the students would get.

Christine's mouth watered. Her stomach reminded her she was famished (French stomachs don't "growl." They're educated to "talk.") She ordered hers to shut up. She had to pay attention to this fellow. Presently, he was pulling her not too gently—not gently at all—toward a door half open in the next house.

The orderly pushed the door angrily. It revealed a big entrance hall. The ornate chandelier was brightly lit. I guess *they* don't have to obey the black-out rules, Christine surmised.

The soldier finally let go of her arm. It was throbbing. Moaning, she rubbed life back into it. She looked up to find herself face to face with one of the most handsome men she had ever seen. Dressed in a dark cashmere robe. Tall. Blond hair. Silvery temples. Piercing blue eyes. Looking at him, she felt very small, and yet suddenly she was no longer scared.

There was mirth in the cultured male voice that inquired, "Pray, tell me, corporal, whom did you bring me to share my breakfast?"

The younger man clicked his heels. He saluted. Silently he waited. At attention.

Christine giggled.

The officer bowed, "Not only very pretty. Educated. You're a student at the university. You speak German, don't you?"

Christine was mute.

"I saw your friend with you several times. Morning and night. Where is she now?" he inquired, looking through the door which had remained open.

"She went on to school."

"Smart girl."

The man's eyes were merry. "Run along, young lady, or you'll be late. We don't want you to be punished, do we?"

"*Danke schön*," Christine mumbled, already outside.

CHAPTER 14

▼

CLAUDETTE CADIVET AND CHRISTINE TOURNEAU WERE serious students who minded all the rules of the school: they were always on time, well prepared for their classes, anxious to get good grades.

One day, Christine got a pass requesting her to go to the headmistress's office. The girl searched her conscience for her sins. Other than funny puns she might have made in class to stave off boredom, she was unaware of blatant misconduct on her part. She handed the pass over to Claudette, who read it and returned it with a shrug of her shoulders and the palms of her hands up in the air in front of her. Her gesture said in silence, "Go and find out."

Standing in front of the president with another junior girl she barely knew, Christine listened to the announcement with increasing confusion and bewilderment when she heard, "Both of you are going to graduate this year. I've had a communication from the dean of the Academy of Caen. It concerns a handful of top juniors who, like you, are allowed to double up on their studies to finish this summer. Everywhere in France we shall need more women teachers in September to do the jobs of the all the men who are gone —those who are absent because they're in the Resistance or because they were sent to work in German factories or because they're hiding somewhere.

"Let me explain. I shall personally tutor you to make certain you'll get the courses you need. It will be hard work. Several long term papers. You might wind up with yet a couple of research papers this summer. You'll get your bachelor's degree then."

She turned to Alice Buisson, "I've already informed your parents. They are pleased. You can go; you're dismissed."

And to Christine, "Stay a moment. It's been decided that you'll teach in a lycée in Le Mans next year."

"In Le Mans?" Christine was not happy. She had hoped to be assigned to a county regional high school, not to a city. She would be on her own. She would make new friends. With her salary spread over the twelve months of the year, she would learn to budget her money. She didn't want to live in Le Mans. She needed to be away from her overbearing loving relatives –- away from her mother–if she was to ever grow up, she needed to be on her own.

Elodie Grabelle missed the hesitant trepidation. She forged ahead, "Because of your high GPA, they want you to take the position left open by Madame Ledou's retirement. Literature and writing classes." When the woman became aware of the look of consternation on the girl's face, she wanted to soothe her. "You can do it, Christine. Believe me, you can. And you'll be living with your family. The Cadivets are there in Le Mans, also. You and Claudette will be able to see each other frequently."

As she walked back to class to tell her news to Claudette. *Surely my friend won't be jealous; she'll be glad for me that I won't have to be alone in Coutance next year.* Christine's thoughts were unsettling. If she had her wish and taught in an isolated country school, perhaps she would be frightened. When she really faced facts, was she ready for a compound of several buildings–classrooms, a gym, a large porch on the playground–housing, foul-smelling toilets, the doors of which could hide an intruder. Was she ready to live alone in a secluded building where German soldiers on the prowl would know a woman's screams could not be heard from far away neighbors?

On the other hand, was she ready to live at home again? She'd been away for three busy years. She was no longer the sixteen year old her mother slapped when she went to the wrong church–the day Madeleine had sent her to represent her and to transmit her condolences to the bereaved who were working for her. That night in her bedroom mirror, a resentful daughter had studied the red marks on her left cheek. She had felt sorry for herself, but more so for the woman who had a short fuse and could not tell she regretted her asinine act of violence.

Christine had matured. She believed what Claudette told her: that Madeleine had really lashed at herself and her daughter had made a convenient scapegoat. Now that Christine would be living at home again, she would make a real effort to talk to her mother. She would tell her how much she loved her. Soon. *Yes, Mom, I love you. I think you love me too, don't you. . .?*

Unbeknownst to the girl, Madeleine Tourneau had promised herself she'd learn to control her temper. Christine was grown-up now. She couldn't be ordered about. Madeleine was very pleased with her younger daughter's academic achievements. Soon, she'd tell her how proud she was of her. Christine had graduated from college at nineteen with a prestigious teaching position in the best lycée in Le Mans–and would likely be promoted to Dean of the School of Literature in a few years. The girl was no longer an absent-minded teenager with nose in a book every moment of the day. *I'll do my best to communicate better with Christine from now on–woman to woman.*

CHAPTER 15

▼

RIGHT AFTER CHRISTMAS RECESS, IN JANUARY of 1944, Mademoiselle Tourneau came to work wearing her heart on her sleeve and a gorgeous solitaire diamond on the ring finger of her left hand. All day long, playfully, happily, she waved it under people's faces, "André and I are engaged. We'll get married as soon as the war ends. It couldn't be too long now. How do you like my ring?"

Inevitably someone ventured, "I'm surprised. I didn't know you were dating."

"I'm as surprised as you are. Almost. We never dated."

They did look perplexed. Fine. She didn't want to enlighten them. It was enough that her students accepted her readily now. No questions asked. As far as they were concerned, she lived in a different sphere. Outside of the classroom, her students and she had no common denominators. That's why she always gave more than one hundred percent, hoping she was reaching a couple of them in spite of the unavoidable distance between teachers and students.

Christine's engagement had been a surprise not only to strangers, but to her father, mother and sister as well. Christine had never let on that her grandparents were in the know. It would have meant trouble.

One evening between Christmas and New Year's, André had arrived as the Tourneaus were about to sit down to dinner. The three women were in the kitchen. When the bell rang at the front door, they heard Philippe greet the unexpected visitor in a voice pleasingly surprised, "Hi, my boy, it's good to see you."

"Hi, Mister Tourneau, I hope I'm not intruding."

"No. No. We're all glad to see you, André. How are your mother and your sisters? Well, I hope. I saw your grandfather yesterday."

"They are. Thank you."

By the time the men had crossed the hall to the living room, the women had joined them. That is, Madeleine and Nicole were shaking hands with André while Christine received the overcoat the unannounced guest had deposited on her arms, "Here, I can tell you want it," he joked.

"Yes. No. Yes." She departed to hang the heavy garment in the hall closet. André had given her time to gather her wits. He had come to ask her father for her hand in marriage. Her heart was beating so fast, everyone must hear it. *He's finally come.*

For once, Madeleine did not immediately tune in to the astounding circumstance. A dutiful hostess, she lamented, "I'm sorry, André. We'd invite you to dinner, but it's very skimpy. We didn't anticipate having a guest, you see."

Nicole glanced at her sister. *Oh, my,* she thought, *the closemouthed little sneak. She's not exactly caught unawares. She's got the look of the cat that caught the canary. It's going to be rather entertaining to find out what went on between those two. But, oh, Mother.*

"Oh, Mother, it doesn't matter," Christine was blabbering, nervously, "André knows there's a great shortage of food this winter. He won't mind sharing the casserole of potatoes au gratin, even without meat."

The man responded affably, "Not at all. You know what a good appetite I have, Christine, I'm starving. I'm always starving. I gladly accept."

Philippe sensed the three women needed time together, "Come, my boy. Let's go to my office. I'll dig up a bottle of pre-war Pernod." Something told him it was a special occasion. He was amused Christine had been so secretive about André. Those two had obviously met not very long ago–where and when?

Mother's question exactly, "When and where did the two of you plan this spur-of-the moment visit?" she asked reproachfully. Not waiting for an answer not forthcoming (Christine could not find words, she was at the same time very cold and deliciously warm all over), Madeleine persevered, "Tell us, Christine, why do you know that the man is always famished. He said you do."

"He came to the camp in Beaumont two years ago, and once again last summer."

"He did?"

"He is the head of the scouting groups in Normandy. He was checking all the camps." Her voice was shaky–her mother made her nervous.

"And Beaumont, in particular, I see. How long did he stay?"

"A couple of hours both times. That's all." She was beginning to be able to speak in a much stronger tone.

"And tonight he comes to pay us a call. He just happened to pass by. That's all."

"Please, Mom," Nicole begged, "let's listen to her."

The sisters exchanged looks of connivance. Sibling affection ran deep in their veins. Although she was irked Christine had not confided to her, Nicole was happy for her. Pleased an older man—as she thought of André Grassin—had fallen in love with her innocent, inexperienced sister. Praying the man will have the wisdom to teach her gently and the restraint to give her time to blossom. But would he?

Another look at Christine told her the young woman was ecstatic. That was enough. Nothing should mar her happiness. The moment was never to repeat itself—one's first love. The first man forever that: the first man, the first love.

Becoming aware their mother had not yet let up, Nicole repeated, "Mom, please, let's listen to her."

Madeleine glared at her daughters who were closing ranks against her, "I'm listening," she hissed.

Christine raised her chin up, "There's nothing to tell," she faltered. Then, suddenly, "Yes, there is. André and I are going to get married."

While the kitchen was plunged in profound silence, Philippe was at the door of the dining room. He called, "Christine, come here, sweetheart."

André put down his half-empty glass of milky Pernod with just a little tap water in it. He was smiling. He moved toward her. He took her trembling hands in his. Seeing uncertainty and hope in the man's darkened eyes, she knew he was nervous also. He looked up from her to Philippe and he settled on her pretty face aglow with anticipation, "I just asked your father for your hand in marriage," he said. As an afterthought, he added, "I hope it's all right by you."

Philippe burst out laughing.

Christine felt the tears running down on her burning cheeks. André searched his pocket for a handkerchief. A big white one. He wiped her face. Gently, he mumbled, "I just asked you to be my wife, darling, and it made you cry."

Philippe laughed again.

Christine's eyes were two shiny gems. Aquamarine today. At other times they were a shade of blue or green or amber. It depended on her emotions and the color of her blouse, André had noticed before. He pulled her to him. Her head barely reached his shoulder. He kissed the blond curls. She smelled delicious. She had not been wearing perfume that day at camp. "Hum," he murmured, "I'll have to learn the name of that." With his thumbs under her chin, he raised her face. He bent down to kiss her mouth.

Discreetly, Philippe Tourneau left the room.

Nicole ran to the garden. She returned with two squishy heads of lettuce—the only kind known in Normandy.

In the kitchen, her eyebrows raised questioningly, Madeleine looked at her husband's face, and for once, she had nothing to say. She heard him make a phone call to the butcher. Yes, for that very special occasion, the man was certain he could send five veal chops right away.

Still silent, her stiff back an indication of her disapproval, Madeleine walked to the pantry. She returned with a jar of peas. Nicole walked in from the bakery next door with a loaf of almost edible-looking bread and the assurance a *Viennoise* would be sent over in about an hour. By then, they'd be ready for a special bottle of Champagne from Philippe's secret cellar shelves.

The following day, at different times, both André's grandfather and mother called their congratulations. At least Charles did. Marcelle Grassin's voice was hostile. Christine was staring at her beautiful diamond, about to tell the woman how much she liked it when Marcelle said, "You can thank my mother-in-law; she's the one who gave you her own engagement ring. It was not my idea. It still is not my idea." She hung up.

Christine kept on admiring her ring. The woman's antipathy did not ruffle her feathers. She was marrying André, not his family. It was a miracle. For years she'd known the miracle would take place. It did. The young woman was so euphoric, nothing could ever mar her happiness.

To assuage Christine's concerns for André's safety, Nicole had told her to concentrate on her plans for the future and to forget that her fiancé was in danger in the maquis. "He made it safely to our house to get engaged to you, didn't he? He was careful. He's not going to let himself be caught by the Germans."

"Dad was amazed he had come to the summer camp in Beaumont twice," Christine added.

"See what I mean, sis? The man's too smart to let the Krauts get him."

CHAPTER 16

▼

THAT DAY, THOUSANDS OF AMERICAN B-17s flew over the city…so many that at nine o'clock, they turned evening twilight into complete darkness. A deep, heavy, continuous sound of a moving cloud of death and unremitting destruction.

Nicole was visiting her fiancé's parents in the country.

Philippe and Christine were foolish enough to go upstairs to view the fireworks in the air. The German anti-aircraft guns were shooting up their rather inefficient defenses. Their searchlights illuminated the sky. The American 'flying fortresses' were sending flares down to frame their target. It was quite a show. Mesmerized, Philippe and Christine remained at the window.

Downstairs, Madeleine Tourneau grabbed a book of store accounts she'd been working on–and her corset–and she started in the direction of the trench Philippe had dug according to the instructions of Civil Defense and his own remembrance of the Great War when he was a young soldier in the Ardennes.

Christine's mother did not make it to the shelter. She was hit in the head by a piece of shrapnel. Because it did not bleed, at first Christine didn't realize the gravity of the wound. After Philippe and Christine deposited her on the couch in the living room, she remained unconscious.

Three days after the bombing, Philippe brought his daughters to his office, "There is something I must tell you, my children."

"We know," Nicole murmured, "Mom is dying."

"Yes," he said very sadly. "And because your mother may only be with us a few more days, I must speak now."

The two sisters waited in silence. Nicole reached for Christine's hand.

They looked at their father, who continued, "Christine, you're going to be very upset."

"What could be worse, Dad, than watching Mother on her deathbed?" the grieving daughter asked, shaking with emotion.

Philippe swallowed hard a couple of times. He spoke slowly and heavily. "Christine, you won't be allowed to send for a priest to give your mother the last rites."

Christine screamed, "You're crazy. What do you mean *not allowed*, Father? Of course, Mom will receive extreme unction."

The man stood up. He moved restlessly around his office. He came back to position himself in front of his daughters. He sucked in a long, audible breath. "We were not married in church. Your mother had divorced her first husband."

"Divorced," both girls said at the same time. And then again, "Divorced?"

Christine hissed, "Impossible. It can't be true."

Nicole speculated aloud, "If the man has died since, Mom would have been a widow."

"He is alive and well," Philippe affirmed. "He, too, has another family now."

Madeleine Tourneau never regained consciousness. She died in the morning of the ninth day. A distraught Christine went to get the advice of the parish priest. Although Mother Superior told the girl not to hope, she accompanied her to her audience with the bishop of Le Mans. Madeleine Tourneau did not go to her last resting place with the soothing prayers of the church. When she divorced her first husband, the woman was excommunicated from the church. Her body was taken directly from the house to her grave in the non-consecrated part of the cemetery. Christine swore she'd never set foot in a Catholic church, ever again.

CHAPTER 17

▼

ONE NIGHT AT THE END OF April, André used the key Philippe had given him to the garden gate. (Just in case he needed a place to hide.) He threw a stone into Christine's bedroom window. Their signal. She glanced at the clock on the nightstand—three o'clock in the morning. In her pajamas, barefooted, her hair uncombed, she ran downstairs to let him into the kitchen.

The man shut the door very quietly. For several long minutes he stood silently with his strong hands clamped on her shoulders. Trying to control his galloping heartbeat. The acrid perspiration of fear and exertion was overwhelming to Christine: the blood rushed to her ears. She felt dizzy. She wrapped her arms around him.

When their eyes got used to the surrounding darkness in the familiar kitchen, the man cursed. "A close call. Damn it. A close call."

Christine waited, silently. Her heart was beating as fast as his.

"A close call. This is Plan B. Thank God, your father gave me the key to the gate."

"Plan B?" she asked softly.

"The Krauts got there much too fast. Plan A was out. The other two guys went their way. I hope they made it. I might never know."

"I heard the explosion. It shook the house. Where was it?" she asked, before she had time to remember she wasn't supposed to.

"We blew up the German Communication Center on Government Square."

"Some people are saying the FFI are making too much trouble too soon," she ventured timidly.

"We can't wait for the Allies to disembark. Our job is to weaken the German Werhmarcht before D-Day."

"D-Day?"

"Soon. Very soon now. Things are about to change," he mumbled in an enigmatic tone of voice.

As if the two of them and their respective families had already talked it over and agreed on a wedding date, the man said suddenly, "We're getting married Friday night. Pack for the weekend. The papers are ready."

"Married? This Friday? At the camp?"

"Father Paul will marry us. We'll have a choice of ready-made witnesses willing to sign on the line," he added, chuckling.

"Married?" Her voice was shaky.

"Be there at six o'clock. The men have planned a real banquet with plenty of wine, you can be sure—and I'll be hungry," he laughed, "For food and for my woman."

He left before daybreak. Daylight would have made it impossible for him to return to the forest of Maneval safely.

At breakfast with her sister and father, Christine ignored her bowl of lukewarm make-believe *café au lait*. She reached across the table for her sister's hand. She squeezed it and murmured, "André and I are getting married on Friday."

Nicole said softly, "I hope you know what you're doing, Sis."

"In war-time, people do war-time things," Philippe said, shrugging.

Nicole said a second time, "I hope you know what you're doing, Christine."

"I do."

I don't believe you do, Nicole thought. *You, my dear little sister, haven't even thought for a moment about what comes after the ceremony. The tall, handsome guy is the answer to your girlish prayers. Your wish. Your dream come true. What do you know of him, Sis? You could be in for a rude awakening.* All she ventured aloud was, "Be careful, Sis, we love you."

At Maneval, at six o'clock on Friday afternoon, Christine didn't tell anyone about her encounter with an enemy patrol just as she was about to turn into a secluded country lane leading to the camp.

"Halt!" the German officer shouted.

She stopped, one foot still on the pedal, the other on the ground.

"*Wo gehst du hin?*" "Where are you going?"

"Food shopping."

"Shopping?" the man's skeptical eyes roaming the field in the middle of nowhere.

Christine was prepared. She stepped down. She opened one of the two bags on her back wheel. It contained a very dead looking skinny hare.

The German guffawed, "Some black market! A puny wild rabbit." With a wave of his hand, he gestured to the soldiers, "Let's go." They departed.

Christine didn't tell André how close the Germans had been. She shuddered to think the patrol could have kept on walking down the hedgerow leading directly to the camp. Perhaps because they'd stopped to question a civilian who was going from farm to farm to scrounge for food, they had turned around. She was promptly surrounded by cheerful, boisterous men in a party mood. Obviously they had not waited for the bride to arrive before they uncorked the wine.

The marriage ceremony lasted a mere five minutes. The young priest was nervous. André was not a religious man, but he believed Christine needed the blessing of her church, even after she had declared she couldn't care less. Because he did not have a wedding band to slip on his wife's finger, he simply turned her engagement ring around. She smiled sweetly to her husband.

Next to André, an older man, who was a town councilman, held the two certificates the witnesses would sign. The legal document was the secular one. The French government does not recognize the religious marriage. Both papers were given to Father Paul for safeguarding at the nearby rectory, where the newlyweds would spend two nights in a guest room.

The wedding guests were warned to keep their voices low. However, after many glasses of the local wines, they were rambunctious. They plied the happy bride with food and drinks. Christine couldn't have swallowed a mouthful if she tried. She'd become aware of the meaning of the crude jokes. *This was her wedding night.* She passed her loaded plates and her full glasses to her new husband, who seemed bottomless.

By midnight, most of the brave men were snoring right at their places, their heads down on the picnic tables. The smart ones had already gone to their tents. Christine was the only female: no mother, sister, girlfriend. She wanted to go home this very minute. She was not ready to continue with this...this marriage ceremony...the approaching bed-time...the stranger who was her husband.

None of the men around seemed to resent the fact their leader would have his woman in his bed. Perhaps it was because Claude's uncompromising attitude and steady fairness had earned him the respect of everyone in the camp.

Some of the warriors were right now making love to their wife or girlfriend. They had sneaked out during the drawn-out dinner. They'd be back before the muted roll call in the early dawn. Their intransigent leader could not have denied the unasked-for permission. It was wrong. It could be calamitous, endangering the whole group if one of the men got caught, but they were gone.

André reached for his glass of wine, miraculously full to the brim all evening long. He stared at the beautiful, shy Mrs. André Grassin on his right. He put a long arm around her and pressed her tiny hand reassuringly. All encumbering thoughts of war, danger, and treason vanished from his feverish mind.

Father Paul stood up. He squeezed André's shoulder gently, "I think you should turn in."

The priest took Christine's hand on one side and André's on the other. He led them to the rectory and to the door of their room.

During the long night, the young woman was kept awake with the ignominious knowledge that in the room next to theirs, Father could hear the springs of the complaining mattress advertise every time her new husband made love to her. So many hurtful times. Christine could not sleep. The man's sweaty body stuck to hers in the middle of the old, uncomfortable feather bed. Several times she tried to pull away, but the slant brought her back to him. He would chuckle and grab her buttocks in his hand.

The next day, being in the midst of all the men made it one of the longest days in her life. She pretended not to hear their crude jokes. She did not wish to catch the furtive looks of concern on the faces of older men. She felt a trickle of sweat running down her back: there would be a second inexorable night. This time she told herself she was ready for the shameful act.

Two days later, the honeymoon was over. Christine Tourneau went back to Le Mans –– Mrs. André Grassin.

CHAPTER 18

▼

No one knew how the army of Charles de Gaulle in Sicily communicated with people in Occupied territory. The old saying "no news is good news" was more than ever a truism. Bad news managed to get through. Philippe Tourneau was informed that his only son, Jacques, had died on the battlefield leading men into a freedom *he* would never get to enjoy. Nicole and Christine huddled for hours in total silence on the couch in the living room where, less than two months before, their mother had lingered between life and death.

A week after her wedding, Christine Grassin returned to the camp in Maneval. A very wet spring, an uninterrupted around-the-clock Allied bombardment, a deep grief, a lack of sleep, and a perpetual worry about her husband...all had glued her brain into a mess of useless wires—she had reached her quota. She didn't feel pain any more. She was numb. She told herself she didn't care what could happen to her now, but she needed André's arms around her. She needed his love. His strength. She knew only that she had to go to him.

The forest of Maneval belonged to a friendly couple she had met several times. The old man had seen her arriving. He'd been expecting her. He put a hand on her bike to stop her. He begged, "Don't go in, girl." Suddenly, Christine came out of her unobservant distraction to realize that the camp had been destroyed.

"I must go and see," she moaned. "I must." Her heart was in her throat. She was choking.

"Please don't go in, child. There's nothing you can do for them now."

"I have to see for myself! I've got to see!"

She let go of the bicycle. Her brain frozen, her mind a complete blank, she stood where the busy camp had been. The place was a tangle of debris: broken branches, tree trunks, strewn camouflage net, pots, boots, pieces of equipment. No human voice. A terrible silence.

The ancient farmer murmured that a division of German panzers had bulldozed the camp the night before. Perhaps first the Germans had captured the Frenchmen and taken the prisoners with them, but no one knew. If the bodies were buried under there, it could be weeks before it was safe to try and find out. The small wood house where the priest had lived was burned. Nothing was left but a pile of ashes.

CHAPTER 19

▼

PHILIPPE TOURNEAU WAS MAKING MONEY. HE loved making money. In his defense, his reluctant sister-in-law told herself Philippe was a robust man. He was a man of action, still in his prime. The world of business was his salvation. It took him from pain and heartbreak to hope for a new beginning.

On the afternoon of June first, Christine walked into her father's office unannounced. Immediately she realized she shouldn't be there. Philippe's secretary was stone-faced, her hand trembled on the ledger, her eyes wide with fear. There was a German S.S. in the room. The protective squads of the Schutz Staffel were as feared as the Gestapo. Both groups had been subjected to continuous indoctrination during the formative years of their adolescence. The men were empty shells. Instruments of terror. Implacable.

Through the window behind her father's desk, Christine saw two Gestapo agents in animated conversation on the patio.

"Ah, here you are, Nicole," Philippe said, too cheerfully. "Those men are waiting to speak to your sister. Do you know where Christine is?"

"No, Father, I don't. I believe she's visiting friends in Avreville," her voice amazingly steady as she walked straight to the back door of the room, pretending to be looking for something she needed. She kept on walking. Through the back yard. Through the connecting alley between her father's office and their house.

All the while, words of one Gestapo man kept repeating themselves in her frantic mind. Unaware that their prey understood German, the policeman had said, "I believe that's the girl we want. They're not fooling me. But we don't have a picture of the two sisters. Let's go. We'll keep on watching the house. We'll get her; it won't take long."

On her magnificent bicycle–huge "balloon" tires, six gears, twin leather bags–Christine pedaled on and on for five hours. She arrived at the beloved old house in Avreville just before nightfall. Blanche and Pascal were waiting for her. Anxious. What if she'd been stopped by the Germans?

They knew their granddaughter was on her way because Philippe and his father had devised a silent communication—three rings on the telephone—if ever the girl had to leave Le Mans in a hurry. The day had come.

Blanche believed Christine should eat a little, but she didn't want food. She wasn't hungry. The adrenaline kick had subsided. She was physically and emotionally drained. Barely able to stand on her shaky legs.

Both grandparents realized the young woman was reaching the breaking point. She looked exhausted, numb, devoid of feelings. When Blanche drew her a bath, without a protest, Christine let her grandmother pamper her just as she had done years ago. Clutching a tiny piece of pre-war soap in her hand, the woman lathered the girl's tired arms and legs. She scrubbed her back. The tight knots of nerves loosened slowly. She did not rush. She could feel the girl unwind. Light slowly returned into her dull eyes.

Finally, Blanche held Christine's hand to pull her out of the tub and onto her feet. She rubbed her dry in a sweet smelling towel. She slipped a fragrant linen nightdress over her head, knowing her modesty didn't permit her to sleep naked. She tucked her in as she had done so many times in the past. Instantly, Christine closed her eyes and fell asleep.

At Avreville, for the next five days, the people never knew whether the sirens rang for the beginning or for the end of an attack… the seconds, the minutes, the hours were a blur of suspended waiting. Planes flew overhead. Bombs dropped.

When, on June sixth, in the roaring of guns and deafening anti-aircraft shooting and earth-shaking tank maneuvers, the BBC told them the Americans had landed on their Normandy beaches, all they could do was wait. Christine and her grandparents waited while more and more Americans disembarked. Four more days went by without real news. They didn't dare venture out of the house. The BBC kept on repeating that the Allies had landed on the shores of the English Channel. That's all they knew.

One morning, Christine stood looking at the huge trees on the school grounds right across from her bedroom. A volley of shots rang out—ran–tack, tack, tack—around the frame of the window, one last shot breaking the top pane of glass.

Before she realized what was happening, her grandfather had pulled her down on the floor. "A sniper," he spat. Snipers were in many trees. Obviously that one had not wanted to kill the French girl at the window, but perhaps rather teach her a lesson in safety.

CHAPTER 20

▼

ON JUNE FOURTEENTH, A TENANT FARMER came to see Pascal Tourneau. "The Americans are only four miles from here. A column of tanks stopped at the bottom of the hill of Saint Mars."

"It won't be easy for them to take Avreville," Pascal explained to Christine and Blanche. He was worried, "There are lots of 'Boches' still in the village. Their panzers are ready to hit the Yanks like clay pigeons the moment they set foot on the plateau. The Krauts have the advantage; they see the Yanks coming up the hill long before they get here."

During the wakeful night, the German artillery on one side, and the liberators on the other side, dug huge craters in the orchard. The old house valiantly resisted. "It's been here for five hundred years or more," murmured Blanche, her arms embracing the girl. "It's going to still be here for your own kids some day."

At dawn, unable to restrain herself any longer, Christine declared, "I'm going to welcome the Americans."

"Don't," Pascal yelled. "Don't. Stay here."

She didn't hear him. She was gone.

She went downhill full speed, her wide cotton skirt puffed up by the wind, powerless to slow down her flight. She literally collapsed into the arm of a man who shouted angrily, "Easy, lady, easy."

The long arm of the man steadied the girl and the bicycle. The American was frowning. He was very irritated. "I wonder what you think you're doing, young lady," he hissed.

"I came to see you," Christine said, nonplussed.

A bunch of soldiers she had not yet noticed yelled at the same time, "She speaks English."

The officer waved them back to their place. "You do speak English, girl. That's going to be helpful," he admitted, somewhat mollified.

51

The soldiers had remained near them. Others joined them. More came. They were gorgeous. So young. Simply gorgeous. Dirty faces. Tired faces. Big white teeth in flashing smiles. Friendly eyes. The Americans.

Christine grabbed the twig the lieutenant handed her. On the dirt on the side of the road, she drew a map of the streets of Avreville.

Very astonished, it seemed, the officer inquired, "What's that road doing here? I don't have that one on my map."

"My grandfather allowed his tenants to build it only two years ago. It cuts through our land. The farmers can get to the silos and the market places much faster than before."

"Well, I'll be..." the man said. The soldiers burst out laughing.

As Christine got back on her bike, the lieutenant shouted, "Stay inside your grandparents' house, girlie, you hear?"

Taking the advice of the American at the head of a column of tanks bearing a star instead of a swastika, Christine pedaled up the hill under cover of the hazelnut bushes in the narrow country lanes. Near the ancient manor house, she called out, "Grandpa, Grandma, they're here, they're here. The Americans are here."

Pascal didn't have the heart to scold her.

CHAPTER 21

▼

WHEN THE SCHOOLS REOPENED IN OCTOBER of 1944, Le Mans city streets were once again filled with men in uniforms. Not Germans. Not French soldiers. Men from another country who spoke another foreign language.

The male scenery had made a complete one hundred and eighty degree turn: the inveterate–or so it had seemed to Christine–feldgrau was gone. The hard, dour faces, the guttural sounds–all had been replaced by the contagious smiles of the American boys and the various intriguing accents of the vast "*Amérique.*" The GI's were good-natured. Chummy. And a girl didn't have to dissemble because she understood what they were saying.

Whereas Christine had kept an uncompromising attitude and a stern face when a German called her "*Gnädigue Fräulein,*" she quickly bubbled with the Americans. They called a girl "honey." A funny term of endearment, she said to them, "It's sticky, gluey, overly sweet." They loved it. They laughed. They were congenial and friendly.

The swastikas were gone.

Place de la République was reborn.

Liberté, Egalité, Fraternité reappeared on municipal buildings.

In the soldiers' clubs, the GI's––short for "Government Issues," they explained––danced with their guests to the tunes of a "stockade band"–the musicians were American soldiers who had been thrown into the stockade by their own military police for various infractions of the military rules. The jazz music they played had been unheard in France until now. The French girls loved the wild dance called jitterbug. The envious French boys joined other inhabitants who stood fifteen deep in front of the building to hear the exhilarating sounds from the Americans blowing their trumpets in the band.

Christine volunteered to be a translator at the American Red Cross Club, Place de la République. It seemed appropriate that the democratic Americans

53

had taken over a beautiful building which the German officers had occupied for years and started using it for their enlisted men. It was the tallest–three stories high–hotel in Le Mans.

Suddenly, it had become four stories high. It took Christine awhile to understand why she would frequently knock on a wrong door. The Red Cross director Lois Latham, a stout, pleasant woman with a slow South Carolina accent, explained to Christine that unlike the French who have a special name for the ground floor (*le rez-de-chaussée*), Americans call the street level the first floor. It confused Christine at first, but not for long. Miss Natham complimented her. "You got it, honey. Don't forget my office is on the third floor." Christine silently corrected the American woman, *Honey goes to the second floor where your office is located.*

Dressed in black from head to toe, Christine remained behind the information desk. She knew she was not to join in the dance. The old biddies on the balcony facing her desk would waste no time reporting her vile behavior to the principal of Lycée Jean Jaurès. They were chaperoning. They couldn't possibly watch every exit door in the huge place, but they sure could keep an eye on a young teacher in deep mourning.

There was no doubt in Christine's mind the chaperones were shocked by her presence. Word had gotten around she was wearing black because her mother and her brother had died in the war. "She should not be here, my dear." There was music. Dancing. Laughter. Young men. "She is in mourning. Her place is at home. Not here."

In her own heart, Christine felt deeply ambivalent. It amused her to realize that if the women knew she was also a war widow, they would be even more adamant. Ready to stone her.

But that, they did not know. Except for Lois Natham, no one in the Red Cross knew. The conflicting emotions in Christine's soul forced her to live a double life. At the club she was cool, composed, detached. She viewed the place as she would a stage set. It brought her a breath of much-needed fresh air. For the duration of an evening, she became a spectator entertained by the unfamiliar surroundings. She was fascinated, transported into a make-believe world.

In her bed at night, she cried and cried ceaselessly. She cursed André for leaving her before they even had time to get to know each other. She blamed the man for his untimely death. For the shattered dream. For the too fleeting moments of miracle —— the love that burned in spite of the odds. Yes, she had had her miracle and it was hers alone to cherish. For one week she had called herself Madame André Grassin.

The next day, once again, she would rise to live in the present. .

.Mademoiselle Christine Tourneau–teacher of foreign literature by day, Red Cross translator by night.

At the information desk one evening, a soldier asked, "Honey, can you tell me what's playing at the theater on the third floor?"

"Hold Me Tight."

She wondered what on earth made the boy jump over the counter so fast to hold her in a crushing embrace.

To the delight of the onlookers.

As Christine had expected, Philippe Tourneau reprimanded his younger daughter for her shameful lack of decorum. (Nicole had decided to remain in Toulouse with her fiancé's parents while they were awaiting his return.) "I don't care what they say about me at the Red Cross, Dad."

"You should, darling. You don't want André's mother to hear your reputation is tarnished."

"Father, André is dead."

"Presumably. You need to wait for the formal death certificate."

"Which I'll never get since there is no longer a marriage certificate. Dad, remember the house burst into flames that night...."

Philippe sighed. His parents and he believed the ceremony had taken place as Christine described. And the marriage consummated. What could one do now except wait?

CHAPTER 22

▼

THERE WERE NOT ENOUGH HOURS IN a day, as far as Christine was concerned. She was always well-prepared for her literature classes. She corrected her long papers on time. She had been irked when a college professor didn't return the students' essays until the last minute. Some never. It was not her style. She was very professional.

Every week she put in twenty hours or more at the American Red Cross. One of her duties was to accompany the Military Police to the scene of an accident between a French vehicle and an American one. The British especially caused havoc with their driving on the wrong side of the road. They forgot the French and the Americans drive, not on the left, but on the right. Several children became victims of British driving errors when the war was over. For those families, the war was not over.

At home, it fell upon Christine to give orders to their daily maid, the laundress, and the weekly cleaning woman. At night, returning from the Red Cross, the girl often entered an empty, dark house. She didn't know where her father spent four or five evenings a week. She never asked. In a long distance telephone conversation, Nicole had said emphatically, "Father does not need us. Neither me, nor you. Stop fretting about him."

One morning, Philippe came to the kitchen looking for his daughter, "I will have two guests for lunch tomorrow. Please, sweetheart, plan something nice."

Certain her father had invited his wife's sister, who also lived in Le Mans, Christine called her Aunt Sophie for help with the menu, and to ask who the extra person might be.

"Darling, I'm not the woman your father is entertaining." After a lengthy pause, in a hesitant voice, Aunt Sophie suggested, "Why don't you ask him?" And again after another silence, "Do come by my house this evening, Christine. I must talk to you."

"Talk?"

"About lunch tomorrow."

Puzzled, Christine agreed. " I'll be in before ten o'clock if that's all right by you."

Later in the evening, Sophie's very angry niece shrieked, "My father has a mistress and he's bringing her to *our* house for me to meet her? Is that what you're telling me, Aunt Sophie?"

"To *his* house, sweetheart. He *is* a widower. Single."

"I won't be there when the woman comes."

"Please, Christine, say you will. It wouldn't change anything, and you'd only create an ugly scandal. Tell Marie to make a pot roast. Buy a few apples for dessert. Make a cup of ersatz coffee. We still can't find any real coffee."

The woman's name was Odette Breau. She was petite, slim, attractive. She wore her thick auburn hair in a contrived knot on top of her head and wore very high-spiked heels. She appeared to be fifteen or twenty years younger than Philippe Tourneau. She came with extra benefits, however: she brought her twelve-year old son named Pierre from a previous marriage. Supposedly, she was a widow. Nastily, Christine told herself she'd never been married and was a low-class unwed mother.

Pierre looked as unhappy as Christine. His brown eyes were dull, afraid, perplexed. When Christine caught him looking at her, he shifted his glare back to his plate. To her credit, the mother also seemed ill at ease. The only relaxed person was Philippe, who coaxed the youngster, "Eat, my boy. You need meat. You're a growing boy." Astonished, Christine got the impression her father was taking this new ready-made paternity very seriously. She was baffled.

CHAPTER 23

▼

BY POPULAR DEMAND, THE BAND OF the stockade came more and more often. Christine's friends joked that *she* was the reason why the Red Cross Club of Le Mans had two or three dances each week instead of one. Every time, Captain Brian O'Connell of the Military Police came to the Red Cross Club: he was on duty.

With the eager help of Lois Latham, the tall, good looking American officer had seemingly convinced the young French translator that she should accept his invitation to dinner at the Officers' Club. Painstakingly Lois and Brian assured Christine that the Officers' Club was in a private house and none of the French women there would look down on her.

And so Captain O'Connell and Miss Tourneau became one more couple who shared tables with other regulars.

The men had stopped asking why Christine always wore a black dress or occasionally a black suit with a white blouse. They all agreed with Brian, that with her light complexion, her feline green eyes, and her blond hair, she was very chic at all times. She was slim, always well coiffed and manicured. So were all the French women at the Officer's club.

Inwardly, Brian was amused when he saw Christine's eyes follow on the sly the quiet exit of a woman and her escort. They'd return an hour or two later for a night cap dubbed "one for the road."

"You're not asking where they're going," he teased once.

She blushed from ear to ear. That's one of the things he liked about her. She blushed so easily. He pushed on, "Well, sweetheart, don't you want to know?"

She stammered, "How many rooms are there upstairs?"

"A great many. Would you like me to show you around the place?" Half mocking, half serious.

"No, thank you," she replied in her prim convent voice.

Brian laughed. Would he have been disappointed if she had accepted? She may have slept with a French warrior a couple of times. She was still in many ways a virgin. He loved what he called her proper manners.

The food at those private parties was superb. Still, Christine could not enjoy it. The smell of the tempting dishes nauseated her. It disturbed Brian. "Force yourself, darling. You're too skinny."

"I'm not skinny. I'm thin."

"Bony. Let's put a little meat on those elegant bones. The war's over. There's plenty where it comes from, believe me. You need not be hungry ever again. Eat."

He pinched her rib right under her heart and tickled her, his hand moving up to hold her breast. She slapped his hand gently. She looked around. Nobody was paying any attention to them. Brian was amused by her reaction.

It occurred to her she was not really in her element. With the exception of one young French girl she vaguely knew, the women in the Saturday night revelry were all quite older and experienced. First the Germans, then the Americans. They were lured by the music, the romance, the food, the gorgeous men, the lust (the money, perhaps), the desire to be taken to the land of plenty where the shelves in the stores would display food, soap, shampoo, clothes, leather goods, lingerie, food, food, food.

To bring her back to the moment, Brian rubbed his knuckles gently on Christine's cheeks, "Darling, don't think. Relax. Try some of the delicious prime ribs of beef. From the great state of Texas."

"Tell me about Texas," she asked. "No, better yet, tell me about Boston."

The unexpected question startled him. Was she leading him on? Brian O'Connell was falling deeply in love with an elusive French woman. Not a woman. A girl. She might have been near her twenty-third birthday, but she was untouched, private, pure, naive. She was natural, authentic, complex. She was a puzzle, an enigma, a mystery: Brian felt he was in love for the first time in his life.

Philippe Tourneau was irked. He did not like to see the big American car parked for longer and longer periods of time in front of his house. He'd been told the officer drove himself nowadays. No chauffeur. Christine in the front seat next to him, naturally. Where did they go between the closing of the soldiers' club at eleven and midnight?

If he had asked his daughter, she'd have dispelled his fatherly worries (or would he believe her?) She didn't belong in the group of young women the GI's at the club called "penicillin broads." They frequently joked about a necessary visit to the military dispensary for which they had other names—not very high class. And about so many—or so they claimed—too-readily-available "chicks." She would have been so vexed if she had known that to them she was an "officer's slut."

The fear of an unwanted pregnancy always lurked in the back of the minds of the "nice" girls who claimed to have been date raped. Still, Christine believed it was the woman who led the dance: *she* was in charge. When Captain O'Connell's hand wandered inside her bra, Christine took it out silently. The man groaned—seemingly both annoyed and amused—then he would usually declare it was time to call it a night.

Sighing with a practiced display of disappointment, he'd reach across the car to push open the door on her side. "Time to turn in, kid," he'd snicker. Always the perfect gentleman, he came out of the car, reached her door as she stepped out. He walked her to the front steps of the house and insisted on a long, expert kiss right under the bright lanterns. The neighbors be dammed. And her old man also.

One morning at breakfast, Philippe declared, "I don't like the fact that people are undoubtedly talking about my daughter."

"They're talking about *me*, Dad? What about you and Odette Breau?"

Philippe had no answer. He stormed out of the dining room. On his way, he banged the door. It reverberated in Christine's heart. While Nicole and she were growing up, their father never shouted at them. Like most fathers in those days, he did not take a great interest in his young children. Madeleine was the disciplinarian. She also made the decisions. She ruled. It allowed her spouse to go through family life with a pleasant, noncommittal smile on his handsome face.

Now that her mother was no longer there to steer each of them in the direction she deemed right, Christine deeply missed the forbidding woman who had never been a companion, nor—God forbid—a playmate. Madeleine Tourneau had been a great example of self-contained vitality. She went from morning to night with purpose. She was fully immersed in her work. She was contented. She was being herself.

Christine realized she had inherited from her mother's ability to take hold of her life. She wanted to live every moment with zest, be it studies, business, relaxation, relationships. She was becoming her own woman. She alone mattered.

CHAPTER 24

▼

THE WEEK AFTER EASTER SUNDAY IN nineteen forty-five, Claudette Cadivet married her childhood sweetheart. For a while, the young woman planned to live with her in-laws. Then Jack's father would retire and the younger man would manage the restaurant "Chez Antoine," rebaptizing it "Chez Jack."

"I can live with this arrangement for a while," Claudette explained to Christine on the day of the wedding, "but not for long. I want my own house to raise the daughter we'll have one day."

"You've got your life so well-planned," the bridesmaid said wistfully.

"Christine, don't be sad on my wedding day, please, or I'll cry with you."

"Let's not feel sorry for little me, Claudette, I'll do all right."

"Please, tell me you're not going to marry the American from Boston."

"I might, if he asks me."

"Don't. André will return from wherever he is. It won't be the first time. We've read lots of stories in literature about soldiers supposedly killed in battle who suddenly came back."

With a trace of bitterness, Christine cut her off, "We're not talking fiction, Claudette."

"I know," she sighed. "Please, Christine, don't go away. Stay in France. You'll meet another Frenchman some day."

"If it makes you feel better, Brian hasn't asked me to marry him."

"And if he does?"

"I might accept. What's to keep me here?"

Claudette pouted, "I refuse to think about it on my wedding day."

"One thing for sure, we shall always be friends. Always. It's a promise," Christine affirmed with deep conviction.

CHAPTER 25

▼

ONE MONTH LATER, ON A VERY pretty day in May, the melodious bells of the little church of Saint Thomas rang for the marriage of Philippe Tourneau and Odette Breau. Christine attended her father's wedding only because her Aunt Sophie had been so insistent. In a long green silk gown, she was walking with Nicole toward the church when suddenly she fainted. One of Philippe's taxicab drivers took her to Sophie's house where she remained in bed for three days, drifting in and out of sleep. She was completely oblivious to the passing of time or to the voices of concern whispered around her. Finally one seemed to bring her to the surface of wakefulness.

"You have a phone call, Christine. Please take it," pleaded Aunt Sophie.

"A phone call?" Christine answered in a drowsy voice.

The woman giggled, "There have been several in the last three days, but I can't answer that one."

"Why not?"

"Listen, child."

Christine took the phone. She sat up on the pillows her aunt was fluffing behind her back.

A male voice asked in English, "Are you still alive, Christine?"

"Of course, I am. Obviously you are aware of that."

"That's good news," replied Captain O'Connell of Boston. And before the young woman had a chance to hang up on him, he added "Are you coming to the Red Cross today, or do I come and pull you out of bed myself?"

"How did you know where to find me?"

I visited with your sister yesterday. She gave me your aunt's address and phone number. So, tell me, what's it going to be? You meet me in Lois Natham's office at five or I come to help you get dressed," he finished with a suggestive laugh.

"I'll be there at five," she answered meekly.

At five fifteen, when she walked into the office of the Red Cross director, Captain O'Connell stood up. He took her hand in his. He pirouetted her around. He was visibly discouraged, "Look at you, you've managed to lose the two or three pounds I worked so hard to put on those bones of yours."

"I couldn't eat."

"Lois, are we going to let this beautiful girl starve herself to death because her forty-eight year old father decided to wed a good-looking widow who's only thirty-five and has a son?" His voice was ponderous and very serious, but his eyes were merry, revealing his mocking intent.

Lois was grinning.

Christine was not amused, "How do you know so much about my family?" she asked, in a daze. Then she remembered the man had spent time at her house with Nicole. She hoped her father had not been at home.

"Marry me, Christine. That's the solution to our problem," the man bent down to whisper in her ear.

"Marry you? Our problem?" Then recovering some of her wits, "What problem?"

"Well, you see, Christine, a man must take care of you. I'm the one to do it. But *you* can't be in Le Mans, France, and *I* in Boston, U.S.A. So we get married; that solves the problem." Apparently he had considered the irrefutability of the argument.

"We get married; that solves the problem," she repeated meekly, echoing his words, not quite grasping the significance of the statement. Or did she?

Brian was already shouting his joy. "Lois, you heard her. We're engaged."

His exuberance was contagious. Both Lois and Christine laughed.

Brian wasted no time, "Let's go see your father."

"My father?" she said without thinking.

"I must ask for your hand in marriage."

"No," she stuttered. "No...don't...do it...You must not do that..."

Very quietly, Lois left the room.

Brian took his fiancée in his arms, "It's all right, darling. This is not a repeat of a previous occurrence. Neither for you, nor for me. This is a first for both of us. This is us, sweetheart, don't ever forget."

She quieted down. Brian kissed the top of her head. He held her silently for a long moment. His breath fluffed her hair. His male scent stirred her. A shiver ran down her spine. She moaned. She said slowly, "Let's go and tell Philippe Tourneau his daughter Christine is going to marry an American lawyer and she'll live in Boston, Massachusetts."

Brian's heart pinched. He hoped to God Christine was not thinking about some sort of revenge. He shrugged; he wanted this woman. He would not probe into her own reasons to become his wife. Perhaps on his part it was lust as well as love, a desire to parade a beautiful, foreign, exotic bride among friends and associates. She would be a useful partner who'd help him accomplish his most secret professional ambitions.

CHAPTER 26

▼

JUST AS CHRISTINE ANTICIPATED, PHILIPPE TOURNEAU was not thrilled by the news. He was bitter, "You're angry with me because I remarried. Because Odette is younger than your mother. Because I have a new son to raise."

Christine stood in front of her father in mute agreement. There was some truth to his allegations. For herself, she needed to add a few more that were hers exclusively: she was anxious to leave France because it would shut a firm door on the past, it would close a miserable chapter of death and more death, it would open a large view on a completely new vista. A new beginning. A new life. And it would be an end to who she was in France.

When she informed her girlfriends she was engaged to marry an American lawyer and move to Boston, Massachusetts, many were envious. Life in Normandy held no thrills. Five miserable years of frustrated womanhood left their indelible traces of boredom, disappointment, sadness, depression. All the young women could see in the near future was more boredom and sadness. They agreed that if Christine was ever going to find the happiness she was entitled to have, it was in the new, bright, enchanted world of "Amérique."

Brian took Christine to buy an engagement ring. She selected a clear, deep-blue sapphire in a modern setting. She had returned André's grandmother's ring awhile back and had received no acknowledgment other than the signed postal receipt. Brian approved of her choice, "It's almost the color of your eyes, sweetheart. It will always remind me of Le Mans where we met. At home, I'll buy you a real diamond."

She didn't want one, but she didn't say it.

Brian elaborated, "I don't wish to spend a lot now, sweetheart. I'll leave all the cash I have with you when I'm sent home. Spend it on your trousseau while you're waiting for permission from the army to join me in Boston. We'll get married as soon as you get there."

Brian O'Connell was jubilant. When his "French woman" was near him, happiness shone in his eyes. Over and over again, he declared himself the luckiest guy in the world. To his many "I love you, honey," Christine replied with a timid, "I love you too."

Wisely, the man didn't ask for more. He was not one to delve into the past. He lived for the moment. The moment was perfect, because soon he would have this beautiful girl in his home in Boston. He couldn't wait to see the looks on his friends' faces. Christine was the asset he needed to move up in the law firm. The perfect hostess. Educated. Decorative. Enticing. Foreign accent. Young enough to be molded to suit his needs.

CHAPTER 27

▼

THAT AFTERNOON, IN THE TOURNEAU FAMILY, Philippe was away on business and Odette had gone shopping. Nicole was packing the rest of her belongings to send to her future in-laws with whom she was staying. The phone rang.

"It's for you," Nicole said, handing it to her sister.

Fleetingly, Christine remembered Aunt Sophie that day, "It's for you." She wasn't surprised to hear Brian's voice.

"Meet me in the Chapel of St. Genevieve in Cathedral Saint Julien at six o'clock'; we're getting married."

Her legs gave way. She was trembling. She was glad the big armchair was right there to receive her when she collapsed into it.

Alarmed, Nicole grabbed the phone from her sister, "Brian, what gives? Christine just about fainted. What did you tell her?"

"I told her we're getting married this afternoon. Six o'clock."

"You're joking." After five seconds, "No, you're not." Another pause. Two bewildered young women stared at each other. Christine was shaking her head to acquiesce. Nicole mumbled into the phone, "Why, Brian? Why today? You told Christine you'd be married in Boston."

"Because I changed my mind, that's why. I'm being sent home day after tomorrow. I want us to be married now. It will be best. When Christine is my wife, she'll get a quick passage to be reunited with her husband. Let me talk to her."

It was three o'clock in the afternoon. Nicole decided Christine would wear the white Chanel suit with an old-fashioned Victorian blouse. In a daze, Christine agreed to everything. She let her sister call their beautician. The woman moved a couple of regular customers to take the bride: hairdo, manicure, pedicure.

In the taxi on the way to Cathedral Saint-Julien, Christine refused to allow herself the tears which threatened to choke her. In disbelief, she was remembering a girl—surely not herself—only a year and a half ago standing next to the Frenchman who had been her crazy childhood dream for almost ten years...the preposterous, incredible fantasy of her naïve girlish days. She saw the surreal image of her wedding in the forest of Maneval. Could it possibly be the same girl who, in a few minutes from now, would be married to another man? *Will this war ceremony tonight make me Brian O'Connell's legal wife? Soon I shall be a foreign woman in a strange land. Alone, but for that man. Is that what I want?*

The look of happiness on Brian's face was radiant enough to communicate itself to the other five people. Two young men from the Saturday stockade band were delighted to be the captain's witnesses. Father what's-his-name was a serious-looking man (in uniform, also) who read from the Bible in his hand.

Smiling, Brian placed a gold wedding band on Christine's finger. The stern chaplain declared them man and wife, "Captain, you may kiss the bride." Brian did. He kissed the bride. Came up for air. Kissed the bride again. The two soldiers applauded. Odette and Nicole were all smiles.

Christine wondered why Brian had to be told to kiss her. Until now, he had not waited for the priest's permission. Or was Father what's-his-name a Protestant minister of one of their innumerable denominations? It didn't matter. She was no longer a Catholic, was she?

Seeing the spark of amusement in his new wife's eyes, Brian repeated the performance. With his arms around her, he kissed her gently, appropriately, thoroughly. She loosened up somewhat and returned his kiss, shyly. For the time being, her husband was satisfied. The "French woman" was now his, for better or for worse. He would teach her to love him.

Dinner was declared excellent by five people. Christine did not notice what she was eating. She went through the motions to please Brian. She drank two glasses of Moët et Chandon, her favorite champagne. She noticed that their four guests were extremely quiet. The American musicians did not speak French. Nicole and Odette knew very little English. Christine was glad she would not have a language problem in Boston.

She told herself that tomorrow she'd have to face another hurdle of communication. She'd have to explain to her dear grandmother, her aunts, her friends that the vagaries of war had again plotted her fate. Repeating to herself over and over again, "I am Mrs. Brian O'Connell" did not make the statement any more meaningful.

Yet, at the hotel, the handsome American officer proudly signed the register "Mr. and Mrs. Brian O'Connell."

And he was shipped home the very next afternoon.

In a hurried phone call from Paris, Brian said, "I'm going to miss you, honey. Let's hope it won't be long before you get the Immigration documents. Be a good girl. I love you. Be good."

Christine's throat was so constricted, she had difficulty whispering, "You know I'll be good. Bye, Brian."

Christine Tourneau was certain she was now Mrs. Brian O'Connell, because an official-looking certificate in a frame on a bureau in her bedroom confirmed she was. This time, the document did indeed exist. And she wore a gold band on the fourth finger of her left hand, next to the sapphire.

CHAPTER 28

▼

THE PRINCIPAL OF THE JEAN JAURÉS High School didn't waste any time. She asked Christine to train the substitute who would take over and finish the school year for her whenever her immigration documents arrived.

To everyone who knew her, Christine was an eager bride anxious to join her husband in the United States. They believed she was head over heels in love with the dashing officer whose picture was displayed in the silver frame on her desk.

What is love? The young woman pondered: love of a child for a grandfather; love between two sisters; loving a very close friend; love for her dog, Cora, the mutt she had picked up at the pound. But love between a woman and the man who would be the father of her children? What sort of love was that? She was so ignorant. Troubled and, at the same time, fascinated. Pulled by a pole of magnetism that lured her forward. Don't look back. Embrace the unknown. The future. Boston. Brian O'Connell.

Once Brian had described his native city as "almost European." What shade of "almost," she had no idea. To begin with, she couldn't fathom what a real American city was like. Brian said, "You'll find French, Italian and even German parts of town—except in politics where it's strictly Irish," he grinned. "You'll find Europe in Boston, honey."

She had asked, "What do you mean by 'except in politics,' Brian?"

He guffawed, "Boston will always remain in the grip of the Irish. That's for sure."

"Is that good or bad?" she questioned.

Instead of answering, Brian kissed her. "That's what I like about you, honey, you ask the right questions. You'll get your own answers." He was delighted with her inquisitive mind. His pert, intelligent "French woman" would have so much to discover in his country.

In her bedroom, Christine O'Connell stared at the picture of an extremely good-looking American officer. Tall, blond, intelligent blue eyes, broad shoulders. Brian said he had been "defensive tackle" in football (whatever that meant). He had a very sweet smile. Indeed, Captain Brian O'Connell was a very attractive, charming man. What was the civilian like in a three-piece suit with a starched shirt and a sedate tie? Ties are so boring. She'd choose his ties for him. But would he let her? What part would she play in his busy life? What part would a Boston lawyer on his way up in his firm play in her life? While he was in Le Mans, Brian had ample time to spend with her. He had no immediate concerns other than pleasing her. The smooth-running operations of the Military Police left him with hours of leisure he devoted to her, but in Boston would he have time for her? Would he have patience?

When Brian had explained to her he hoped to be made a partner soon, she did not understand why it seemed so very important to have his name added to those of Sager, Fishban and Murphy. They all worked mostly with bankruptcy–that she understood. Foreclosures and garnishments, she did not. She would learn. She would learn very fast about the new country she was about to adopt as hers.

In the first week of November, Brian called to inform his wife her immigration application had been approved; her travel papers were on their way. She would sail from Le Havre to Boston on December twelfth on the *USS Seattle*.

Christine made short visits to her aunts, her grandmother, Claudette, and the good sisters of Saint Vincent de Paul. Visits made short by suppressed sobs, heart-palpitations, lots of tears. Promises to write. Promises to return frequently. Promises and tears.

On the twelfth of December 1945, Philippe, Odette and Nicole accompanied Christine to Le Havre. The old Peugeot had been put back together, piece by piece, like an interlocking toy. After four years of forced respite in a barn, it was still dependable. Although nowadays Philippe Tourneau owned several Citroëns, three Renaults, and a couple of liberated German army vehicles, the man favored their old, dependable, comfortable Peugeot. Christine wondered if it reminded her father of their crossing the Loire River on a pontoon bridge five years before. Since Philippe had returned from a business trip to find that his young daughter was Mrs. Brian O'Connell, he had had very little to say to her.

In the back seat, Nicole held hands with her sister. Both young women were trying hard not to let tears flow. They too had very little to say.

Christine only had two large suitcases. No trunk. A few pictures of her relatives and friends. Her diplomas. Her legal documents for entering the U.S.A. Nicole promised to send her shoes as soon as leather was once again available. Christine didn't particularly like the American shoes she had seen:

they were worn by the army nurses. They were ugly flat shoes. Old women's walking shoes. Christine liked high heels, no less than two and a half inches. She reminded her sister of her shoe size: five. Extra wide.

On their way to Le Havre, they encountered one of the rare icy days in Normandy. As they were passing cars stranded on the side of the road, Philippe ventured those people wouldn't make it to the harbor. His Peugeot was valiant. Reliable as always. It moved forward.

Deep down, Christine was telling herself silently that if the big car didn't make it on time, and the ship left without her, it would be a sign she shouldn't go. More and more often she wondered what an American man was like at home. She had only known men in uniforms. War time. Soldiers. Officers. What would Brian be like in civilian life? In reality, Christine had dated only one man––Captain Brian O'Connell. She felt she was still a pre-schooler when it came to men.

When she thought of her father and mother in prewar time, Philippe was "dad" and Madeleine was "mother." It didn't help her to imagine them as husband and wife––much less as lovers.

In Le Mans, the Red Cross club's men flirted with her all the time. They were happy to be alive and in one piece. Brian delighted in the banter. There had been times when a fellow officer accused Captain O'Connell of robbing the cradle: Brian enjoyed seeing Christine stand up straight, her eyes blazing. She'd sputter, "I'm not a child. I'm twenty-three years old." They declared she was very cute. "I'm not 'cute'; I hate that adjective. I'm not the blond with no brains." The men then called her "delicious"–something as stupid as cute. At that moment Christine felt she'd be accepted by the men–especially the ones who had fought in France–but what about the American women? Would they befriend her or would they ostracize her and make her feel like an intruder?

The harbor was swarming with Americans in uniforms. They were going home after several years away from their families. By now the various groups of GI's kneeling over a boisterous craps game with piles of French money exchanging hands were a familiar sight. Brian had been very mad one day when he'd lost a lot at a poker game. Americans sure were gamblers.

It occurred to Christine that perhaps she also was a gambler. She tried not to see the French girls who had lost: they were sobbing, their arms around the neck of a departing lover.

Nicole spotted a group of French women who were conversing in jovial tones. She surmised that, like her sister, they were on their way to a fiancé or a husband on the other side of the Atlantic Ocean. She pushed Christine toward them. An older woman (late thirties, early forties) greeted her, "Where to, darling? I'm going to Boston. Suzanne here is going to North Dakota. Marcelle to Colorado. And you?"

"Boston also."

Philippe couldn't take much more. He hugged his daughter. His eyes bright with tears, he murmured, "Promise to come back if things don't work out. Remember, you have a job waiting for you anytime." He did not add, "and a home."

For two cents Christine would have turned around to go back. Right now. This very moment she felt ambivalent deeply troubled, nauseous, filled with conflicting emotions. Yes, she wanted to go, but her heart was breaking. At the instant of separation with her country, Christine tasted her profound love for France.

The hand of the sympathetic French woman, who called herself Yvette Tanguy, pulled her forward, "Comm 'on '*chérie*', we're not turning back now. Let's go see what's awaiting us over there."

Yvette faced the distraught father, "I'll take care of her. I'll watch over her as I would my own daughter. Don't worry, we'll be fine. I'm going to Boston, also."

She pushed Christine toward the narrow gangway where American Navy personnel were checking the boarding passes of some fifty war brides, "I don't speak English. Christine, ask the guy if we can room together."

"Sure, no problem. We'll put you both in 'R' two hundred and five."

They followed a jolly sailor to their home for the next ten days: a very crowded inside cabin with four berths–two over two.

"It's so small," Christine deplored.

"Showers and toilets down the corridor over there," the sailor added with obvious glee.

"How will four of us be able to get dressed in here?" Christine asked, perplexed. Discouraged already. She shouldn't have worried. The other two passengers never showed up in 'R' two hundred and five. Yvette explained to her bemused roommate the women were 'grabbed' as soon as they set foot on board.

"Grabbed?"

"Grabbed. Quickly. I guess the men could tell when they looked at them..."

"Could tell what?"

Yvette shrugged, "Those guys offered them more spacious quarters for the duration of the crossing."

Christine's mouth gaped. She was so astonished, she couldn't believe what she heard. "You mean they'll sleep with other men while their husbands are expecting them?"

Yvette was not a naïve twenty-year old. She had one daughter who was a nun in Brest. She had lost her husband in a work camp somewhere in Germany. Their son was killed when landing in Sicily. She was now married to an American widower who worked for the railroads making good money, big benefits, and a pension. She didn't regret her decision. She certainly could use a change of scenery. So could her new friend, she believed. The poor girl was so young. Inexperienced. Not stupid. Far from it. But oh, so vulnerable. She would need a mother. *If the lawyer she's married to doesn't have one, I'll be her mother. I'll watch over her,* she thought, pleased to have a French friend in the city of Boston.

Christine mumbled under her breath, "How can a girl who's promised, or even married, sleep with another man?"

"Lust, chérie."

"They're sluts. That's what they are."

If Yvette was tempted to agree, she didn't. She kept her own counsel. She chortled, "I saw two or three who were very obviously pregnant. There might be more before we dock in the Boston harbor."

"'Lust' as you call it, Yvette, is for the coupling of animals. People make love to create their children. A man and his wife must be faithful to each other."

Yvette shook her head from side to side, "That's what you and I believe, darling. Not everyone agrees. Instant gratification is becoming the rule. Never mind the consequences. Let's go, love, I hear the announcement for dinner."

The December Atlantic Ocean was choppy. It had been pitching wickedly from the first minute the ship left the English Channel.

Christine was seasick. She could not stay on her bed within the four walls of the windowless, tiny cabin and watch the coat on the peg on the wall cover one hundred and eighty degrees, swinging all the way up to the ceiling to the left, and back again to ceiling to the right.

She felt a bit better if she remained mummified on a lounge chair on deck. Yvette wrapped her in several heavy blankets and left her there while she went to eat, "I'm not missing a meal ever again," she jibed. "From now on, I go through life with a full stomach." She was annoyed with her young charge, "You should make an effort, Christine. You wouldn't feel so bad if you had something to upchuck," she giggled. "Force yourself to eat something,"

"All right," Christine acquiesced–being surprisingly docile because she was weak and dizzy–"when the teacart comes around at four o'clock, I'll eat something."

The old sailor was pleased to see the young woman wanted food. He offered a choice of what sounded like "cold cats" or perhaps a hot dog. He covered his ears when she started wailing in protest, "Go away. Turn this boat around, I want to go back to a civilized country. Even when we're dying of starvation, we don't eat cats or dogs."

The four or five souls brave enough to dare freezing on the deck couldn't contain their laughter. "Did she say 'cats and dogs'?" a man repeated . "Poor kid. She'll have to get used to the Boston accent. Cold 'cats' on the menu—and hot 'dogs' wouldn't be my idea of a gourmet meal either!"

CHAPTER 29

▼

It was only the day before they were to disembark that Christine realized the *USS Seattle* was not going directly to Boston.

"It's taking the passengers to New York City," Yvette said, displaying her documents.

Christine took her papers out of her suitcase and verified the information: indeed they were heading for New York Harbor. She was unable to comprehend why she had been mistaken. She wasn't worried. *No doubt Brian knows and will be at the pier waiting for me*, she thought.

When the ship pulled into the harbor in the wee hours of a bitter cold December dawn, on deck long lines of silent people watched the awesome Statue of Liberty in the distance. "Our gift to them," murmured Christine through the lump in her throat.

The ship moved so slowly, the motion forward was almost imperceptible. Until it stopped between two piers three hours later. No one spoke. Everyone was mesmerized. There was so much tension in the air, Christine could feel the quivering throb in the thick silence. Numerous returning GI's who, but for the grace of God, might not have been here this morning. Much older. Wiser. Their personal joy tainted by keen anguish, increased by a touch of senseless guilt. Some immigrants of war-torn Europe—each with their own amalgam of emotions: excitement, anticipation, anxiety. And the war-brides. In a singular moment of time, Christine's heart knocked in her chest. A melody vibrated from heart to heart. A once in a lifetime fleeting brotherhood. They were in America.

Suitcases in hand, Christine walked toward one of the immigration counters for non-citizens. The unfriendly man who took the papers she handed him snarled, "You go sit over there until someone comes for you."

Twelve hours later, Christine was still seated at the same place. Another French girl was also there on the hard bench next to her. Forgotten—both of them. They watched each other's meager luggage when one went to the bathroom. They didn't talk.

When it became too painfully obvious Brian O'Connell had not come to fetch his wife, Christine placed her winter coat on the floor. She curled up on the cold tiles, on her side, with her head on her arm. What were 'they' going to do? Put her in jail? Toss her on a boat returning to France? She didn't want to think. Sleep. She'd sleep. Nothing to do but sleep.

A kind soul she didn't see covered her shivering body with a rough army blanket. Grateful, she wrapped it around herself and dozed on and off throughout a very long New York night. She was too demoralized to have coherent thoughts. Between intermittent dreams, when she was swimming under icebergs or eating a chewy morsel of dead cat, she stared, unseeing, at the hellish, cavernous hall, wondering why she was there.

When she looked at her watch, it was nine o'clock the next morning.

Drowsy, empty-headed, nauseous, she was pulled up to her feet by a tall civilian she barely recognized. She wasn't sure she was glad to see Brian O'Connell.

So he had arrived. Only twenty-four hours late after all.

Christine didn't turn around to look at the other girl. Dazed, she walked between Brian and another man—each carrying one suitcase. Each holding her hand.

The stranger on her left looked sheepish.

On her right, the other man avoided looking at her. He was wearing a pair of brown corduroy trousers and a heavy plaid jacket. Even in civilian winter clothes, Brian O'Connell was still handsome. She sighed. She stumbled. The two men tightened their hold on her hands at the same time. Brian still not looking at her. Ashamed, she presumed. He should be. She had spent her first twenty-four hours in *Amérique* on the filthy floor of Ellis Island. In a repulsive barn from which unwanted people would be shipped back like cattle to where they came from. She had come to accept it would be her fate. It was not. At that precise moment, Christine Tourneau didn't know if she was glad or not.

The man on her left spoke first, "She's about to collapse, Brian. Why don't you pick her up and carry her?"

O'Connell mumbled, "We're there." They stopped near a big car. Christine was exhausted and too much in need of a hot bath to notice the vehicle, or she'd have declared it ostentatious. Great length. Overabundance of chrome. A flamboyant shiny blue chassis.

Disoriented, she sat between the two men. Their presence assuaged her resentment. For having imagined the worst, her relief was overwhelming. It nearly erased the fears of the previous night. Not the vexation. Not a big dose of indignation.

She waited for an explanation.

None was forthcoming.

The stranger at the wheel grinned, "Her pictures don't do her justice. You're a lucky stiff, O'Connell."

"She's mine. My very own 'French woman'. Back off, guys, she's off limits."

"Cool it, buddy. She is your wife; still, she's a beauty."

"That she is, isn't she?"

In spite of herself, Christine piped up, "If you two characters continue to talk about me above my head as if I didn't exist, I'll yell so loud, you will have to shut up."

"I'll be dammed," the driver bellowed.

Brian agreed, "You will be, Sean O'Neil. Have no fear." Soon their bantering no longer registered: the young woman was sound asleep. Two childhood friends smiled. Brian put his left arm around Christine, and with his right hand he brought her head down gently. With a sigh of satisfaction, she curled up, her dirty feet on Sean's right knee, her fanny on the seat, and her head on her husband's lap.

She dreamed the ship she was on was being tossed wildly from bow to stern. To Port. To Starboard. She hung on the bar of the berth—unaware it was Brian's arm. When she didn't feel the swell of the ocean anymore, she raised her head. She gazed ahead at a parking lot full of cars, "Where are we?" she inquired.

"Ho-Jo. We're stopping for lunch," Brian informed her.

"I'm hungry."

He laughed, "First time I heard you say it."

"She probably had nothing to eat yesterday," Sean ventured. He was looking at her. If that was a question, she was not going to answer it. She did not ask why they had not showed up on time the day before: a vague look of repentance on their faces told her they were not very proud of themselves. She would wait for the right time to get her answers. She had never openly questioned her parents' actions either, nor their orders.

They entered a busy restaurant filled with bright yellow and orange splashes of color: on the counters, on the stools, on the booths, even on the uniforms of the waitresses. Christine blinked. She giggled, "Cheerful place."

The men chuckled. They were studying the yellow and orange shiny menu—three or four pages of suggestions. Overwhelming.

Christine stared at the pages. She lifted her face when a middle-aged woman plopped three tall glasses of ice water on the table without being asked. It must be the American way, the French girl thought, bewildered. She drank her water in one non-stop gulp. Not asking his permission, she switched glasses with Brian and emptied his promptly. Sean placed his glass in front of her. She drank that one, also.

The waitress watched her with an amused look and raised eyebrows, "Thirsty, aren't you, honey? Rough night, hey?"

Yes, *Honey* was very thirsty. Dehydrated. She thought, *"Rougher than you think. Not what you're insinuating, though."*

The contrition on the faces of the two men confirmed the woman's suspicions. One beautiful young girl and two handsome guys. She shrugged, "Ready to order?"

Softly Brian demanded "What'll you have, sweetheart?"

Christine didn't have the faintest idea, "Order for me. What are 'you' going to eat?"

"A cheeseburger. Fries. Make that two cheeseburgers. A glass of milk," he told the woman who wrote it down.

"Same for me," said Sean.

"And you, honey?" asked the waitress.

'Honey' did not know. She murmured, "My first meal in America."

"What does she mean?" Interested. Prying.

It was Sean who explained, "She's just off the boat, you see."

Ann–her name was printed on the pocket of her uniform–peered from one man to the other. Curious, "Whose girlfriend is she? What country is she from?"

Cutting off their answers, Christine made up her mind, "A ham and cheese sandwich. With lettuce and mustard. No mayonnaise." She was always amazed by the amount of 'mayo', as they called it, the GI's slapped on their bread. She preferred butter. But, then, she was a Normandy kid.

"Good," said Ann. "Ham and cheese." She paused to write. She enumerated quickly, "On white bread, rye, pumpernickel, rye with seeds, hard roll, soft roll? Do you want the bread toasted, or not?" The choices confused Christine. In France before the war, there was only one kind of bread. She opened her big, green eyes wide. She asked innocently, "Can you say that again slowly?"

The waitress groaned. The men roared. On each side of their booth, people stood up to take a peak. Uproarious. "What a cute accent!" Where is she from? A Frenchie, I bet."

As soon as he managed to stop laughing, Brian rescued his wife, "On rye bread, toasted. No, make it white. They have not had white bread in France for three or four years."

Christine was relieved. The heat on her face made her uncomfortable. "She blushed," someone at the next table said. She felt she was in a theater. Strangely, she was the entertainer. It was not a comfortable position.

The waitress left to get their order.

Chapter 30

▼

After lunch, they filled the big tank with gas. Then Brian took the wheel. At first, Christine sat prim and proper between two Bostonians. The three of them silent. Then sleep closed her heavy eyelids. This time, Brian got her feet when Sean O'Neil pulled her head down on his long thigh. The front seat of the car was so wide, the slender girl's butt nestled happily there. She didn't see her husband's hand slap Sean's paw when the driver discovered it laid on his French woman's derriere. In a far away mist, she heard a man chuckle and another growl.

In her somnolent state, Christine was content. She had found her happy-go-lucky Americans. Tomorrow, she would telephone her father to tell him she was in Boston. He would call Nicole, Grandma and Claudette. That would give her time to find the nearest post office to buy the necessary stamps.

At six o'clock, they stopped for dinner. In Le Mans, Christine had learned the American meals were backward: a light lunch and a heavy meal at night. She would have to get used to it. Brian had explained they often had less than an hour for lunch. The workday finished early. Around five o'clock. They had a long evening ahead.

Whereas, the French canceled everything at noon—even the post office and the banks closed for two hours. Some of the stores for longer periods of three or four hours. Noon was the main meal for a French family. It meant school lasted until six or six-thirty in the afternoon and many places of work closed even later.

Christine believed she'd like the shorter workday, but she told Brian a heavy meal of meat and potatoes so late in the day was not good. The lack of exercise must hinder the digestion. Brian surmised the French people must be sleepy on the job after a big mid-day meal. Christine admitted it was frequently the case. She added that very often, a family waited until eight or nine to have their supper. Many times while she was trying to do her homework, her stomach protested. She was so hungry she couldn't concentrate on her books.

Madeleine Tourneau wanted to wait for Philippe. Three times each day, the five of them sat at the dining room table to eat their meals together. Often enough, the conversation between her parents and her siblings became very animated while Christine was mostly listening. She kept her own counsel. At night, in their study, Nicole and she replayed the salient facts and rehashed the disputable opinions.

Christine would get used to the American meal schedule. She believed it would be awfully nice to quit school at three in the afternoon. Yes, she intended to teach in Boston. Somewhere they'd need a French instructor, no doubt.

During dinner, she watched the men eat grilled steaks. Huge steaks. She was no longer surprised by their size. She'd seen the Americans eat that much meat at one time in the Officers' Club. A heaping plate of mashed potatoes. A big mixed salad. Bread and butter. Two cups of coffee. An enormous slice of what was called 'cheesecake'. The very idea of a sweet dessert made with some kind of cheese puzzled her. No thanks. She didn't want to taste it. Not now. She settled for a bowl of vegetable soup, a roll with butter, and a glass of water. In France, she had tasted the soldiers' sweet sodas. Sickening. No orangeade. No sarsaparilla. No root beer for her. Water, please.

For four years in France, Christine had lived in total darkness from twilight to the next morning. A slight infringement on the blackout requirements, a crack of light in a window would mean a heavy fine from the German Kommandatur. They could not send Philippe or Jacques to pay for fear they'd be detained, so Christine had gone twice to face the enemy, money in hand. Glad, awfully glad, when she was out of there. "We were scared. Always scared. Afraid to talk. Afraid to breathe. We never knew what their next move would be," she had told Brian and the others around the table at the Club. "At the end, we mistrusted our neighbors–even a relative or perhaps a friend. The Gestapo was everywhere. When a civilian was arrested by the Nazi state police, other French people burrowed themselves deeper into the darkness. They attempted to become invisible, therefore ignored and hopefully safe for a while."

And now the road in America. The endless road from New York to Boston.

The numerous towns and cities were lit with thousands of street lights. Storefront lights. Many a theater marquis. Fluorescent neon signs. The houses and even the stores had no closed shutters. Every window was ablaze with brilliant light. And the countless bright headlights of cars. Everything blazing. A very radiant new world. Lights, movement, adventure, laughter. Cars. Gasoline. Food and more food. Laughter and more laughter. Christine had truly arrived in fairyland.

CHAPTER 31

▼

THE ENTRANCE TO THE APARTMENT BUILDING where Brian O'Connell lived was a gigantic hall of mirrors reflecting the silhouettes of people half a dozen times. It made Christine dizzy. She was drained. She barely noticed the exotic green plants which reached the high ceiling. She staggered when Sean O'Neil removed his strong hand from under her elbow. "Easy, girl," he said. "You're home."

With a deep laugh, "So long," to Brian, "Good luck, honey," to Christine. A wink. Sean O'Neil departed.

Brian deposited both suitcases on the carpet on the floor. He groped in his right hand pocket for his keys. He unlocked the door. He grabbed the bags, pushed the door with his foot and turned to his wife, "Stay where you are, sweetheart. Don't move. Don't go away," with a chuckle.

Puzzled, Christine froze on the spot.

Quickly Brian returned to the door left open. He picked up his bride. She wrapped her arms around his neck. He carried her over the threshold.

"Just like in the American movies," she whispered, kissing his neck. "Don't you dare drop me," she giggled nervously, all the while tightening her arms around him. He firmed his grip on her backside, a movement that raised a conflagration in her. "Not a chance," he grunted in a hoarse voice and opened his mouth over hers.

He could tell the French woman was much too tired to look at her new surroundings, "I'll draw you a nice, hot bath, darling, and it's beddy-time for my baby."

She was grateful. Vaguely relieved. She took out her vanity-case, as the French women call it. (In Madame's boudoir, there's also a vanity table.) Vanity. Not tonight. She hung her white, linen nightdress on the peg behind the door.

Surreptitiously, Brian rummaged around in the overnight bag. He hung a pale green see-through gown on top of the other one. He remained standing at the door, looking at her. At what he could see of her under the foamy, fragrant bubbles. She pouted, "Go away, Brian, don't stand there. I don't want you to watch me."

Amused, he taunted with loving tones, "Darling, we're married. Remember?" *Remember our wedding night in Le Mans. Time also to remember why Sean and I didn't meet the ship on time...*

Deep down, Brian was glad the expected explanations had to wait. "I'm going to take a shower. I'll be in the bathroom across from yours, sweetheart. Holler if you need me." As an afterthought, he jibed, "Don't go under in the tub, honey. I can just see tomorrow's headlines: 'French war bride drowns on her first day in America'. No, please don't!"

She giggled. The truth was, she was exhausted, light-headed, unsteady. She could easily fall asleep right now or faint. She would not allow herself the luxury of a long bath. She mumbled to herself, *Not my first day in America, Mister O'Connell. Where were you yesterday?*

In the shower, Brian O'Connell rejoiced that his gentle, well brought-up wife had spared him the vociferous fight another woman would've started upon his arrival at Ellis Island. Someday he would tell her about the lost twenty-four hours, before Sean—or someone else—would have their own version.

Brian O'Connell, attorney, with the firm of Pager, Fishban and Murphy had been granted two days off to go and meet the *USS Seattle* in New York Harbor.

Sean O'Neil naturally decided his place was with his best friend. "We'll share the driving. Long round-trip. While I'm at the wheel, you can cuddle your French...your French lady."

"Watch your language, O'Neil, in the presence of my wife."

"My language? My language is always proper, decent, elegant."

"In court."

"Out of court, also."

"You're entitled to your opinion, O'Neil, but as far as I'm concerned, make believe you're in court when my wife is around. And the rest of the guys, also. Remember, we're all educated Bostonians."

Remember.

Somewhat chagrined—and he should be—Brian remembered the sequence of events: since the ship was due to dock in mid-morning on Tuesday, the two attorneys decided it was no use arriving at the pier before four o'clock in the afternoon. It would take that long for them to be allowed on board to claim Christine O'Connell. It meant they took their rightful place at the weekly poker game on Monday night. With boiler-makers drowned with beer, they forgot to watch the clock. At four in the morning, well-fortified, they left Boston.

At four o'clock in the afternoon, less than eighty miles from New York, the Connecticut State Police pulled them over, "You guys going to a fire?"

"No, to a ship to pick up his wife," Sean said meekly enough.

The state trooper turned to the second officer, "Boston lawyers."

"Boston lawyers with a bottle of Scotch between them. We're right across from the police station. You two gentlemen follow us, please."

That's how O'Connell and O'Neil arrived at Ellis Island on Wednesday morning. Sober. Chastised. Mortified. Not really sorry. Fortunes of war. All's well that ends well.

By the time Christine O'Connell found out, she would not remember how terrified she was. She would have fallen in love with her good-looking husband all over again. Brian would have rekindled the magic. *Just like in the movies*, Brian told himself as he tenderly deposited his sweet wife in their marriage bed.

CHAPTER 32

▼

WHEN CHRISTINE WOKE UP THE NEXT morning, she was disoriented. She was in a very wide bed, much wider than a French bed. She was wearing her silk nightgown. She looked around the unfamiliar bedroom. She was in America; the new Mrs. O'Connell. She quickly jumped out, anxious to see her new home.

She read the note Brian had left on the night table, *Welcome home, darling. I'll call around noon. Will take you out to dinner this evening. Look pretty.* Delighted to be alone to look around her new home, Christine replaced the flimsy green nightgown with the comforting Victorian house dress.

In the small kitchen, she played with a pot which perked her coffee—somewhat similar to the cauldron the women kept boiling on the laundry boat on the river in Le Mans. A miniature one, of course, made of aluminum. Fascinated, she stood watching the bubbles on top of the lid turn darker and darker, until the color and the smell invited her to pour herself a cup of the brew. Just right. Perfect. She would buy that gadget for Nicole and one for Claudette.

There was a toaster made to accommodate the thin, even slices of American bread. All soft. No crust. The opposite of a baguette, which is mostly crust with very little soft dough inside. She pulled open both doors. She placed one slice on each set of electric wires. She turned them around to toast the other side. Great. She would buy one for her father. Philippe would have to get an adaptor because electric currents do not match, but he would not have to light the coals in the kitchen stove every time he wanted a piece of toast.

She found butter and jam in the refrigerator. A good breakfast. She loved jams. All kinds of jams. Her grandmother made the best ones because she picked the fruit in her own orchard. Her mother's jams were not bad, either. Fun to make in the huge copper pots. Only no jams in France in the last three years because there was no sugar. That's why.

She wandered from room to room: a big living room tastefully decorated.

A good sized dining room. Two bedrooms. Two baths. She played with a switch on the small television. She was fascinated by the black and white picture on the screen (they had no televisions in France).

She took a long bath. She sampled four different cakes of soap, trying to decide which one she liked best. She walked barefoot on the thick carpets. She dressed in a two-piece linen outfit. The apartment was so cozy warm, she did not need to wear a sweater.

Back in the kitchen she examined every shelf, reading the labels on the cans of food. After all, she was neither indiscrete nor trespassing. . .this was her home. She discovered some strange things. One box said 'corn flakes'. What on earth were corn flakes? She shook a few out on the palm of her hand. She put four or five in her mouth. 'Tasteless', she declared aloud.

The refrigerator, with its two doors, fascinated her. In Le Mans, they had no refrigerator. Not even what Brian had described one day as 'an ice-box'. They kept the perishables in a screened cupboard anchored to the thick wall of their very cool cellar. The underground room was always much colder than the rest of the house. Miracle of miracles. Brian's refrigerator held a couple of trays with ice cubes. Real ice. What progress! And comfort! She would write that to her friends.

At noon, Brian called. He sounded so far away, so professional, so business-like. A man she did not know was at the other end of the line. He was concerned about her, "Are you all right, sweetheart?"

"Yes. Yes. I'm fine, of course. No, I won't go out today. No, Brian, I will not take a nap. I'm not a bit tired. Don't worry about me. I found *Gone with the Wind* on a shelf in your den. I'll read it."

CHAPTER 33

▼

AT FOUR O'CLOCK, BRIAN CALLED AGAIN. Definitely, he was irked. He almost shouted at her, for God's sake. He was going to be delayed and would not get home until eight or eight-thirty.

"Brian, we don't have to go out to dinner. I've been looking around this American kitchen all day. I've found I could easily fix a meal for us if it's okay by you."

Her husband's voice sounded much happier now, "Great, darling, that's my girl. Surprise me, honey. And put a bottle of champagne in the ice bucket," he laughed.

A couple of cans of crabmeat, eggs, milk, a chunk of yellow cheese—cheddar–from Wisconsin. *I must remember to ask Brian for a map of the forty-eight states. I'd like to learn where Wisconsin is. Where does he keep the flour? In a canister, of course. A quiche. A crabmeat quiche.*

In the bottom drawer of the refrigerator she found a funny looking head of cabbage. Closer inspection turned it into a head of lettuce. It was huge and almost as hard as cabbage. She never saw one like that before. She remembered Brian had told her the squishy stuff they have in France–the only kind available there–is called 'Boston lettuce' here. Funny. She made a vinaigrette in the bottom of the salad bowls–the way her mother did..

No doubt Brian had shopped for her, or perhaps his cleaning lady or a friend had done it, because there was a big basket of fresh fruit on the dining room table. Brian knew she liked to finish her meal with an apple, a pear, or an orange. In Le Mans, the Americans had brought her oranges for the children in the hospital after she told them the young kids there had never seen an orange–if they did, it was so long ago they didn't remember.

One night when Brian and Christine sat in the big officer's car in front of her house. Christine asked about his parents. She was taken aback when the man declared abruptly that she wouldn't have trouble with in-laws. There was no one but him. His mother had remarried. She lived in Florida. She never wrote. Never called. He never wrote. Never called. Better that way. He had one sister. Older. She lived in Chicago. Never wrote. Never called.

Timidly, Christine had asked, "Will you let them know we're married?"

"No." He pushed open the car door and stepped out. End of conversation.

CHAPTER 34

▼

DURING THE LONG OCEAN CROSSING, CHRISTINE had pictured herself the Good Samaritan. She would bring the members of the O'Connell family together. In the car between New York and Boston in her drowsy state, she heard enough to realize Brian would not allow her to try a reconciliation. "No way, man. Positively *no*," he had stated in response to Sean O'Neil's inquiries about his mother and his sister.

Christine was determined she would at least get to know some of her husband's friends here in Boston. He promised to take her to meet them on the weekend. She could hardly wait.

The next morning, Brian handed Christine two twenty dollar bills and a set of keys: one for the front entrance of the building, the other for their apartment.

"Don't go and get lost," he teased her. "I know you're eager to explore. Stay in the neighborhood, please."

To her surprise, the O'Connells lived on a street not very different from that of a middle-class district in any French city the size of Boston. Several small stores—the owner's living quarters on the upper level. Narrow, two-storied old brick houses with front steps and a basement apartment. Christine could have been in France walking on cobblestones.

Before shopping for supper, she entered a beauty parlor. She no sooner opened her mouth, all the women in the place turned toward her at the same time. *So, that was the French girl that good-looking lawyer brought back from the war.* Tongues wagged. Obviously they didn't think she understood English too well. There were no smiles in Christine's direction. "With dozens of single attractive Irish girls around, why on earth did some guys bring home a foreign woman?" a nasty customer asked very loud. A shiver ran down young Mrs. O'Connell's spine. Would Brian's friends feel the same way?

Two hours later, she was once again well-groomed. She liked the reflection of the perfectly-coifed slender woman in the mirrors of the entrance hall. What did she care about the gossips under the hair dryers. They were not Brian's friends. Brian's friends were going to like her.

CHAPTER 35

▼

FRIDAY EVENING. SEVEN O'CLOCK. BRIAN O'CONNELL whistled. His wife laughed. She had chosen to wear a straight, blue linen dress, split on one side along her calf. Three-inch high heeled blue pumps. Hand bag a shade lighter. On her shoulders, a colorful Parisian scarf. A short jacket matched the dress. She was ready to face her husband's friends. The men would goggle. Not new. Unimportant. The women? The women mattered. She wanted to be accepted by the female circle. She needed to be accepted. She would charm the girlfriends and wives.

For years, Brian O'Connell, Sean O'Neil, and seven or eight of their friends–all former choir boys in Saint John Catholic Church–met at Conolly's bar on Friday night. Looking around the parking lot, Brian burst out laughing, "Well, well, full house tonight. They all want to meet my French woman."

One who came over with open arms was Sean O'Neil's girlfriend, Cathy McGee. A vivacious red-head with the freckled face of the Irish girls Christine knew before the war. "I heard you talk when you arrived, Christine. You don't sound French," she said by way of welcome.

"What do I sound like?" Christine was intrigued

"Well, I expected you to *speek thee Eengleesh* language with long vowels and no 'th' sound, like my *mozer* and my *faazer*..."

"Like the chambermaid in the movie?" Laughing.

"You sound more Irish than French. You've got a brogue."

"I spent time in Ireland during the summer when I was 12 or 13 with one of the nuns in our school. Then my Irish friends came home with me a couple of times before the war. My mother wanted me to improve my spoken English."

"That explains it."

"I don't know if it does. I suspect the 'brogue' comes from my own vocal chords. I've been asked if I am a heavy smoker, but I don't smoke."

"She doesn't even like wine," Brian piped in. "Her only sin is that she loves me, don't you, hon?" he grinned wryly.

"Tonight, I'll have a glass of champagne, please," Christine said to her husband.

Promptly, Sean and another guy went to order French Moët to toast the new Mrs. O'Connell. Christine giggled, "I'm amazed; in an Irish bar in Boston, they have my favorite French champagne."

As far as Christine was concerned, the evening was a success. The 'girls' all promised to call her and to take her shopping. All but a pleasingly-plump brunette who never said a word all night. On the sly, Cathy McGee whispered, "Don't pay any attention to Maureen Crawford. She had high hopes about Brian...I'll tell you later."

Well, Christine didn't think Brian had lived the life of a celibate monk until he met her. As a matter of fact, she had never given a thought about it until tonight. It was of no concern. Their marriage was a new beginning. A blank page. It started the day after she disembarked on the east shore of the United States. From now on, Brian and Christine would develop the plot together, the two of them.

Christine felt confident it wouldn't be dull. A dull life was what she ran away from. She was more than ready for bright lights, surprises, action. Invigorating action in an exotic locale.

Not war-time action. That chapter was closed. No more death, grief, tears. A new country. A new language. A new life. A rebirth.

After the pleasant evening at the bar, Christine was content to relax in the comfortable car. She was repeating to herself the names of the women, trying to match them to their respective husbands. All of a sudden, she realized Brian was exasperated with her. In an ominous voice, he boomed, "Return to earth, girl, I'm talking to you," with a biting sidelong glance.

'Girl'? What was he so angry about? She didn't speak. She waited, confused.

"Why on earth did you tell those women you'd baby-sit for their kids? You did. I heard you," he went on, not toning down his anger.

Christine's stiff back relaxed somewhat. She was not guilty of a crime. "I've got lots of time on my hands. Morgan and Rose said it was difficult to find someone to stay with their children for just a couple of hours. I said I'd do it."

"You won't."

"I won't?"

"No. My wife doesn't need to work for fifty cents an hour."

She was peeved by his childish reaction. She stammered, "I don't want money. I'm doing them a favor."

"Don't. I don't want you to."

She choked back her next question. No use pushing him. He'd had more than his share of Scotch. She recalled that in the Officers' Club in France, someone had wisecracked about the great capacity of Captain O'Connell to hold his liquor. He did not hold his liquor silently. He became rambunctious, eager to argue, ready for a fight. When it happened in Le Mans, she had told herself it was the other belligerent who was inebriated.

Well, Brien was not about to pick a fight with her now. She wouldn't let him.

She glanced at the man's red face. Too many highballs. Too many draft beers. She was uneasy. When her father had imbibed several glasses of wine during a meal, he became talkative. He told a few off-color jokes her mother disapproved of, but he was never pugnacious. He was witty, amusing.

Perhaps, after all, tonight Brian had been nervous about introducing his war bride to his childhood friends. Still Christine was perturbed, alarmed, obscurely apprehensive...

CHAPTER 36

▼

ONE EVENING THAT BRIAN WAS NOT supposed to be home for dinner, he walked in unexpectedly. Christine was already in the pale green negligee after her evening bath, curled up on a couch with *Gone with the Wind*, which she was reading for the third time.

A look at her husband's very angry face brought her up to her feet immediately.

"That's right. Get up. Make me supper," he snapped imperiously. He did not kiss her. He crossed the room on his way to changing his clothes, she presumed. She was stunned when the man turned around to inquire in a malicious, mean voice, "Have you played Madame de Pompadour in that get up all day or were you expecting company, perhaps?" He paused near the bedroom door. "Or did you have a visitor this afternoon?"

Christine opened her mouth, hesitated, then closed it. The question was unworthy of being answered. She walked to the kitchen silently. When Brian's moods were morose or sullen, she didn't rebuke him. No use adding fuel to his incendiary temper.

While she reheated the beef bourguignon, she boiled some rice. She fixed a salad. She never had visitors in since Cathy McGee had come in one day. That night, Brian had a fit. A very nasty burst of fury. Enraged, screaming, he forbade her to entertain anyone. He repeated forcefully, "Not anyone, you hear, while I'm not at home."

She complied. She had no choice.

So naturally, she did not tell him when she and Cathy met for lunch once or twice a week. That was before Christine got the job. She saw an ad for a waitress in a section of town where she hoped no one would know her. The hours were just right—eleven to two P.M. The trouble was, the Greek owner of the run-down luncheonette declared he couldn't hire her if she didn't have a social security card.

She called Cathy who gave her the address of the nearest social services.

The female clerk asked her name. She said, 'Tourneau'. She spelled it out for the woman. Christine Tourneau. Address? No time to waste, don't hesitate. She gave their house number, two-nine-seven, South...and finished with the name of the street that angled with theirs–two-nine-seven South Congress Street. The woman never asked what Christine's credentials were. She didn't ask if she had a green card or a visitor's visa. There was no reason for the dread in the pit of Christine's stomach. It was all legal.

Five minutes later, she was outside, staring with disbelief at her brand-new social security card. It had been so easy. She returned to the 'Greasy Spoon'–thus baptized by Cathy–and she got the job.

She left the house at ten in the morning and walked an hour to get there. She returned on bus number thirty-five, which cost her a nickel and left her two blocks away from the apartment. Every evening she was afraid her husband would say he'd tried to reach her on the phone at noon and demanding to know where she was. He never did, thank God.

She didn't dare open a bank account. She kept her meager earnings under a piece of white paper in a shoebox. She loved shoes. She bought them on a whim. She owned too many. At first, Brian teased her about what he called her foot fetishism. Now he did not tease her about anything. He rarely spoke to her at home, except to yell. He was usually courteous, even attentive, however, on the rare occasions they met his friends at Conolly's Pub.

Presently, the man came into the kitchen, wearing the long wool housecoat Christine liked. In it, he looked even more smashing. Such a handsome man. Funny, but he also seemed more formidable. More intimidating, more dangerous. No social amenities between them. The closeness palpable. If he wanted to, he could...She shuddered. At the office, things didn't go as he wished. He never spoke to Christine about his job–in fact, he hardly ever spoke to her at all except with impatience. He was often irascible. When he was truly waspish, she shook her head in silence to pretend she shared his view.

Under her quiet ways, she was deeply disappointed. She felt unfulfilled. She was unhappy. She was thinking of slow caresses. Of knowledgeable male hands on her bare skin. Of murmured foreign words of love. She didn't dare tell the man she pined for more than his powerful body inside hers. She wanted a return of the tenderness of their first weeks together. Patience. Sweet desire. She wanted to be loved.

Because this man now was unfamiliar, unknown and estranged, she became more and more alienated. She was tired all the time. She became depressed. Then indifferent. Then hostile.

Standing by the kitchen counter, to be at his beck and call, she watched Brian pour half a glass of Scotch on two ice cubes. No water. Steady hand.

A glassy look in his eyes. He downed it non-stop. Poured himself another. He picked at the food. Got up to dump the rest into the garbage can on the side of the stove. He stumbled to one of the couches in the living room. Two seconds later, he was snoring heavily.

Christine picked up the afghan on her chair. She covered her husband with it. She carried her book to the guest room. She spent a troubled, sleepless night.

The next morning, she woke up later than usual. Brian was not a breakfast eater. Neither was she, but she believed they should start the day together with a cup of coffee. At first he seemed to like the idea. That morning, however, he had already left for work. Obviously, he had stayed on the couch all night. Their bed had not been slept in.

From that moment on, Brian drank more and more. He arrived intoxicated and kept on filling his glass to the top. He never staggered. He did not talk to his wife. He just stared at the small black and white TV until they went to bed after the eleven o'clock news. Yet, he obviously didn't have trouble getting up in the morning.

Sean O'Neil told Christine the whole bunch of guys stopped at the Irish pub for a couple of drinks after work. On Friday night, they often stayed to watch boxing together on the TV screen of the bar. "That's all there is to it," he swore. "The other guys are single. Brian forgets he's a married man. Have no fear, girl, your husband is very professional on the job at all times."

Professional on the job. A mean, screaming maniac at home.

CHAPTER 37

▼

ONE NIGHT BRIAN O'CONNELL REFUSED TO pick up the phone when O'Neil called. "Tell him to drop dead," he yelled at Christine.

"You don't have to repeat what the son of a bitch said; I heard him." O'Neil hung up.

Brian had declined to engage in a vociferous exchange with his best pal. They had previously rehashed the situation on the pavement in front of the gold-domed Massachusetts State House. No need to scream on the phone. There was a very available scapegoat within reach. The man walked toward his wife. He grabbed hold of her hair in his left hand, and the novel she was reading in his right hand. He threw the book across the room. It landed on the dry sink where it scattered broken chunks of precious China figurines. Christine couldn't quite thwart an involuntary moan.

A handful of blond hair stuck to her husband's fingers. He stared at it, "For Christ's sake, woman, let your hair down. Have a drink. Have two drinks. Relax. Miss Tourneau is always so proper. You never let your hair down, do you, Miss Tourneau?"

Christine told herself his derision shouldn't hurt her because he was so obviously in his cups. Tomorrow he would apologize and bring her a box of candy or a new book. Tomorrow...

Years ago, a sunny Sunday afternoon. Another world. *Let your hair down.*

Her mother had done it once while her fascinated young daughters were watching her. That day, Madeleine Tourneau washed her fabulous hair and she sat on the Roman steps on the courtyard–brushing, brushing, brushing. Her long, long hair. Soft. So shiny. A beautiful woman. So vulnerable.

What kind of a woman? What was Madeleine like in bed with a man? With Philippe? My father. Did he caress her magnificent auburn hair covering her shoulders and her breasts. Was he gentle? For sure, Philippe was never violent.

Ah, but her mother's first husband was another matter. A drunkard. A wife beater. A tale repeating itself. Family history. Secrets. Shame. Heartbreaks. Mother and daughter. The mother: proud, brave, so private, had accepted the excommunication of her church, the rejection of her peers, the sneers of the righteous elders. To save a life. . . her own.

Sadly, Christine's inner voice whispered: *It was in another world and another time. Mother was deeply wounded by unjust criticism. If I ever leave Brian, I'm just as vulnerable. I, too, will be a divorcee. Good Christian people will not welcome me into their judgmental church.*

CHAPTER 38

▼

CATHY MCGEE ENTERED THE RESTAURANT JUST as Christine was about to leave. Depositing three dollar bills and two quarters in her purse. Her tips. She had planned to go to the Laundromat across the street to wash her uniform. She never took it home.

Surrounded by the drove of washers and dryers in action, the two friends were alone in the place. Christine murmured, "Has Brian always been a heavy drinker?"

"His sister saw him push their mother around one time too many. Just as their father did so often when they were growing up. That's why neither woman wants any part of him now. That's why they've never contacted you. They're still afraid of him. Both Brian's mother and sister have asked me what you're like."

She paused. For a knowledgeable moment, her sad eyes met Christine's above the clothes they were folding. "Mrs. O'Connell thinks you should leave before it's too late."

There was a long silence. Christine's blue eyes were filled with fright.

Cathy stammered, "Christine, has Brian ever..."

"Hit...hit me?" The young woman halted repetitions paused and started again. "Beat...beat me? He pulled my hair. Several times he pushed me hard. Once he held my arms so tight I had to wear sleeves to hide the black and blue marks." She clenched her teeth. She repressed the sobs she wasn't going to allow. *Not here. Never. Oh, Mom. You. Me. Mother. Daughter. Oh, Mom.*

Aloud, she continued, "At times I believe I must go before he looses control completely. But where? I can't return to France now. It would be too easy for him to find me."

"Perhaps you should go to the French Consulate. They might be able to help you."

A minute of hesitation. Then a confession. "I went."

"You did? What did they suggest?"

"That I watch my step."

"Some help."

"Something like, 'You're joking, lady, if you think we'll tangle with the powerful Irish Mafia of Boston.'"

"Oh, dear. What now?"

"I suppose I wait until I'm carried to the hospital on a stretcher."

That very same night, Brian O'Connell came home sober, charming, attentive. The old Brian. Captain O'Connell sans uniform.

For a couple of days, life was uneventful. Pleasant even. Christine strove to maintain a belief in happy-ever-after marital bliss. They went to Copley Square for a succulent dish of baked scrod. They tasted the unique beans of Durgin Park. They walked hand in hand. They stopped to sample Indian pudding. "God knows how many silversmiths and bookmakers ate here," Brian quipped, with a youthful titter. "To put myself in their place takes me way back in American history."

Christine suffered pangs of remorse. She shouldn't divulge marital secrets to a sympathetic woman she barely knew. She resolved to be very discrete from now on. Cathy McGee told her Brian's first wife, Mary Ann O'Connell, could not get witnesses to come forward on the day of the divorce because all their neighbors were afraid of her husband. A powerful attorney. His name in the *Boston Globe* a couple of times since his return from Europe. A man on his way up in the firm of Pager, Fishban, and Murphy. It would serve no purpose to come too close to Cathy, who couldn't really do anything for her anyway. Sean O'Neil kept his girlfriend—not a fiancée, no promises—obedient to his wishes. He wasn't ready to get married. Although, deep down, Cathy was miserable, she let the whole world know Sean O'Neil was the one and only man for her. "Sean is too wrapped up in himself, too selfish. I'm sorry I'll never have any children, but I accept that it's my fate."

At that time, Christine didn't reveal that Brian also had declared he did not want any children.

One day in July, Christine called the only friend she had in Boston. She was crying. She sounded hysterical. She could barely get the words out of her mouth. "Come here, please! Make it fast. I'm not going to be here long."

Christine hung up the phone. When Cathy arrived, she was horrified. "How did he do that?"

'*That*' was a shiner the size of an apple. Dark blue. Horrible.

"And *that*, and *that*." Christine stuttered, baring her forearms, her back, her thighs.

Slowly she began to explain. For a few days, things would be well. Brian stayed mostly sober. Then, with no warning, he would explode. Last week he came home very drunk every night. "On the phone, around four o'clock in the morning—it made it nine over there—a man called from Ireland."

"From Ireland? Are you sure? How do you know?'

"I'm sure. I listened on the phone in the kitchen. I even know the place. He was calling from near Donegal. It's a school in Northern Ireland. I figure my American husband is involved in 'International Trade'; that's why the French consul wants nothing to do with me and my troubles."

Cathy was as pale as a ghost, "If Brian ever suspects you know..."

Christine tittered bitterly, "I'm not going to wait around long enough for him to find out."

"You're leaving?"

"This very minute."

"How will we stay in touch?"

"We won't."

"Christine, you don't mean it."

"Too dangerous. For you. And for me. If you don't already know, Cathy, I could tell you things about Donegal. Your boyfriend and my husband are involved in deals the French Consulate is aware of, no doubt. Dangerous games our men are playing."

Cathy McGee's face was very pale. She stammered, "Christine, you can't just disappear like that."

"I'm going to make a good try at it."

"What about your French friend here in Boston? Is that where you're going?"

"No." A second emphatic, "No."

"Just tell me her name, in case."

In a weak moment, Christine mumbled, "Tanguy. T-A-N-G-U-Y." She pushed Cathy away from her after one long minute of silent embrace. Cathy—dear, sweet Cathy—must never, ever discover the murderous drop which had made the glass overflow.

No tears.

No tears, Mother.

Five minutes later, carrying the same suitcases she brought from France a few months prior, Christine entered a Boston taxicab a couple of blocks away from the apartment of Brian O'Connell. Out of earshot of curious neighbors and suspicious tenants, she enunciated clearly, "To the Greyhound bus station, please."

Chapter 39

▼

For all her precautions, Christine was startled when the cabby asked in a derisive tone, "Going away, kid?" Was she becoming paranoid? She had two heavy bags. She was on her way to board a long-distance coach. A simple question. Or did all Irish guys between thirty and forty know one another? She suspected in this part of Boston she was "the French broad" O'Connell married in Normandy.

She had never inquired about the schedule of Greyhounds departing for New York City. Until last night, her plans had been nebulous. On some remote back burner. Likely never to be put into action.

Until last night…

Brian was away on what he'd called a "business trip" – "four or five days," he had said. After his departure, Christine had looked in the drawer of his bureau where he kept his passport. Gone. Brian O'Connell was most likely in Ireland.

At about eleven o'clock, when Christine was stretched out in front of the T.V., the doorbell rang. Puzzled, not really alarmed, she opened door and O'Neil barged in. Obviously very drunk, but still able to perform, the madman raped his best friend's wife all the while declaring, "It was my turn to go. The bastard monopolized the job, so now I captured his French trophy."

The next bus didn't leave until one o'clock in the afternoon. It meant arriving at Grand Central Station in New York at three o'clock in the morning. There was no turning back. She bought a one-way ticket.

She shared a seat with an old woman who was bent on unraveling her long life into the captive ear of the girl on her left. At first Christine tried to pay attention. It should help calm her tumultuous emotions. Her thoughts were sparkling in a myriad of directions. What would Brian do this evening? Would he report her missing? Do the police care about runaway wives? How would the sisters of Saint Vincent de Paul greet her? Would they bang the door in her face as the French consul had done in Boston? Where would she go with her meager cash if they did? She knew no one in New York, nor anywhere else in America. *Don't panic. The sisters will take me in, if only for a few hours. Then what??* She put her head on the back of the seat. She shut her eyes. The monotonous drone of her travel companion soothed her. *Don't think. Too late to change my mind. Trust my guardian angel. . .*

The bus went in and out of the many cities all along the Atlantic Coast. It made good time on the highway, but in the maze of the old historic towns, it took forever to reach the repulsive, dirty stations. Passengers popped in. And popped out. The old lady left in a town called Whitehall. "That's my Whitehall," she said, laughing, glad she had arrived. "I believe there's a Whitehall in every state of the union," she informed Christine on her way out.

At six o'clock, when the vehicle pulled into one more nameless bus station–Christine was by then thoroughly lost–the driver stood up. "That's the end of the line for me, folks. Your next driver will be in soon. You have a half hour to grab a bite. Don't forget to use the facilities while you're here. I don't have to tell you there are none on the bus."

Christine's stomach reminded her not too gently she had not eaten in the last twenty-four hours. She walked to the counter. She stood in line. Since she would not bite into a so-called "hot dog," she bought a hamburger and a cup of coffee, both of them vile. The man next to her shoved the catsup her way. "It will make it go down easier." She didn't want it. She forced herself to eat the roll and to drink the black, tepid water.

Back in the same seat, she slept fitfully on and off until they were in New York City. So many lights. So many cars. At that hour in the middle of the night, there were quite a few people in the bus station.

Carrying her heavy suitcases, she walked slowly to a waiting room–the only place to go at three o'clock in the morning. She sat next to other stranded travelers. She was unable to ignore the uneasiness in the pit of her stomach. Even if it was too late to turn back, it was time to think seriously about her predicament.

Time to think–Time also to remember. . .Another bench–Another terrifying wait. . .The last time, she had been rescued a day later–no rescuer this time.

In Le Mans, the nuns got up at dawn to hear Mass. At six o'clock, Christine decided to walk toward the Convent of Saint Vincent de Paul on Twenty-third Street and Ninth Avenue. She believed the sisters would be up.

She changed her mind. She couldn't manage. She didn't know what direction to take. She was wearing high heels, the only kind of shoes she owned. She was exhausted physically and emotionally. She hailed a cab.

After she paid the man and gave him an extravagant tip (she could tell from the obsequious bows and too many thank yous), she stood by her bags on the New York pavement.

New York City at dawn.

Few people on the streets in that part of town.

She looked up, up, up.

Towers of glass and stone with thousands of windows rising toward the sky. Dizzy façades of curving walls.

When Christine's eyes came down from the roofs that touched the slow-moving morning clouds, she was trembling. She had to steady herself before she could bend down to pick up her suitcases. Except for the Eiffel Tower in Paris–so fragile-looking against the blue mist–she could never have imagined buildings (real buildings) of such gigantic height and such exuberance.

At six-fifteen, she rang the bell of the convent, which was dwarfed between modern skyscrapers. A younger vision of Sister Agnes of Le Mans opened the door. The wings of her fetching cornet danced around her pretty face. She smiled, *"Entrez, je vous prie."* She picked up one bag and turned around in the hall, walking fast with a purpose. Holding the other bag, Christine stood there, unable to move. Mute. Choked up. What was there to say?

The greeter came back. She extended her free hand to the newcomer, "I'm Sister Jane."

"Oh, no, you're not," Christine burst out foolishly.

"I'm not?" the young nun inquired with a mischievous smile.

"You can't be Sister Jane."

"I can't? Why?"

"Because Sister Jane is..." Christine paused, searching for the right words, remembering only that the "Sister Jane" she knew from France was mean and ugly and this beautiful nun was lovely and sweet like the Sister Agnès she so fondly remembered. She sidestepped, "You're more like Sister Agnès. Sister Agnès is very nice."

"I see," Sister Jane chortled. Her intelligent eyes lit up with pleasure. "Sit on that bench, won't you. I'll go and tell Mother Superior you're here. What's your name?"

"Christine."

"Christine?"

"Christine Tourneau from Le Mans."

Christine stared at the white walls in the hall. She was well acquainted with all the reproductions which adorned them. All historic portraits in gold frames. Saint Vincent de Paul in the act of nursing the sick in a hospital. Marguerite de Valois. Anne d'Autriche. The seventeenth century paintings soothed the girl. She was home. She was in well-known territory. No longer frightened, her spirits rose. The sisters would take care of her.

Sister Jane-Agnès returned, "Mother Superior will see you. She has been expecting you. Follow me."

The kind face of Reverend Mother broke into a wide smile. She stood up. With outstretched arms, she embraced the slender girl, "Christine? Christine Tourneau? I'm delighted."

She backed up. She took the girl's hands in hers. Held her at arm's end, "You're just like Sister Agnès described you. I expected you'd come."

"You did?"

"Not under these circumstances, dear child. Sister Agnès wrote three times since you arrived in New York–six months ago? Eight months? She was certain you'd drop by some day to visit us."

"The French don't realize how big the U.S.A. is and how far Boston is from New York. I was on the bus fourteen hours."

Mother Superior's face became very concerned, "That bad, child?"

"Worse, Reverend Mother."

"Sit down, tell me about it."

"My husband drinks...a lot..."

"He hits you, doesn't he?"

No answer to the question. The young woman's gaze traveled guiltily toward the commiserating nun, "I wanted so to make it work. But last month, Brian told me he doesn't want a child. Never."

"He's a lawyer, yes?"

Forgetful, Christine stammered, "How did you know?"

"In her letters, Sister Agnès told me about you." *A lot about the girl's husband in the Forces of the Interior, her brother, her mother, her dear grandfather.* Slowly the compassionate older woman said, "When your father remarried, you could not go on believing he needed you. Your whole world had collapsed."

"I never thought I was so very anxious to forget the past. In Boston, I asked myself many times why I had to shut out the past so much. Now I know I wanted to erase the war years."

"That's human, child. Please, tell me, you do pray?"

"I guess you also know I refuse to enter a Catholic Church, Mother."

"Some day. Do you pray, Christine?"

"I suppose it can be said I do. Outside. By myself."

"That's praying, also, child. God is listening." After a pause, Mother Superior added, "*You* also listen, Christine. You still believe in your guardian angel or you wouldn't be here right now." On a different road altogether, she inquired, "Is there any way your husband can trace you to this place?"

"No. I am sure I never mentioned Saint Vincent de Paul to Brian."

Relief. A warm smile. "You can stay here, Christine. Three dollars a day. It includes the meals and a bed. Can you pay? If you can't, don't worry."

"I can, Mother. I have almost two hundred and fifty dollars."

"You're rich. Ten times what some girls have when they arrive here."

"Other girls?"

"Several. All of you foolish young women who trusted a complete stranger."

"Brian is thirty-one. He's educated. He has a good job. Friends. A very nice apartment."

Mother Superior sighed. Softly she mumbled, "Charming. Smooth talker. Very handsome in uniform. A captain, wasn't he? Charismatic, no doubt."

"All of that," Christine agreed sadly.

And still you're here today, Christine Tourneau. The lost lamb. Completely on your own. In this vast country, you are alone in the midst of strangers, except for us in this convent. We won't be able to sustain you very long. I shall have to shove you out in the cold, cold world very promptly. If Brian O'Connell cannot connect his estranged wife with us, perhaps someone else can. She stared the young woman in the eye. Very seriously, she asked once more with the exact same words, "Christine, is there any way someone else in Boston can trace you to this place? Think carefully. Do you believe someone in Boston can find out you are with us?"

Christine didn't hesitate to say no. She needed to believe it. She had to be safe. She shook her head, let the memories come. She thought of the times the orphan girls in the School of Saint Benoit accused her of being the nuns' favorite student because her parents gave loads of money to the Saint Vincent de Paul Society...One never boasts in public about their good deeds. God forbid, what bad manners, Madeleine used to say. If you have more than your share, give unselfishly. Silently. Anonymously. *And here I am today. An orphan in a foreign country. Gathering the rewards of my parents' generosity.*

"Sister Agnès wrote that you have a college degree, child. We won't have trouble finding you a job with a place to stay. If you're willing to teach in a girls' private school."

"Yes, yes, of course."

"Good. It won't take long. I'll give you the address of our placement agency. They're in need of a French teacher in the suburbs. Somewhere in New Jersey."

Christine's face broke into a big smile. She was saved.

Mother Superior was startled by the quick change of mood. *The girl's so young. She'll bounce right back.* Aloud, she informed Christine, "Room and board. Pleasant surroundings. Near enough so you can come and see us from time to time." She was certain Christine barely heard: It was clear that the girl's relief after the recent terrible fright was overwhelming. The nun thanked God the poor lost child had been smart enough–and brave enough–to come to her. And God answered promptly. . .lucky for her.

And so Mademoiselle Tourneau joined the faculty at Ave Maria School for young ladies in Englewood, New Jersey. A sin of omission. Nobody–not even the head mistress–asked the new French teacher if she'd object to going to chapel at seven o'clock every morning. She was a protégée of Mother Superior, wasn't she?

And so Christine recited her prayers in Latin as any fervent Catholic would at the dawn of each school day. Silently she never failed to add her grateful thanks to the benevolent God who had rescued her from a momentous female error of judgment and guided her into a safe, feminine haven.

On the one weekend she was off each month, Christine visited Sister Jane. They were good friends. Christine at sixteen was undecided whether she was in love with André Grassin or whether she had the vocation. To be dressed in Sister Agnes's habit, to wear the attractive cornet, to descend the abrupt thirteen century streets in long flowing robes, to be saluted by almost everyone on the pavement, that would be great. Her fate was decided when André popped up in the Boy Scout camp that summer. It was out of her hands. Some day her childhood dream would come true. She would marry André Grassin.

For herself, Sister Jane revealed that at times she was strongly attracted to a certain man–a mortal sin when the man was a Catholic priest. Aggravated by her reluctance to confess a stirring of lust, she admitted to Christine shyly.

What if their lives had been reversed? Christine born a poor fisherman's eighth or ninth child in Britanny; Jane the pampered daughter of rich parents. They pondered those questions and many others seriously. With great earnest, the two women attempted to grasp the aspirations of their inner souls. They talked philosophy, war, life and death, desires, wants, beliefs. By tacit agreement, they never discussed a failed marriage. One day Christine told Jane perhaps she would go back to France at the end of the school year. The young nun advised her to stay in America awhile longer, "Don't give up too soon. As a matter of fact, maybe you could bring your sister over. The school headmistress has told Mother Superior they're in need of a nighttime proctor in one of the girls' dorms. Would Nicole come to be with you?"

It was worth a try. Christine wrote to Nicole. She knew she was lonely at the home of her future in-laws where she waited for her fiancé to return from the agitated French colony of Indochina.

To her delight, Nicole accepted immediately: Christine's descriptions of the American paradise whetted her appetite. Since her passage was paid by the school, she'd get her passport and a six-month visa, with no trouble.

CHAPTER 40

▼

NICOLE ARRIVED IN NEW YORK CITY in November of 1946. Her pockets were full of the good bread they served on board. "Look at it. White bread. Can you believe it, Sis?" Obviously in France things were still far from pre-war opulence. Christine was going to be very happy showing Nicole the U.S.A.–what she knew of the U.S.A. That was a small acquaintance with Boston (better forgotten). The fascinating city of New York. A pleasant, upper right-hand corner of prosperous New Jersey. The great George Washington Bridge. And most of all, stores filled with all kinds of goods.

From the very first day, Nicole was disappointed by the Academy of Ave Maria. She didn't let on right away. The two sisters were delighted to be together–especially on their day off when they strolled in and out of places in New York City. They soon discovered the great bargains of Fourteenth Street, the leisurely walks in Central Park, the Metropolitan Museum, the Cloisters in Upper New York where a surprise awaited. It displayed, among other treasures, the doors of the eleventh century monastery of their natal village. With its outrageous, indecent wealth, the New World bought the old one: imported European culture! Transplanted medieval history.

In school, Christine was Mademoiselle Tourneau–the French teacher–and Nicole was Mademoiselle Tourneau, the housemother–too-young-to-be-a-housemother.

Christine's room was spacious, with a four poster bed in dark mahogany, a matching set of drawers , called by the funny American name of "bureau." A bathroom was shared with the Latin teacher next door.

Nicole had a tiny space to herself partitioned from an immense dormitory containing sixty beds with sixty unruly fourteen-year-old girls who made fun of her French accent. The mischievous, spoiled, rich daughters of business tycoons and government officials were as well behaved in class (where grades were given) as they were miserable creatures after curfew. It was hard for

Christine to believe the stories Nicole told–until they switched places one night. After that, Christine and Nicole plotted to leave Ave Maria as soon as they found other jobs.

Meanwhile, the Tourneau girls made the best of what they had–knowing it wouldn't be for long. They were secure. Away from danger. Well surrounded by educated women. Good manners. Delicate attentions. Respect. A roof over their head. Fabulous meals. Money to buy clothes, leather shoes, and gifts for relatives in France. They packed many boxes with cans of tuna fish, salmon, soups of all kinds. Sugar. Coffee. Soap. Toothpaste, gloves, socks. Many, many packages to Philippe and Odette, but twice as many to their grandmother, Blanche Tourneau, who distributed the manna to her tenants and their children.

The academy for proper, young American females was a restorative oasis. A refreshing period. A tonic Havre-de-grace for their battle-scarred souls. They spent the Christmas holiday at the convent with the friendly nuns, who were all ears when Nicole and Christine talked about the Nazi Occupation. They shopped for their New Year's Eve banquet along the French district of Eighth and Ninth Avenues: pâtés, 'rillettes', oysters, *Buche de Noël*. Even champagne!

Mother Superior was extremely diplomatic. In several telephone conversations with the headmistress of the Academy, she managed to have Nicole dismissed while Christine would keep her contract until the end of the school year in May.

The girls settled in a furnished apartment on Grand Avenue, five minutes from the school. Christine went to work at seven thirty. She had lunch in school. She returned at three-thirty in the afternoon. She was pleased with the arrangement and the freedom. Although she no longer had to cover study hall in the evening, the trustees had instructed the dean to let her keep her salary. If her sister and she were careful about their tight budget, they would have the money for the rent.

Nicole, however, no longer had means of her own. She had too much time on her hands with nothing to do. She was still unhappy. She was irritable, impatient. She wanted to make money. She needed a job.

To get a job on her own, Nicole must have a social security card. *No sweat. I'll get my sister a social security card. Then she'll get a job.* A repeat of a previous scenario while Nicole waited in a diner with a cup of coffee. Social security card in the name of Nicole Tourneau.

A couple of friendly guys in the apartment adjacent to theirs befriended the French girls. Pierce Hundley (the taller) and Jack Smith (the mulatto) took Nicole and Christine to their favorite diner in a nearby town of Montville where two Greek brothers promptly hired Nicole. The two men liked her. They loved her accent, her smile, and her bright, intelligent eyes.

From the very first day, Nicole made a lot of money. The customers—mostly truck drivers, electricians, masons, and male office clerks—were all very generous with the "Frenchie" at lunch time. Mother Superior found her another well-remunerated job waitressing in the Italian restaurant in the late afternoons and evenings.

Life was good. A rose garden. An adventure. They were living life one day at a time as it should be lived. Finally, they were enjoying peacetime in the land of plenty.

Until Christine called Yvette Tanguy in Boston one evening. Not certain why she was doing it out of the blue, or what she expected to hear.

Yvette picked up the phone on the first ring. "David's in the shower. Say nothing. I'll speak fast. I'll hang up fast. David forbade me to talk to you."

"Forbade?"

"When you suddenly left him that day, your husband showed up here at three o'clock in the morning. An enraged bull. Out of his mind. He shoved David out of his way. He pushed me against the kitchen counter. He threatened us."

"At your place?"

"You obviously left our address there. David was about to call the police, but when Brian had looked under the beds and in all the closets, he went out screaming that he'd get you sooner or later."

"I'm very sorry."

"Are you all right?"

"I am. My sister is visiting. She's with me."

"Good. Take care." Quickly, Yvette added, "If I ever hear anything about Brian, I'll forward it to the sisters." She hung up before Christine finished saying, "Yes, thanks. How did you guess?" Lamely. They must've talked about Saint Vincent de Paul during the ocean crossing two years ago.

"But I didn't think I left Yvette's name in the apartment," Christine mumbled.

"Did you forget an address book there?" Nicole asked, alarmed.

"I didn't. I had packed all the papers I would take if I ever left." Perhaps Brian got the Tanguys' whereabouts from the immigration officials.

"It probably was easy enough for him."

"Yes, I guess." Her eyes feverishly brilliant with the horror of a new concern, Christine blurted, "On the morning I was leaving Boston, I called Cathy McGee."

"You did?"

"Stupid. I know. I showed her the bruises on my body. She made me give her the name of my friend on the *USS Seattle.*"

"Christine!"

"I was not myself. I was..." Nicole cut her off. "I know, Sis, don't blame yourself. If Brian had the address of the convent of Saint Vincent de Paul, he would have been there six months ago."

"That's what I tell myself. Yet, at times, I still dream he finds me. He drags me back to Boston by the hair. My scalp comes off in his hand. I'm bald like the women-of-the-night after the war when the Frenchmen dragged them naked through the streets."

"Stop, Christine, stop right now."

"Okay, Okay."

"Don't keep on flagellating yourself, Sis. Get rid of the hair shirt. You've not done anything wrong." After a pause, "No more than Mother did when she divorced her first husband."

"That's what I tell myself."

"Then start believing it."

Nicole told Sister Jane, who told Mother Superior. The nocturnal visit to the Tanguys, thank God, was six months earlier. By now, Brian O'Connell had likely given up on finding his wife. Mother Superior would call the Little Sisters of the Poor in Cambridge to find out if the man had been there. She was praying for the safety of her own flock. And for the safety of Christine Tourneau. Who would have thought so many husbands would turn out to be violent men who drank too much, and who battered their spouses, emotionally and physically? Could it be they were unhinged by the carnage of their years at war? In their cocoon in the convent, the nuns knew nothing of the turmoil the American GI's went through. Nor of the ravages of the souls of the European women under fire. Their youth lost. Their loved ones killed. Murdered. Their hearts shattered every time. It was remarkable that Nicole, Christine, and unknown others picked up the pieces and moved on.

Barely a month after her sister's phone call to Yvette Tanguy, Nicole received a thick envelope from Sister Jane. It was a message from Boston, so she had wisely mailed it to Nicole.

Christine was just arriving back from school. "May I?" she asked, her arm outstretched. Silently, Nicole let go of the letter, staring at her sister, waiting for her to browse both the handwritten page and the newspaper clippings.

A couple of minutes ticked silently. Nicole finally managed to whisper, "Sit down, Christine. I'll get us a couple of drinks while you read."

The Boston Globe. May 8, 1947 (another May eight).

Brian Patrick O'Connell, well-known attorney in the firm of Pager, Fishban, and Murphy, was killed in a brawl in Conolly's Pub yesterday after closing hours. Shortly after 2:00 A.M., some witnesses confirm. The police are investigating. Captain O'Connell of the Thirty-Seventh Artillery Division and the military police had no immediate family in Boston. His estranged wife could not be reached. Patrick John O'Connell –uncle of the deceased–took the body to Ireland for burial in the ancestral family vault.

A weekly paper, *The Free Press*, published the same devastating news with a few added details: The pub was closely watched at all times by the CIA. It was believed to be a meeting place for men involved in Ireland's internal affairs. It was known that Captain O'Connell had visited Patrick O'Connell in the vicinity of Donegal several times during the war. There were sly innuendoes as to the presence of the Irish politician in Boston on the night of the shooting. It had to be more than a coincidence. Why was Brian O'Connell gunned down that night of all nights?

Brian O'Connell's best friend, Sean O'Neil, stated that eventually he would be able to contact the widow through her family in Normandy, France.

The Tourneau sisters sipped their cognac in complete silence–each deep in their own thoughts.

It was no surprise to Nicole when Christine slept non-stop for forty-eight hours after she managed to stammer on the phone she was too ill to teach her classes. With great difficulty, she wrote down some exercises her students could do with the substitute. Since her colleagues knew nothing about her sister's life before she came to the school, she did not enlighten them. Mademoiselle Tourneau had caught a bout of intestinal flu or some such likely-to-be-short malaise.

A week later. Yvette Tanguy mailed another letter for Christine to the convent. It contained a copy of Brian O'Connell's death certificate. Yvette had deliberated a few seconds before sealing the letter. Should she also send her condolences…her congratulations…her best wishes? She abstained from comment.

Mother Superior was shown the newspaper clippings and the death certificate. She shook her head slowly several times from right to left and left to right, "It is not for us mortals to try and comprehend the Lord's will. His decisions must not be questioned. We must accept them with the greatest humility. The Lord is our shepherd. Praise be the Lord."

"Amen," the nuns answered.

"Amen," the Tourneau sisters echoed.

"I am a widow for the second time," Christine repeated to herself over and over again. Not certain she believed it. It must be her overworked imagination. It couldn't be true.

She'd reach for the clippings of the Boston newspapers to assure herself she was not making it up.

In her feverish dreams, the face of André Grassin replaced that of Brian O'Connell for a few seconds. It was so long ago. She could barely recall what André looked like. Would the Boston lawyer disappear that quickly from her heart? Time would tell.

CHAPTER 41

▼

BAD NEWS NEVER COMES IN ONE...A second calamity soon followed.

Either the immigration officials were a lot more efficient than they were believed to be–or some cantankerous soul from the academy turned Nicole in as being illegally in the U.S.A. One afternoon, a couple of immigration agents came to the Greek diner to arrest not only Nicole Tourneau, but also a half a dozen men in the Greek kitchen who had jumped ship to work in America. The two brothers who shared ownership of the restaurant were outraged. Needless-to-say, they blamed Nicole for their troubles.

Because they were angry with her sister, they did not call Christine. When the phone rang at eight o'clock that night, Christine expected it would be Nicole saying she was working late at the Italian restaurant. Fabulous tips. Or perhaps Nicole was going to the local theater to see a movie with a couple of friendly waitresses. That week they were playing a western with Hopalong Cassidy.

Instead, a deep, male voice inquired, "Is this the home of Nicole Tourneau?"

"Yes."

"Are you her sister?"

"Yes," Christine murmured. She sensed trouble. She waited.

"She was taken to jail in Newark this afternoon."

"Jail? Did you say jail?"

"That's what I said."

"Why?" in a shaky voice.

"Because her visitor's visa expired six months ago."

"She has a social security number."

A faint laugh, "We'll have to talk about that some other time."

Christine was dumbfounded. Nicole in jail. That was so weird. She mumbled, "What happens now? What can I do?"

"Get hold of a lawyer. Make certain he can get to court with you in Newark before noon tomorrow with five hundred dollars."

"Five hundred dollars?"

"Yes, the judge will give Nicole time to gather her belongings before she goes back to France. You'll get your bail money back."

"The judge?" She was discomfited. She murmured, "Jail, bail, judge. My sister's in jail?"

Concerned that she didn't grasp the gravity of the situation, the caller asked skeptically, "Christine, are you sure you can get hold of an attorney on such short notice?"

I knew one rather well but he died. She persisted timidly, "Do we really need one?"

The stranger's cultured voice sounded as if he were bewildered by the question.

"Yes you do," he informed her forcefully. More softly, in a controlled voice, he went on, "Any lawyer will do, Christine. The judge will only have eyes for you and your sister." The man did not give his name, nor why he was so anxious to help. He hung up. Christine never thought to ask who he was. After she wrote down more clearly the address of the courthouse she had scribbled, she went next door to find out if the French professor could help her.

Pierce Hundley had a lawyer friend right there in Englewood who would be available the next day. Christine had the money in her bank account. She would put up the bail.

The middle-aged judge took some time with the case of the French girls alone in the U.S.A. He questioned Christine first. In the car on the way to Newark, Pierce and the lawyer had warned her to answer the questions 'yes' or 'no'. Not to volunteer any unrequired information. Your name: Christine O'Connell. Your husband's profession: attorney-at-law. Your sister's name...

When the stern judge asked Nicole if she liked America, she answered that she did, but she was ready to go back to France where she was about to marry Lieutenant Maurice Marcet.

All of them could see the judge did not really believe a pretty French woman did not want to hook up an American husband and remain in this great country. "Your sister's happy with us, Nicole. She wants to live here. You'll change your mind about leaving. I'm granting you an extension of six months. And by the way, you are permitted to work. I know you want to shop in our stores. They're filled with things women want. Things they don't have in France right now."

Joel Rubin, the attorney, Pierce, Christine, and Nicole were guests of the generous judge at lunch time–an exchange of reminiscences because the lawyer and the judge loved France. Pierce Hundley looked uncomfortable. He had to teach a class that afternoon. He kept looking at his watch. He suggested they should return to Englewood. Joel was irked. Good thing Hundley wasn't a lawyer, or he would know one can't be impatient with a benevolent judge. After all, there had been no mention of war or heroic acts in battles. They had conversed about Paris, the city of lights–not a threatening subject.

CHAPTER 42

▼

NOW THAT SHE WAS IN POSSESSION of legal papers, Nicole lost interest in making more money. She had already bought innumerable clothes and gadgets. She had filled two big trunks. She declared she wanted to go home. Christine did not argue. No point in trying to make her change her mind. She had come for a visit and the visit was over.

One day in July, Nicole was accompanied on the French ship *Europa* by two government agents who were there to make certain she was not escaping through the nets of immigration. Christine refused to go with them to the pier on Forty-Fifth Street. She was crying. From behind her upstairs window through a veil of tears, she watched her sister get into an unmarked black sedan. She did not observe that one of the men kept his back turned. She was unaware she had glimpsed him a couple of times in front of the TV at the Clinton Inn. If she had gone as far as the car, she might have recognized his voice–the man on the phone the day Nicole was arrested.

Once again, Christine was alone in the world. Alone in a foreign land. No relatives and no friends. Except for Mother Superior and vivacious Sister Jane Agnès, whom she saw about once a month for a couple of hours. She knew she had to keep busy. She should never sit down long enough to start feeling sorry for herself. From the minute she woke up until she fell in bed, exhausted, she was on the go. The kind headmistress of the school offered her a couple of extra study halls and duty. She accepted. While she was in the midst of people, she had no time to think about her loneliness. When she arrived late in her empty apartment, she was much too hollow to mope around. She only wanted two things: a warm shower and sleep.

Keep your chin up, girl. Get on with your own life, she heard Madeleine Tourneau whisper to her.

"Yes, Mother, I will," she answered aloud. She went on alone as if it didn't matter, but she felt her heart was breaking one more time.

119

CHAPTER 43

▼

TOWARD THE END OF THE SCHOOL year, Pierce Hundley took the forlorn French girl next door under his wing. Almost every night, he dropped in with an excuse. A good book. A special dish he had made. A movie Christine should see with him. A new restaurant. Christine was grateful.

By now she was waiting on tables at the Inn almost full-time. The tips were extravagant. The dollars kept pouring in. The habitués loved her accent and her contagious laugh. Her Friday night and Saturday night "drinking tables" in the bar brought her in one evening more than the school paid her for a full week. Her bank account was growing by leaps and bounds.

Although the president of the academy told Christine she could have her job in September, she was unsure she wanted to sign her contract. Pierce had put a bee in her bonnet: he believed she should enroll at Columbia University to get an American degree. She liked the idea. She was tempted. She figured if she took a roommate to share the rent and kept as many hours at the Inn as she could, she'd manage financially. The catch was to get accepted at the university. With Pierce's help, she'd give it a try.

"First things first," Hundley declared. "Go to the French Cultural Embassy in New York and get your diplomas translated into credits."

"Credits?"

"American colleges grant points or credits for each course that's completed with a passing grade, about 30 credits in one year. One hundred and twenty and you have a diploma from that university," the man explained.

Surprised, Christine asked, "A student doesn't have to take an exam at the end of four years to get a diploma?"

"No, no. One accumulates credits."

"That's great. Do you think Columbia University will grant me credits for my Pierce hoped so. He didn't know for sure how foreign students were accepted. For them, there was an entrance exam of some kind. That revelation could wait. Let Christine return with a translation of her French master's degree first.

The adjunct to the French consul seemed perplexed. He held Mademoiselle Tourneau's diplomas in front of his face for what seemed like a very long time. He deposited them on his desk. He stared at the young woman. Then suddenly he grinned, "I'd say, Mademoiselle, it's going to be difficult to do justice to these." He pointed out the parchments in front of him.

Christine was puzzled. The man seemed to be making fun of her. She was not conceited, but she was proud of her academic accomplishments. Timidly, she attempted to justify her achievements, "During the Nazi Occupation, there was nothing one could do except study. I did four years in three."

"You entered at sixteen, didn't you?"

She felt the blush on her cheeks. "The nuns got rid of me, my father said."

The Frenchman bellowed, "I can well imagine..." He stopped in mid-sentence.

Christine finished it for him, "Imagine that I was a pain in the neck."

They laughed. They were friends. Then, seriously, the fatherly representative of France added, "We'd better do this right, Christine."

"Is that difficult?"

"Yes and no. The American system is very different from ours. It will be hard for the people in the admissions office to accept that at nineteen you had a bachelor's degree, and at twenty a master's. But I'll do my best. By the way, congratulations. We're all proud of you."

Professor Hundley was also proud of his candidate for admission. He ironed out the wrinkles. He presented his neighbor with a date for the exam. On August twenty-first. A formality. "Christine, with your academic background and your knowledge of English, it will be a cinch."

A cinch, perhaps, mentally. A very uncomfortable four hours straddled over hard bleachers in a cavernous gym. Surrounded by young and not-so-young people who were all attempting to get an American college education. It was obvious the fifty or sixty men and women were parked there because they were foreigners. Americans would have been given desks. And a ten minute break to stretch their cramped muscles. Every so often, Christine straightened up her shoulders and rubbed her back. She'd tap a foot that went to sleep.

Somewhere in the recesses of her memory, she saw herself facing the first irascible agent at Ellis Island. The callous treatment was reserved for those who weren't born on the blessed U.S. soil. The agents all conveniently forgot where their parents or grandparents had hailed from–unless of course they were all descendants of "Native Americans," as the redskins were starting to be called. She giggled. People stared. They began to laugh, also. She stood up. She articulated loudly, "Seventh inning stretch." Everyone near her stood up. Then others did, also, The four proctors didn't look thrilled, but they said nothing. Christine sat down again. She went back to her science test.

The day she got the results of the entrance exam, Christine opened a bureau drawer and threw the paper into it. She slammed it shut. She decided to forget about Columbia. She regretted she had not accepted the teaching position at the academy, but comforted herself with the realization she'd soon have an impressive bank account. Meanwhile, she'd decide what she should do next. She had no intention of waiting on tables the rest of her life. What if immigration officials descended on the place once again? What if it was declared that since she wasn't an American citizen, and she had no husband to look after her, she would have to return to France? She was confused and bewildered, afraid to ask for advice. The only person who might be able to help her was Pierce Hundley, but she felt she didn't know him well enough to burden him with her very personal dilemma.

Professor Hundley had returned from vacation. He had spent a couple of weeks at the French island of Martinique, where his roommate, Jack Smith, was visiting his relatives. Pierce knocked on his neighbor's door, "Well, Christine. About the exam?"

"Forget it."

"You didn't take it?"

"I did."

"Then?"

"I don't want to talk about it. I'm not going to Columbia, that's all."

Pierce was perplexed. He thought something was strange there, "Let me have the test grades, Christine."

When she hesitated, he got annoyed. He was not to be dismissed so fast. In a firm voice, he repeated, "Let me see the grades, Christine."

Reluctantly, she handed him the grade sheet.

Now Pierce was really baffled. "All right, Christine. So you changed your mind. Can you tell me why?"

"I'm not going to struggle with grades of C, that's why."

Professor Hundley roared. The coffee cups on the table trembled. Christine was offended. "It's not funny at all," she said.

"Yes, it is, honey. You didn't know such exams are graded on a scale of eight hundred. You thought your score should be ninety-eight or ninety-nine, didn't you?"

"Eight hundred?" in a dubious voice.

"My dear girl, get yourself to the admissions office at Columbia tomorrow morning. I can't wait to hear what they'll have to say."

What they said was an embarrassment to Christine Tourneau. But only because when they saw the seven hundred and ninety on both her math-science and her language-art they did not allow her to stay in the waiting line with all the other hopefuls in the hall. She was in and out in a few minutes, her course permissions signed. Congratulations. Delighted to have you in my class.

Like a proud papa, Pierce took her to the New York Palace on Madison Avenue for an elegant lunch.

In Professor Hundley's French seminar, Christine Tourneau never said a word. She was rather well-acquainted with the philosophers of the Age of Enlightenment. That made her popular. She was in great demand because she passed the answers to the right and to the left. On the day they were studying Montesquieu (briefly). Christine realized most American students at the large oval table did not have the background of ancient Roman history necessary to understand the *Spirit of the Laws.*

Professor Hundley was careful not to notice Christine Tourneau's much-appreciated help. The two of them went on pretending they didn't know each other out of class. They made certain no one saw them get in his car together on the nights he stayed in his office waiting to take her back to Englewood, along with Jack Smith, who was also getting a teaching degree.

On other evenings, Christine took a late bus. At night, the view of New York City along the Hudson River was breathtaking. She never got tired of it.

All day Saturday and Sunday—and a couple of evenings when she had no class—Christine waitressed at the Inn. Because she was well-liked by the patrons, she was allowed to keep her textbooks and her homework on a tiny table in the corner of the pantry: she made very good use of her time. Not only on the job, but also back and forth on the bus to the city. Even when she pushed the vacuum cleaner around the apartment. Pierce and Jack told her they could hear her talking to herself. At times, inside the elevator, she recited history dates and scientific formulas aloud. If other tenants found her weird, that was their problem.

Nicole and Claudette wrote frequently. They urged her to come back to France. She could have a teaching position from the first day. The Academy of Caen had not crossed her name off. She was still officially on the payroll of the French government–with a temporary leave of absence. Should she return to Le Mans? To be deported from the United States would be a terrible humiliation. It certainly would be less traumatic if she went back on her own accord.

She didn't want to go back. She loved the U.S.A. That's where she wanted to live. She told herself that anyone who was lucky enough to live in this great country would never want to return to the country they left––except maybe for a visit to hug relatives and dear friends.

Even when Philippe Tourneau called his daughter on the phone to beg her to reconsider her foolish decision, the answer was still, "Father, I wish to remain in New York. I'm fine. Don't worry about me."

Between her studies and her job, Christine had little time to herself. She was rarely lonely nowadays. Either Pierce or Jack dropped by to ask if she needed something. The two were good friends–like brothers, she told herself. Each man did his chores smoothly. Pierce did the food shopping and the cooking. She knew he was a great chef because he brought her samples of his dishes. Jack cleaned the apartment and did the laundry. Although Christine had never set foot inside their apartment, she got the feeling it was run very efficiently.

Christine told them she was afraid to go alone in the spooky basement where the washing machines and the dryers were located, so Jack called her when he was going there. One day, he offered to take her clothes to spare her the trip. Because she suddenly blushed uncontrollably, he teased her, "Honey, underwear is underwear, and yours is exquisite."

At times, unexpectedly, Jack's fiery temper would explode. For peculiar reasons: because Pierce and Christine went out for a drink on their way home; because when Jack arrived at their apartment, Pierce was next door chatting with his neighbor; because Jack didn't feel included in their Columbia circle of friends. Perturbed, Christine wondered if the young man was jealous. She decided to put some distance between herself and the two men. From now on, she would accept an occasional invitation to go to a movie with another waitress. She never accepted one from a male customer in the bar. It was a joke between her and the bartender, Jack Vernano. "That's a smart girl," Vernano jibed. "Ask me, kid, before you let one of those guys buy you a drink. I know everyone in here. I've worked in this place for over thirty years."

Thanksgiving was the following week. To her surprise, the French waitress got an invitation from a woman she did not know who had come to lunch that day with a group of friends. "Ask any of your bosses; they all know me," she said

Christine went to the one brother who'd be more likely to give her time off. The other two were less amicable. Reluctantly, the man agreed. He didn't want to offend the president of the Tenafly Women's Club. It seemed to Christine the woman who issued the invitation was the kind who wouldn't easily take no for an answer.

Obviously pleased, her hostess said, "I was worried Jim may not let you off the hook on such a busy day." She chuckled, "You'll miss generous tips on Thanksgiving Day, I'm afraid, Christine. By the way, I'm Gina Jordano. This is my address and phone number. About four o'clock. My husband or my brother will pick you up right here. Be ready."

"Yes. Thank you."

Christine was glad. It would be nice to visit with an American family in their home on Thanksgiving Day. The American holiday with no equivalent anywhere in Europe. Christine knew it celebrated the unofficial birth of this land of plenty. It was really great to be included in the festivities. However, she was puzzled by the invitation. She had never met Gina Jordano before today. Perhaps she shouldn't be so astonished. Cathy McGee had told her she would have been received warmly in Boston if it were not for Brian O'Connell's attitude. She had assured Christine that as a rule Americans were very hospitable. Christine refused to dwell on the unpleasant Bostonian memories.

That same night, a very interesting, handsome man at the "Friday TV table" said his first words to Christine, "I'm told you're having Thanksgiving with us, young lady. At my sister's house. I'll pick you up here after the first shift at four o'clock." At first, surprise kept Christine rooted in place, her voice locked somewhere deep in her throat. Then, still mystified, she acquiesced. The taciturn man, who exuded an air of danger and an aura of mystique, had never spoken to her before. His brown eyes—so dark—followed her when the other guys teased her and she gave tit for tat. She felt he enjoyed the game. On the rare occasions when he smiled at her—a potent expression that only intensified the tightness she felt when she was near him—she almost wished he would remain less warm and teasing. It was easier to ignore him when his rugged features were stern and serious.

She turned to the bartender, whose raised eyebrows and friendly grin told her he hadn't missed much. She mumbled in a petulant voice, "Jack, stop laughing. I don't even know his name, and he didn't say it. That's the first time he ever spoke to me."

"He's here often enough lately, kiddo. More than he used to be. His name's Nick. Nick Tarzini. I wouldn't be surprised if he planned this little get-together." The bartender was obviously amused.

"Where does he live?"

"He used to live here. He grew up here. All those boys at that table over there went to Tenafly High School together."

"They're not *boys* anymore," she giggled. "Where does Nick Tarzini live?"

"I don't know for sure. Some place in Virginia, near D.C. His parents moved there during the war. His father died last year."

"Why is he here so often?"

Vernano's smile widened, "Good question, girl."

Christine felt uneasy. Nick Tarzini had certainly stared at her during the boxing nights. At times his eyes held a friendly gleam mixed with a hint of puzzlement. Nobody could accuse him of being loquacious. He examined her with disconcerting thoroughness. While Christine was somewhat intrigued, she did not wish to know more about the dark man with the strong chiseled features. *I don't give a hoot what he's like. Or who he is, really*, she kept telling herself.

Good, because she didn't learn much about him at his sister's place on Thanksgiving Day. There were many people. The big house resounded with adult laughter and children's playful voices. Christine's lonely heart suddenly swelled with joy. She was part of the noise, the confusion, the laughter. For a few brief hours, she relived family feasts in the old days in France when she was growing up.

Immediately after pumpkin pie and apple pie à la mode, "Uncle Nick" went to the den to watch TV with the men. The "girls" cleaned up the dining room. They did the dishes together. They chattered non-stop about their kids, their neighbors, their spouses, politics, movies, books, the cost of living and, most of all, the relatives who weren't there.

When it was time for Christine to take leave and thank her hostess, Nick Tarzini was nowhere in sight. It seemed he had gotten a call to go back to work, wherever that was. Gina and her husband took Christine home. She didn't try to figure out why she felt a little disappointed.

CHAPTER 44

▼

THE DAYS FOLLOWING THANKSGIVING WERE HECTIC. Not only did Christine have a couple of long research papers to do, but Pierce Hundley was constantly in the way. He was at loose ends. Jack had returned to the Island of Martinique. Christine listened to Pierce's laments with a faint touch of exasperation, "Won't he be back? He can't just walk out and not complete the semester at Columbia. It puts you in a bad light. I wouldn't do that to you."

"We had a fight."

She nodded, "I've already guessed that much."

"It's not the first time."

"The boy's volatile. But you're very patient with him."

"He needs his diploma to teach on the island. He wouldn't have had a college education without my help," Pierce admitted with a touch of acerbic recollection.

"He's so close to the end. He'll return."

There was a lengthy, uncomfortable silence. With seemingly a great deal of effort, unsure how to continue, Pierce Hundley murmured, "Marry me, Christine."

She staggered, "Marry you?" A wave of dizziness overcame her.

Pierce grabbed her arms and steadied her.

We're getting married on Friday in the maquis camp in the forest of Maneval...

Come to the Chapel of Saint Genevieve at five o'clock. We're getting married... All obstacles had been swept out of the way for two spur-of-the moment wartime ceremonies.

And now, a third time...in the U.S.A.

In Englewood, New Jersey. *Marry me, Christine.*

A deep lethargy enveloped the young woman. Everything blurred. Fatigue dulled her mind. How could this be happening a third time? Why would she allow it to happen?

"*Marry me,* Christine. You'll get your citizenship papers quickly when you are Mrs. Hundley," the tall, educated gentleman insisted, convincingly.

Through the tightness of her throat, the young woman whispered, "Your mother will be happy. She told me she wanted grandchildren. I think she likes me."

"There you have it. You get your citizenship papers and my mother's happy."

Christine noticed fleetingly that her fiancé didn't say, "My mother will get the grandkids she wants."

A few days after Thanksgiving, Myriam Hundley took up residence in New York City in a friend's apartment facing Central Park. She had come from California, she explained, to help Christine shop for her bridal outfit and to plan the wedding reception. On the two or three occasions they had previously met at Pierce's place, the two women had become friends. Myriam was a tall, elegant lady with exquisite manners and definitely lots of money.

Since Christine was alone in the world, her delighted future mother-in-law took it upon herself to make sure the long-expected-never-really-anticipated event was going to be a perfect day. Myriam took Christine to an exclusive second hand store on Madison Avenue which had been highly recommended by her friends. There Christine tried on one bridal gown after another, each one more magnificent than the last one. Each dress had been worn once by a young woman with a large bank account. Myriam insisted it was the thing to do—a two thousand dollar outfit for five or six hundred dollars. She wanted Christine to accept one as a wedding present.

As she modeled the gowns and paraded around the place, Christine went from tears to suppressed laughter, back to tears, more laughter. One clerk murmured, "The usual case of nerves." Myriam agreed. Christine was tickled they couldn't read her thoughts. *I'm getting married in church in a wedding gown. I'm getting married in church in a wedding gown. There will be photographs of a happy bride at the arm of her very handsome, new husband.*

She tried one exquisite gown made of beaded French Chantilly lace over satin. The bodice with mandarin collar had long sleeves. There was lace appliquéd on the gown and the hemline. It was exquisite...

She tried on an enchanting A-line chiffon gown: enchanting...

Next was a silk taffeta ball gown with French bustle and cascading roses. It had a detachable chapel train: gorgeous...

Then an elegant *peau-de-soie* sheath she really liked: so very chic...

Myriam preferred the silk duchess satin with trumpet sheath. On Christine's head there would be a short trimmed veil attached to a headpiece and nosegay. What if Christine thought it was garish, showy. Myriam Hundley was paying...

So be it, she sighed silently.

Hiding the silent hysteria that threatened to choke her, the happy bride-to-be let her mother-in-law make the final arrangements.

While Myriam Hundley, her New York friend, and the manager of the store were oh-oh-ing and ah-ah-ing over each gown, Christine's mind wandered. She was already twenty-five years old. Brian O'Connell had not wanted children. She would convince Pierce that fatherhood would bring him great joy. There's no doubt marrying him was the answer. After she became an American citizen, she'd relax.

The timid voice of her past life whispered, *You could've returned to France. It was a great country before the war. There are some educated single Frenchmen left. In the Great War, most of the mature men were killed or maimed. In this last one, civilians were killed while the Germans promptly made prisoners of the soldiers who have since returned home.* She caught herself as she heard her own voice declare aloud, "But I don't want to go back." She looked around. Nobody was paying attention to her.

On December 8, 1947, Pierce Hundley took Christine Tourneau (it was the name on her French passport) for his wife. Their union was blessed in a chapel at the Cathedral of St. John the Divine by the Protestant minister of the campus of Columbia University in the presence of several teachers, a handful of students and Pierce's jubilant mother. Christine made a superhuman effort to concentrate on every moment, but she felt strangely disconnected from the proceedings. Her mind was devoid of coherent thoughts. If it were not for Pierce's tender look as he gazed into her misty eyes, she would not–she could not–believe the unreal scene was taking place.

Joel Rubin had escorted the bride in. He gave her away to his friend, Pierce Hundley. A professional photographer hired by the groom's mother took pictures–many pictures.

After the happy couple had been congratulated by the two dozen people there, the delighted matriarch took everyone present to dine at Chanterelle in Greenwich Village. Not only did Myriam Hundley pay the exorbitant bill without batting an eyelash, upon kissing her new daughter-in-law goodnight, she pressed money in the palm of her hand. With a smile, she forced the new Mrs. Hundley to close her fingers on several five hundred dollar bills. "Go shopping, darling," she suggested with elation. "I told my California friends you have that French *je-ne-sais-quoi*. You're always so very chic, honey. My son and you will always be the best-looking couple around."

There was no doubt in Christine's mind she had married the handsomest man—so, so good-looking. Attractive enough to be a movie star. Gregory Peck. Gary Grant. Rock Hudson. And educated. Sweet. Considerate. A perfect gentleman at all times.

Before the end of January 1948, Christine Hundley became an American citizen. She bought a heavy, old-fashioned, silver frame to hold the much-coveted official document. *Even better than a marriage certificate*, she whispered to herself.

After exams, young Mrs. Hundley stood in front of a college wall in Low Library, along with a crowd of boys and girls and some middle-aged students. They were scanning lists of identification numbers. Next to the secret number, known only to the student, was a grade.

In the midst of an apprehensive silence, out of the blue, a high-pitched female voice screeched, "She's got nothing but A's. Two A's and three A pluses." The screaming shrew was pointing a finger at Christine.

Professor Hundley had just arrived. He stopped dead in his tracks, just in time to hear his spouse inquire in a sweet, soft voice, "Do grades come in other letters of the alphabet?"

Pierce remained on the side until Christine spotted him and went towards him.

As they walked quietly away, side by side, Christine laughed, "It was a repeat of the day I got accepted at the University of Caen."

Pierce squeezed her arm. "Don't let other people bother you, honey. Be your own woman."

Christine turned her face to hide her sudden distress. She might be her own woman. An American woman, even. She was also a married woman. Legally married to the most gorgeous man who lived in his own apartment across the hall from hers.

CHAPTER 45

▼

BECAUSE THEY WERE BOTH TIRED AND in great need of a rest, the newly-weds did not go on their delayed honeymoon during the end of the year recess. Instead, they stayed in New Jersey. With daily trips to New York—Radio City Music Hall for the yearly Christmas pageant—Broadway shows—museums—restaurants—Fifth Avenue stores—Christine was delighted and Pierce was generous. Everywhere they went, women drooled with envy. God bless him, Pierce really never noticed.

It was at home in *her* apartment Christine became more and more disconcerted. For one thing, Pierce had not yet moved his clothes in. He shuffled back and forth between *his* place and hers. When she asked him why he didn't get rid of the superfluous rent, his answers grew vague. If she insisted it didn't make sense to have two addresses, his smile hardened ever so slightly, "Since the yearly contracts on both places run to the end of June, there is no immediate rush," he would reiterate, irked that she mentioned it again.

Christine felt a discontent that grew and grew. One day, she realized they were fighting very frequently, just as Pierce and Jack Smith had done. And because her new husband had yet to share her bed, her muddled brain demanded to be heard. The young woman lived in a state of mental confusion. Not really willing to accept. Too late to deny. To refuse the facts was insane. To acknowledge them was equally demented. She tried to keep her disturbing feelings at a tolerable level. She was in denial.

One evening, embarrassed and confused by her rampant thoughts, she declared to herself she'd go mad if they did not talk. She did. She found Pierce staring at her incredulously.

"Certainly, on the day we got married, you knew what kind of relationship we would have." He thought it was a fair bargain. She got her American citizenship. He squashed the nasty rumors about Jack and himself. He was told he'd get the promotion he deserved at the university. He was very pleased.

"Next year, I'll be the dean of all the Liberal Arts departments, darling. That's what I want."

Christine realized only a woman as naïve and inexperienced as she was would have been taken in. Was it too late to salvage the pieces? Perhaps not. She could foresee a day when two men or two women would be allowed to live together as so-called normal couples do. Pierce would come out of the closet where society forced him to live. He wouldn't need the sham. Jack or a new lover would materialize. Christine would go her way.

When finally Pierce murmured, "I thought you understood...," she interrupted him.

"I didn't."

"Christine, you're a very intelligent woman."

"Not when it comes to men."

"Stay with me, honey. I love you."

"You don't."

"There are all kinds of love, sweetheart. I do love you."

"Like a sister?"

"Like the beautiful woman you are. Your brains. Your thoughts. Your tastes. Your education. Your appreciation of every discovery you make."

"It won't be enough."

"For the moment, let's pretend that it is. Intercourse is not everything. We share so much. We are a twosome. If and when you meet another man you fall in love with, I'll let you go, I promise."

The man himself was not certain what he wanted from the relationship. He had reached a place where his emotional life was on perpetual currents. Draft after draft left him disoriented and frustrated. Unsatisfied. Disgruntled. To his own ears, he sounded neither convincing nor convinced.

Both Pierce and Christine knew in their hearts that the point of no return was getting closer.

Before the start of the spring semester, three Columbia couples decided to go spend a week on the beach at Martinique. At first, Christine declined, but then Pierce seemed certain he would stay by his wife's side every minute of the day and the night. He wasn't even sure Jack Smith was there. If he was, Pierce would prove to his wife that if she was strong enough to remain chaste, so was he. Christine was not as disassociated from Pierce's dilemma as she would have liked to believe. She loved him. She wanted to help him. She felt she herself could live up to the terms of their unusual agreement. But could he?

Their rented car took them from Joséphine de Beauharnais's birthplace to every sugar plantation. They visited all the rum distilleries. They dined in Creole restaurants in the charming capital of Fort de France. They strolled through the fantastic flower gardens. The height of the flamboyant orchids and the amaryllis kept Christine spellbound. She deeply inhaled their suave perfume. She watched (blushing) the lascivious movements of the dancers–a belly glued to another belly, pliant bodies swinging languorously from side to side in time to the mesmerizing Caribbean rhythm.

After a potent rum *maracuja*, Christine put her head down on the one twin bed, her senses filled to the brim with sunshine, colors, sounds, smells. Her body pleasingly relaxed, she told herself she was content.

When Pierce would decide to call it a day, he'd slip into the next bed quietly, not to disturb her.

From the furtive looks the other couples gave her at the end of the evening entertainment, she suspected Jack Smith had appeared on the scene as soon as she left. Bits of overheard conversations replayed in her memory. "Of course she knows."–"She agrees with the arrangement."–"His mother went back to California, happy."–"Christine must be playing the field."–"Do you think she's one, also? Women as well as men, you know."

Upon their return from the island, Pierce no longer attempted to pretend he was satisfied with the status quo. He became despondent. He missed teaching one class or another. He lost weight.

His wife suggested he should consult a psychiatrist. He refused.

She offered to go with him to speak to a marriage counselor. He refused.

In her heart, Christine loved the man. She wished they could go on living together. Two very good friends. Sincere interests in new horizons. Intelligent travel companions. Art lovers. Movies. Plays. Books. A platonic relationship. Why not? They could do it. *She* could do it, she was certain.

When in the middle of May, right after the end of the spring semester, Pierce packed to go to La Martinique, Christine knew she had lost the battle.

A week later, Jack Smith called the university with the shattering news. In turn, they informed Christine Hundley that her husband had drowned on the volcanic beach of Anse de Fortune on the French island he so loved. All they found on the beach that fateful day was his wallet inside his towel.

Looking at the face in her own mirror, Christine studied the pale features of an unknown woman. Now for the first time, she realized how distant she had become from Christine Tourneau. Her intent blue-green eyes hovered for a second on the oval face framed by blond curls. "Move over, Scarlet," she murmured. "Only twenty-five years old and I'm a widow for the third time."

CHAPTER 46

▼

COMPARED TO THE LENGTHY CHAPTER IN her life of girlish dreams about André Grassin and to the O'Connell episode of deception and violence, this last act in a tragedy of misguided conjugal ties was more gratifying than sad.

Indeed Pierce Hundley was a generous man. While they were married, he paid the two rents from his own pocket. Not only did he finance food, entertainment, utility bills, but he also bought his wife a car. "Now that you are Mrs. Hundley, darling, you don't have to pay for your studies at Columbia, you can afford to have a car of your own."

His wife loved the little Renault Dauphine a soldier had shipped over from France. When the seemingly eternal New York snows finally melted, she got brave. She drove across the George Washington Bridge to park on Columbia Avenue and One Hundred and Sixteenth Street.

In June, Myriam Hundley emptied her son's apartment. The gentle woman found time to be solicitous of Christine. In her motherly grief, she was thoughtful and kindhearted. She tried to convince her daughter-in-law she was the angel who could have turned her son's life around if Pierce had let her. She insisted Christine accept the beautiful dining room set and the gorgeous Chippendale sofa. Her parting words were cryptic. "Joel Rubin will be in touch with you. If you move, let him know where you're going."

Christine had no desire to move. Where would she go? She still had her job at the Inn. Between the long waitressing hours, her summer courses at Columbia, and the extra education classes at night in another college, she was mentally and physically exhausted all the time. She was emotionally barren. Spent. Drained. And yet, at the same time, she was content to be who she was and live her own rather unexciting days. For the first time in twenty-five years, she remained in the shallows of life, no longer tempted to seek out the depths and excitement she had previously craved.

Until she was fifteen, Christine had been pampered and cherished. She had no choice but to obey the pre-established rules: church, school, the nuns, her mother, her loving grandparents; all had kept her in a well-protected cocoon no intruder could ever reach and penetrate. Even during the five long years of war, she had always felt she could count on the dear people who loved her.

Death itself would eventually remove, one by one, huge fragments of the fortress. Pascal. Madeleine. Jacques. The three of them, much more so than André, who had been more fantasy than reality. After he vanished, Christine pushed open the gates leading to adulthood. She had done it at first very timidly. She had promptly fallen into the arms of a second male protector who would take her to the Garden of Eden.

When it turned out Boston was, for the wife of Brian O'Connell, a far more dangerous city than Avreville or Le Mans—occupied by the Nazis and the murderous S.S.—once more, she staggered out to try and become a woman who could stand on her own two feet. She was proud that it was not Brian O'Connell's death which had made her free. She had done it herself with fortitude.

Certainly along the way, the kind hands of Mother Superior had sustained her trembling first steps toward self-reliance. She remembered the nightmarish evening on the Greyhound bus. Where would she have gone if the sisters of Saint Vincent de Paul had refused to shelter her until she found a job that suited her? What pit would have opened to receive her? Thinking about that moment, she shuddered every time she read in her newspaper about exiled girls who became streetwalkers to stay alive.

When she married Pierce Hundley, Christine demonstrated what a bright student she was. The harsh lesson she learned during the turmoil of the Nazi Occupation was called survival. It had taken her a while to recognize that her mother was the one who had taught her all along–Germans or no Germans, Gestapo or no Gestapo–that it was natural to want to outlive adversity. Some people who are best fitted to the conditions in which they're placed will strive. Christine was grateful she had inherited Madeleine's intrinsic ability to endure misfortune and pain.

Christine had eagerly clenched the rope Pierce had thrown her. The lifeline was her second and final swim toward the U.S.A. With her American citizenship, she was now firmly anchored where she wanted to be forever. She asked herself if she had become wicked. Was she lacking human emotions of grief, regret, sadness? Why didn't she feel a greater amount of pain? Perhaps she had used her quota before she turned twenty-one. Indeed she was aware she had kept her part of the bargain with Pierce (a bargain it was, after all) and she had been so very eager to give Brian all the love he was unable to accept.

One day, Pierce's attorney called, "Joel Rubin here, Christine, when can I come? I've got important papers for you to sign."

Early Sunday morning. Joel brought the bagels. Christine made the coffee. Condolences were unnecessary. Joel had lost a good friend–a friend of long standing. Christine had lost a different kind of friend. They had no need for words. Joel's long hands patted Christine's tiny ones silently on the table. Softly the man murmured, "He loved you very much." "I loved him very much." "It wasn't to be." "*You* manage to have a home and children." Pierce had said she was perspicacious, intelligent, kind, gracious. She was nevertheless a real surprise. Tears ran down the man's cheeks. "Christine, even under these circumstances, I bring comforting news." "News?" "Look at this." He placed a check next to her coffee cup. Ten thousand dollars. The bearer, Christine Hundley. The giver, Pierce Hundley.

Before she found her voice to speak up, Joel answered her, "The week before you got married, Pierce gave me that sum to put in escrow in case something happened to him. He wanted you to go on with your studies. Don't let him down, honey, get your master's degree. That was his desire."

"So much money. I'm astonished."

"Use it, Christine, to make yourself happy. It's also Myriam Hundley's wish."

She *would* use it. She would stay in the apartment in Englewood. She would drive to New York and to Teaneck. It would save a lot of time. She would continue to work at the Clinton Inn in Tenafly and she'd be so busy she wouldn't ever look at another man. She would no longer have a weakness for bondage. No broad shoulders to cry upon. No hand to hold hers in the unknown, but also, no male commands to obey. She would be–she *was*–her own woman.

CHAPTER 47

▼

AT COLUMBIA, ONLY A VERY SMALL group of Pierce's friends knew Christine Hundley. To everyone else, she was Christine Tourneau. At the Clinton Inn, she had always been, from the first day, Christine Tourneau. When she married Pierce, she saw no reason to inform anybody of her new identity. Three months later, she knew she had made the right decision. Her private life should be of no interest to anyone there. If, human nature being what it was, someone cared to gossip about the French-girl-at-the-Inn, let them use their imagination. She chuckled inwardly. No one would possibly have enough creativity to come close to the truth. None of those people's inventive powers would endow the secretive Christine with three—not one, not two, but three—very attractive husbands, would they?

Three husbands in four years. Well, not at the same time. A trigamist she was *not*.

In June, it occurred to Christine she never saw Nick Tarzini at The Clinton Inn any more. The thought came to her on the day she waited on a table of members of the Tenafly Women's Club, whose president was still Nick's sister, Gina Jordano.

Gina remarked she hadn't seen Christine since Thanksgiving day at her house. Where had she been hiding the whole time? "Right here," said Christine. "I guess our paths didn't cross. I'm working on my master's in foreign languages at Columbia. I need the tips to pay the college tuition, my books, and the rent.

"Bravo," exclaimed Gina. "That's the thing to do. Women must become independent." The members of the club all agreed. "Smart girl. You can do it."

Chapter 48

▼

Speak of the devil. Nick Tarzini appeared at the Friday boxing match that very week. Same old silent act. The man didn't speak. Or when he did, Christine was not around. When she collected the empty bottles and returned with fresh drinks, he simply grinned in lieu of verbal thank yous. It was not exactly as if he made Christine feel practically invisible, it was more that she had the impression she was of very little interest to Nick Tarzini.

Whenever inadvertently she touched his arm as she deposited a bowl of peanuts in front of him, she was always uneasy about the flash fire of desire that filled her. She admonished herself. She was grown up now. She was no longer a dizzy girl who fell in love every time an attractive man looked her way. She was a mature woman making her way in life alone from now on. She had learned her lesson. She was not going to create a new disappointment for herself. Deep down, she couldn't help it; she was intrigued. Nick Tarzini's dark eyes held her under their magnetic charm. They seemed to say, *I know so much about you.* It was at the same time exhilarating and troubling.

Curious, she stopped to eavesdrop in the pantry. Fran, the stern manager, and perk, flirtatious Susie were at it again. "He's the strong, silent type, isn't he?"

"For the fifteen years I've worked here, I never heard him joke with a girl."

"What does he do for a living?"

"That's the clincher, no one knows for sure."

"Some of the guys at that table must know."

"They are evasive. They say he's based in Washington, D.C. and he travels a lot."

"I know John and Richard are either in the FBI or the new CIA. Nick Tarzini might be in some branch of Interpol."

"Perhaps he lives on his old man's Mafia money. There's enough, I'm told, to go around."

The only word Christine retained was 'Mafia'. Once, she'd married into the Irish Mafia. She wasn't sure she knew what the word encompassed with the epithet Irish in front. Wasn't a Mafioso a son of Sicily? She had no doubts Brian O'Connell was engaged in illicit trade—a lawless lawyer. It taught her not to judge a book by its cover. Or did it? In hindsight, she also saw things that should've clued her in to Pierce Hundley's true colors. How would she ever trust the next man when the ones before him had been anything but trustworthy?

Who was there to trust? Something in Nick Tarzini seemed to want to keep Christine at a significant distance. If occasionally he glanced at her with a thoughtful expression, if she sensed he might be attracted, for whatever reason, the man did not allow himself the possibility of a relationship. He had a frequently distracted look. In the far-away mood, no tentative joy would blossom. Then, perversely, there would be a devilish sparkle in his intelligent eyes. Yes, she told herself, the haughty, aloof man fascinates me. When I'm close enough to him, I can almost feel the strength of his big hands.

She would force herself to relax. She concentrated on the other customers at his table. She did not look at him. Still, while she was taking away empty beer bottles and bringing fresh ones, she reminded herself silently that once, in war-time France, she had been attracted to the magnetism of a tall, dark, dangerous man named André. A man who also kept his thought to himself. A man as mysterious as Nick Tarzini.

The inner voice whispered, *Christine Tourneau, you didn't do any better with two very handsome blond men, their brilliant blue eyes and devastating smiles...*

CHAPTER 49

▼

THAT NIGHT, CHRISTINE'S LITTLE RENAULT WAS at the garage for a check-up. When she got ready to go home, she saw four or five of the drinking buddies in animated conversation in the pouring summer rain. Nick Tarzini was wearing an olive drab, epauletted officer's raincoat stretching over the wide breadth of his massive shoulders, his strength palpable. Although Christine whispered to herself she was not ready to deal with this, she was intensely aware of the man. She tried to push those errant thoughts out of her mind. She couldn't do it. She knew that deep down she was dead-set on making him take notice of her.

She dropped her umbrella back in the stand by the door. She walked quickly to the bus stop at the end of the parking lot. From the Clinton Inn to her apartment, it was a ten-minute ride. She could hop either number fifteen or twenty. In a pinch, number twelve was close enough. She turned her back every time a bus she could use came around. It didn't stop. She was more and more drenched. Her limp hair stuck to her skull. Wasn't it rather obvious she was waiting to be picked up? She changed her mind. She would get on the next bus.

"Christine, is that you? Are you still here?" said a modulated, low, male voice. It thrilled her in spite of her resolve not to care. Irrationally, perversely, for a few seconds she felt trapped.

What does it look like? she was about to answer, angry with herself. She must be a sight. Her clothes glued to her, her hair a wet mop, her eyes, nose and chin dripping faucets. She managed to mumble, "No bus. Must be because of the rain."

Nick had gotten out of his car. He stood in front of Christine, wiping her face with a huge handkerchief, which smelled of aftershave and tobacco. "Come on, get in. I'll take you home." He held the passenger door open for her. He bent down to tuck the hem of her long skirt under her legs. He shut the door. Walked around the car. Sat behind the wheel.

Under his intense amused scrutiny, Christine felt an instant response—both discomfort and awareness. He must know she'd been waiting for him. She was almost certain he did when he shot her a wicked grin, "Where to?"

"Grand Avenue. Englewood."

While her insides had jolted as she stepped inside the car, she didn't blink. She was supposed to be irked by the unpredictable bus schedule—not congratulating herself. She straightened on the seat, all her senses heightened.

Having caught a whiff of her enticing French perfume and a hint of her womanly warmth, Nick drove silently. Christine chattered non-stop. About The Clinton Inn. About Columbia University. About the rain.

Nick braked to stop right in front of her apartment when he remembered he wasn't supposed to know where she lived. He passed the building. Christine ceased her nonsensical monologue, "Back there, number two hundred and ten." Nick parked where he was. They ran hand in hand under the lukewarm shower. Laughing.

In the entrance hall, he was considerate of her safety. "I'll see you to your door. It's late. Do you often come home this late?" He reached to brush wet hair from her face, the action incredibly intimate. He didn't like to think of her walking the long, deserted halls on her tap-tap-tap high heels. The tenants would know she was coming home alone. He waited until she'd opened the door. Glad to see she had two locks. He bent down. Kissed her on the cheek. "Good night, baby; be good." His actions were performed so smoothly, so easily, she wondered if he was even aware he'd touched her.

The rumble in Nick's own voice astonished him. The urge to just hold on to her there by the door was startling. Her hand was still in his, her eyes so wide. Again, he reached to brush back the stray tendrils of hair that had come loose around her face. He had to force himself to let her go. It wasn't easy.

There was a heavy pause. Finally, he said, "Good night, Christine." He was pleased with himself because his voice sounded determined and firm. He left.

CHAPTER 50

▼

FROM SEPTEMBER 1948, UNTIL MAY 1949, Christine went on with her harrowing schedule. She couldn't get out of it. She wanted to have her master's at the end of the school year.

One night at the Clinton Inn, Gina Jordano invited her to dinner on her free evening. At first Christine said she worked seven nights a week: either here as a waitress or at Columbia, or in a small college in nearby Teaneck to transfer what she considered rather non-essential education credits. She explained she'd be fully certified to teach in a public school in May. Gina congratulated her. She reiterated her invitation.

Perversely aware she was treading on dangerous ground, Christine took Sunday afternoon off and met the Jordanos for the second time–her heart going a mile a minute when she heard the beautiful masculine voice, "Did I see Christine's car out there?"

It became a Sunday ritual. The owners of the restaurant let her go at three o'clock. The girl was pushing herself too hard, and it wouldn't ingratiate them to the powerful Tarzini family if they didn't give Christine her Sunday afternoon.

More and more often, Nick shared his sister's family's Sunday dinner. When Christine got in her Dauphine to drive to Englewood, the big man accompanied their guest to her car. He bent down to kiss her on the forehead or on a cheek. He shut the door on the driver's side, "Bye, baby, be good."

Returning to Gina's house, Nick battled with his own mixed emotions. He knew his sister was guilty of attempted match-making. He told himself he had never succumbed to a woman's manipulative behavior before–he wouldn't start now with his sister, even if everyone in the family was on her side. He reentered the living room, poised for battle. He chuckled and said to himself: *Who am I fooling? They all know I'm head over heels in love with a complicated French woman...*

By the second Thanksgiving at Gina's house, Christine had met the friends and relatives of Nick Tarzini. That day she also met his mother, a sweet soft-spoken, short Italian lady, whose beautiful dark brown eyes she had bequeathed to her only son. There were, no doubt, speculations about the French guest. They were passed on with apparent innocence. The children were more open than the adults. Eight-year old Phyllis tugged Christine's skirt, "Are you Uncle Nick's new girlfriend?" In the sudden silence, blissfully unaware she was trespassing, the girl continued, "You don't look Italian; you have blond hair and blue eyes. You even have freckles."

From the living room where he was bouncing his two-year old nephew to touch the ceiling and to fly up and down like an airplane, Nick's laughter roared back to the kitchen, "See, Christine, that's how reputations are made in an Italian family."

CHAPTER 51

▼

PURPOSELY, CHRISTINE HAD TAKEN A BUS to work in the morning. When Nick drove Christine home later, as usual, he walked with her inside the building. But he didn't stop at the door of the apartment. He put his foot inside to prevent her from banging it on his face as she had done several times in the past–leading him to wonder whether she also felt a discontent about their parting with a chaste kiss on the cheek.

Nick went in. "Nice," he said, appreciating the big room. His roaming eyes took in the massive dining room table (she kept it without the leaves in it, but it still was impressive), the beautiful Chippendale couch, the tall green plants, the lovely knickknacks. "Nice," the man repeated, not really looking at the furniture.

Christine felt her cheeks grow hot. *Don't overreact again,* she admonished herself. *I won't give him a hint of how confused I am. It doesn't make sense. Anyway, I'm in control. I'm perfectly relaxed.*

Nick's arms swept around her waist, holding her against him. Her body was lithe and firm and fit nicely against his own. The top of her head reached his shoulder. Softly, tenderly, he kissed the perfumed short curls.

His manly, very personal smell clung to him. Mixed with the hint of tobacco (he was a heavy smoker, she'd noticed), the scent was appealing. With a thumb under her chin, he raised her face toward his. He kissed her long and hard. He came up for breath. He kissed her again. His voice seemed to carry a note of reproach (to whom? to him or to her?) when he backed up toward the door, "I'd better be going," he sighed audibly.

Her eyes were bright with unshed tears. She had lost her voice. She watched him leave. While she turned the double lock behind him, she sniffled the sob in her throat. Once more, the world around her was spinning. *Don't fall in love again,* chided the voice inside her. Was it already too late?

Nick sat behind the wheel of his new Ford, not moving. He was beginning to feel a little more on track, but his mind was still in a whirl. He felt giddy. Until today, he had never been so much in love. He was thirty-four years old. The first time he fell in love, he was twenty and in college. With hindsight, he knew his libido was at its peak then. It was lust more than love. He had grieved for many seasons after the little bitch had two-timed him. Being in love now was a kind of stupidity. In love with a foreign girl who was here today and might be gone tomorrow. He knew very little about her beyond the devastating smile and the flash of warmth that lingered in her eyes when she looked at him. And the way her body became sinuous and fluid in his embrace. In such moments he wondered what thoughts were running through her mind.

Nick Tarzini was in a suspended state of euphoria. He didn't want to put a stop to it. It was so wonderful he decided to remain in it. Yes, that was it. Why try to deny it: he was in love.

CHAPTER 52

▼

THROUGHOUT THE WINTER MONTHS, CHRISTINE FORGED a semi-convincing story for Nick's disappearing and reappearing acts. It made her heart soar that when he was in town, he gave up Friday at the Inn to take her out to a late dinner or a movie. When three or four weeks went by with no news, she concocted excuses. His job kept him away. He couldn't tell anyone where he was or why he went there.

That morning, the long-expected phone call had set her world right again. The now familiar voice asked casually, "Hi, babe, how about I pick you up after work tonight? What time?"

Whenever they were together at the Inn, he would be on a stool in the bar and they wouldn't talk to each other. His eyes full of mischief, he would shake his head imperceptibly to let her know enough was enough: she must stop flirting with this guy or that guy. He knew she was doing it to aggravate him, to make him pay for his lengthy silence. How could he know that when he was near her, she felt contented simply by being in his presence, in the same place with him? She would swallow with great difficulty. She would struggle to slow the rapid beating of her heart.

Because of the early phone call, she had taken a bus to work. Nick drove around the block to where she was waiting. He reached her door with his long arm and opened it. She slid into the seat. He pecked her left cheek, a simple action that incited instant longing. Deliberately she sat far away.

"Come closer, baby. Don't be angry. I couldn't help it. It's the job."

"The job *you* say," with an audible touch of petulance.

"I wish I could tell you," he murmured with a lightness he didn't feel. His voice deepened, "You have to take my word for it, honey. That's the way it has to be."

"You could've called."

"No, sweetheart. I cannot ever call you. You just have to believe me," he snapped, irritated by his own remorseful reaction. How he had fantasized what it would be like to have her near him every day. He pressed on the gas pedal angrily. He tried hard not to let her presence in the car unnerve him. He'd sworn he'd never let a woman break his heart again.

Christine was not appeased, "The job you say, Nick, your job or a woman?"

"No other woman, Christine. My heart is yours. You occupy the whole place when I'm away, believe me. You, baby, only you."

They were driving along the beautiful Hudson River, going toward the George Washington bridge. New York City lights on the skyscrapers created a fairy land they both reveled in. Nick pulled Christine very close to him. His touch had a tremendous effect on her. She sighed contentedly. She was discovering her body was finely tuned to his caresses. He drove with his left hand, leaving his right arm around her shoulders, holding her in a tight embrace. He told himself he could handle the situation, he would never lose his grip on reality, he was in full control here.

Christine was blissfully contented. *If Nick is telling me the truth, I will be happy with the moments stolen from the job. As long as I am not sharing him with another woman. As long as I am the one girl he kisses so deliciously.* His kisses were heavenly. She never had enough of them. And he was so strong. She basked in the man's strength. Until today, she had expended too much energy resisting the attraction.

CHAPTER 53

▼

WALKING DOWN THE HALL ON THEIR way to her apartment, Christine handed Nick her keys. Opening the door, he swept her up in his arms and shut the door with his foot. He carried her to her bed and laid her down on the pale, blue spread. The open windows let in a fragrant smell of lilacs. It was a sensuous spring evening.

Christine's lips were still on fire, crushed by Nick's masterful mouth, but she whispered limply, "No. Nick. No." She was aware that what she said and what she wanted were entirely different.

Nick's voice dropped to gentle and loving tones, "Yes, baby, yes."

She knew perfectly well she was trying to delay the inevitable: she could see it in his eyes gazing at her with a compelling mixture of male arrogance and tenderness. He was so determined and sure of himself; she breathed a small sigh of surrender.

He felt her tremble when he placed his hands on each side of her face. He wondered if she was going to cry. He never dreamed the kind of love he had for her was possible. All these years he had always been too wrapped up in his work. Now, wherever he was, he couldn't keep his mind off her. For the first time in his life, he had learned the meaning of the word loneliness. He counted the days, the hours, the minutes, until he could hold her in his arms again.

For her part, Christine had made a valiant effort to convince herself she did not want to ever fall in love again. Tonight she knew she did not wish to walk forever alone without a man–this man–to take the love she had to offer. She had a need to nurture. She had fallen in love with Nick Tarzini the first moment she saw him.

Nick undressed Christine slowly, stopping to kiss every inch of bare skin where his eyes roved with a thoroughness that made her feel warm all over. He covered her modesty with the blue bedspread and quickly joined her between the sheets. She felt the heat emanating from his naked body. She saw the shards of gold in the depths of his brown eyes. Her fingers touched the subtle shadow of beard along his jaw. He kissed her with raw passion. When he paused to catch his breath, timidly she traced the line of his bottom lip with a fingertip. The mounting passion spread like a wave through her body, followed by the moving of the earth....

The morning after Nick made love to her, Christine wavered from torment to panic to bliss. No remorse. She was no longer a naive twenty-year old. She had known that Nick's lips closing down on hers, searching, demanding were not a culmination. The man needed more. She, too, wanted more. She wanted to make him as happy as she was.

CHAPTER 54

▼

IN MAY, WHEN CHRISTINE GOT HER diploma, she started to look for a teaching position in a public high school in New Jersey. Nick arrived one evening full of what he considered to be good news. He was accustomed to having his decisions accepted,

"I spoke to my friend in Warrenton in Virginia. He has a job for you in his school: French, Spanish, German. Just what you want, Christine. You can live on our land, in a caretaker's house. Couple of empty ones. You'll have a choice. They're nice. You'll like them."

She shouldn't accept without questioning. She should stand on her own two feet. She should decline the offer.

She remained silent.

In June, she moved into the coziest cottage imaginable. A huge stone fireplace in a living room with dark beams. A second floor banister encircling a bedroom and bath. A dream come true. The hilly Virginia country was the touch completing the picture of the perfect place to live. To marry. To bring up children.

When he was home, Nick came to dinner. Jokingly, he said his mother was glad to get rid of him. Christine knew Amelia Tarzini wished to see her son married. Like herself many decades ago, the girl Nick was in love with was alone in this country. She returned his love, a mother could tell. She'd make him a good wife. What on earth was he waiting for? Soon he was going to be thirty-four.

CHAPTER 55

▼

THEY WERE SEATED ON THE RAMBLING porch, admiring the magnificent sunset, when Nick turned to Christine, "I never asked, but you do have a safe deposit box in your new bank here in Warrenton, don't you?"

"I mean to get one, any day."

"You do have your birth certificate, your diplomas, your citizenship papers, your husband's death certificate, don't you?"

"I don't have my husband's death certificate. Joel Rubin has asked, but he didn't get an answer yet. I think I should translate his letters into French. The island of Martinique is an administrative division of France."

Special Agent Dominick Tarzini's rigorous training and discipline came to the rescue as he hid his emotions–astonishment and dismay. Nick was a voracious reader of murder stories, the gorier, the better. Right now he could not recall the case of a wandering corpse, from Boston, U.S.A., to Ireland, and from there to a French island in the Caribbean. He stared at nothing, his mind a dance of question marks. Unaware of the turmoil her words caused, Christine asked with loving concern, "Do you think you should go to bed soon, darling. Remember, you have an early plane to catch."

Still dazed, Agent Tarzini kissed his lady goodnight on the cheek. A small kiss. He vanished into the darkness between his lover's cottage and his parents' mansion. Much later, in the middle of the night, Christine realized that Nick knew nothing about Pierce and their unconsummated marriage of convenience. She shrugged. She would explain it. Nick would believe her.

CHAPTER 56

▼

CHRISTINE LIKED HER NEW JOB. THE teachers in Martinsville High School were friendly. Colleagues and their families were her social life. Christine received many invitations to dinner. She also took many meals with Amelia Tarzini at the big house or in nearby restaurants, so she was never alone for long periods of time. Just enough to appreciate the time to herself. Time to read–mostly recent novels, biographies, history. Getting reacquainted with classics. She was never bored.

It was only when the days and the weeks stretched without the presence of the man she loved that she became lonely at times. Then she'd call Nick's mother. They played endless games of Canasta. They talked at random about France before and during the war (Nick had landed in Cherbourg on D-Day plus three), about Italy forty years ago, about the U.S.A.–they never lacked topics of conversation. Amelia Tarzini was intelligent, always pleasant. She had a great sense of humor. The two women laughed a lot together.

In December, Nick returned from wherever he had been with souvenirs for everybody, as usual. He delighted in giving his two sisters, his nieces and nephews, his mother and Christine presents he had bought thinking about them in the foreign countries he worked. Christine knew better than to ask where he had been. She didn't need to, she could tell from the gifts.

Nick told Christine that this time he was holding on to his souvenirs; they would be his Christmas presents. They'd remain a surprise until then. He stood in front of her, smiling, his probing gaze on her face. He loved to watch her emotions reflecting on her intelligent hazel eyes. She didn't have a poker face, that's for sure. Why today was she putting some distance between them? On each return, he welcomed the powerful attraction flowing between them. Until he met her, he was not prone to go berserk over a woman. Now he was putty in her hands. Why didn't she rush into his open arms this evening?

"Speaking of Christmas," he said, to give himself time to unravel the mood of the moment, "this afternoon after I left the headquarters, I browsed in town. Remember, honey, the ring you admired in the window of Holtzman Jewelry Store? It's still there — would you like it for Christmas?"

She was piqued. And she dared, "The only ring I want from you, Nick Tarzini, is a wedding band."

"Certainly," he replied undaunted, never out of his depth for very long, "I'll make an appointment with my friend, Bill Leonard."

"Bill's a doctor," she was both deflated and confused.

"In this country, honey, a man needs a certificate of good conduct, or more precisely, of clean health, before he can tie the knot."

CHAPTER 57

▼

CHRISTINE HUNDLEY CHANGED HER NAME TO Christine Tarzini with the help of a Justice of the Peace, who, naturally, was a good friend of Nick's. Ann Contini and her husband Pete were the witnesses. Without reading the documents presented to them, the four of them signed a couple of official-looking papers which Nick and his friend brushed off as merely a formality.

"I now pronounce you man and wife," the magistrate declared with a beaming smile. "What God has joined together, let no man put asunder."

"God," Christine mumbled, unaware she'd said it aloud.

Nick guffawed, "Don't worry, sweetheart, we *are* married. You're now Mrs. Dominick Tarzini–all very proper and legal."

Christine told herself she was imagining things when she thought she detected a suspicious hint of unease in her new husband's voice.

Perhaps the touch of constraint was on her side. For the first time God had nothing to say about this wedding ceremony. Later on, the bride would not ever be able to refer to it as her fourth trip down the aisle: there had been no aisle and no priest.

When Christine looked up into Nick's merry eyes, she saw a blend of joy, mischief, tenderness. Not an iota of doubt on her part either. The right article, the genuine one on this day, their wedding day. Nick Tarzini and Christine would be lovers forever and ever.

The happy bride declared she was ready for the feast.

All the guests were in a very jolly mood. In Amelia's house, the caterer displayed mouth-watering dishes. French pâté. Snails. Lasagna. Italian breads. Biscottis. Huge salads pungent with olive oil. Roast pork with a powerful garlic odor. Lots of wine. Lots of laughter. Two good reasons to rejoice: it was three days before Christmas, and Nick was married today.

Many pictures were taken. Not official ones. No professional photographer. When Ann had suggested one, Christine had vehemently objected. Too forcefully. She saw the bewildered look on her future sister-in-law's face. She did not elaborate, "I'm sure there'll be plenty of cameras and I'll put all the snapshots in a special album," she explained tentatively. She did not want to think about the double frame on Myriam Hundley's piano. She was certain it was still there and would remain there forever and ever. In a letter a couple of weeks after Pierce and Christine were married, a happy Myriam had written that on one side there was a picture of Christine alone in her gorgeous bridal gown, and on the other side, "the most handsome couple on their wedding day."

Christine had destroyed every picture of her three previous husbands. Her life began when she met Dominick Tarzini. The happy guests tonight would provide for a thick wedding album. The only one. The one she'd pass on to their children and grandchildren.

Today, the bride wore a two-piece outfit. Old rose. Taffeta. Long skirt to her ankles. Not too full. She loved the sheen of the silk. The fabric was both stiff and supple. Everyone could hear the feminine rustle of the pleats with her every move. Nick approved. He was so obviously pleased with his new wife.

And she with him.

He was very handsome and seemingly unaware of his dark attractive looks. A big man. A tender man. Her lover. Some day soon, a father—both of them wanted children. This was the happiest day of Christine's life.

The newly-weds were asked where they were going on their honeymoon. Christine giggled, "Nick doesn't want me to tell you."

Nick had had his share of wine and highballs—not to mention the champagne after the wedding cake—his eyes lit with tender amusement, "My bride is well trained." His face crumpled into a rueful grin, "We're hibernating in the cottage. If anyone—anyone—darkens our front door, I'll skin them alive."

CHAPTER 58

▼

NICK HAD SOME VACATION TIME COMING to him. He spent two months at home with his wife and introduced her to some of his Virginia friends. She in turn invited a few colleagues to dinner. She became better acquainted with Nick's sister, Ann (her mother called her Anna). Ann Contini; her husband Pete; and their two lovely children–Anthony, six; and Amber, four–lived in a new house built for them on the property, a mile down the narrow path meandering at the foot of their mountain.

A while back, Christine believed Ann did not like her. She was aloof. She seemed cold at first. In reality she was just like her mother, full of mischief. Easy laughter. A lot of fun. "I didn't know what to make of you, either," Ann explained to her new sister-in-law. "When Nick dumped you here in July, Mom and I believed you'd get married immediately. As time went on, we were angry with him and with you."

"Angry with me?"

"A woman should be able to make her man propose, especially...," she stopped in mid-statement.

"Especially when they're practically living together in view of everybody?"

"Not exactly," Ann retorted merrily. "Nick never moved all his clothes into your house. For all purposes, he was living with my mother in the mansion." She paused, smiled, "Close enough, I'd say."

Christine murmured, "I was ashamed. I shouldn't have let things go so far. I tried to tell Nick your mother was upset, but you know your brother; nobody can tell him what he should do."

She stopped. She didn't look at the other woman. She sighed, "I was so much in love with that man, I would've followed him to the end of the world...I never told my father or my sister that my new address in Virginia was also Nick Tarzini's address."

"Will they notice it now that you're married?"

Christine shrugged, "It doesn't matter any more. I'm Mrs. Dominick Tarzini," she finished with obvious contentment.

"So you are. We're glad. Finally, my baby brother settled down. And with the kind of woman we all wished for him. He was hard to please. So spoiled by women: his mother, his sisters, his girlfriends."

Uncertain if she should continue, she glanced at Christine. Telling herself the French girl was sophisticated enough to have accepted a liaison with her brother next door to their mother, she went on, "Nick dazzled all my friends. They found him so attractive, so charming, starting when he was in high school." She persisted, "Even when he never ever made a commitment—or perhaps because he didn't promise anything, some girls were determined to hang around until he proposed." She stopped, "I talk too much, that's what Pete says."

"Ann, I used to ask Nick where he had left his wife. I couldn't believe a woman had never gotten him."

"A woman did once."

"The one in college? I saw his yearbooks. That girl and he were in pictures together many times in his senior year."

"That's the one. We never met her, but my brother was head over heels in love. When she dumped him for the next captain of the football team, Nick didn't look at a woman again. At least at home he didn't date. Or rarely. He became a confirmed bachelor."

"Unconfirmed nowadays," Christine laughed gleefully.

Ann laughed, too, "We're so glad he married you, Christine. You'll be happy together. Nick has always been a nice brother and a loving son. He will be a good husband and a great father."

CHAPTER 59

▼

AT FIRST, CHRISTINE BELIEVED THERE WOULD be no wedding presents from France. Philippe, Nicole, Claudette, and Blanche were all extremely mad at her. They had hoped she'd return to them. When she got married a fourth time, they gave up on her. She'd made it clear she didn't want to live in France. "The American" she was. "The American" she'd stay. With the French touch of superiority and sarcasm, they seemed to have forgotten D-Day. If they didn't quite forget–how could they–they persuaded themselves the war was good for the economy of the huge country suffering from the depression. Sure the Yanks came to die on their soil, and they were grateful. Still, the French were envious. It would be a long time before France enjoyed a quality of life equivalent to that of the U.S.A.

When the wedding presents from France finally arrived, Christine realized they had been thoughtfully selected. Nicole and her husband were in the French-occupied section of Berlin. They sent a cuckoo-clock from the Black Forest. They knew Christine's love of clocks. Blanche had not forgotten either. She wrote her "American" granddaughter that the antique grandfather clock was on its way to her. Christine cried with joy. The tall clock was part of her childhood–so much that she knew she'd never part with it, no matter how long she lived. It was made around eighteen hundred. In those days there was no TV, no radio, no digital watches, no electricity, so when it rang in the middle of the night, a sleeping farmer wasn't certain if he counted three or four rings –– should he get up? Could he turn around on his pillow and continue his dream? –– the clock rang a second time a minute later. One, two, three, four. Darn. Time to get up. Yes, the beloved clock would make Christine feel closer to her grandparents. She would cherish it forever.

Christine would never know who had decided to send her parents' bedroom set. Perhaps Odette Tourneau preferred to exile a reminder of Madeleine Tourneau. Likely the four-poster twin beds were not to Odette's liking. She preferred very modern furniture. Perhaps Aunt Sophie had shamed her brother-in-law, "Philippe, why don't you give my sister's daughter something that belonged to her mother?"

Claudette sent a set of dishes a century old. She wrote there were so many sets in her in-laws' restaurant, she distributed them to their friends as wedding presents. She had not forgotten Christine's taste for the lovely hand painted Côte d'Argent. The primitive colors–blue, yellow, green, just a touch of red–were enhanced by any tablecloth Christine put under them. It needed the heavy tableware which arrived in a wooden box a month later. Christine gasped, "My mother's silver," she told Ann. "My father's second wife parted with it. She sent it to me. Look at it, the T for Tourneau is now the T for Tarzini," she laughed.

Mirth was mingled with affection in Ann's voice, "Your grandkids won't know which side of the family bequeathed this heavy, old silverware to them."

Christine had grown up surrounded by the Tourneaus' lovely antiques, so she took them for granted. They were handed down from generation to generation. In most cases, they already were in the farmhouse or the manor when the newlyweds moved in. Each new family added to them. The occasions for carefully-selected gifts were plentiful: Christmas, birthdays, christenings, first communions, betrothals, weddings. The three Tourneau women had loved to shop together. Philippe was generous, not only with their designer clothes and soft leather Italian shoes, but also with presents. The French liked to outdo one another with whimsical items–often destined to be a conversation piece. Now that ancient treasures were arriving in Virginia, Christine and Nick were delighted. The man himself collected beautiful foreign souvenirs during his treks all over the world.

Already, the cozy cottage looked as if the Tarzinis had been living in it for years: nostalgic pieces of furniture and familiar objects created a downy, snug nest that sheltered their precious love.

CHAPTER 60

▼

IN HER LETTERS, AUNT SOPHIE WAS explicit. Odette Tourneau got rid of everything that reminded her of the first Mrs. Tourneau. "She's a lame brain. She lives from morning to night–and no doubt, night to morning–to please her formidable husband. Naturally, your father gobbles it up. A man likes to have his wife at his feet. She tells everyone she adores him. As you well know, he never was tight-fisted, and he is very good to her son. Odette is no Madeleine. She has nothing to do all day except pamper herself and shop. We may not have much in our stores, but somehow the woman finds what she's looking for. Money opens the doors. Money buys anything. You won't believe your eyes when you come home, Christine. When, darling? I'm not getting any younger. Your grandmother also wants to see you before she dies. Sorry if it sounds like the emotional blackmail that it is. When you see the house on Avenue Rhine and Danube, darling, you'll be glad your dear mother never lived there."

When?

At times–when Nick had been gone too long–Christine was so homesick she cried herself to sleep. She couldn't tell Amelia, who had never wanted to go back to Italy. And never did. A couple of times her husband went to visit his relatives in the Alps, north of Genoa, but his wife did not accompany him.

Christine was not quite ready to go to France. Not yet. Some day. First, she wanted a baby. No, first she wanted to hear Nick say "I love you." He loves me. Why can't he say, "I love you." Is it because I'm a dysfunctional partner in bed. I don't bring him the thrills the trashy modern novels describe in near pornographic terms.

She dared–almost dared–to voice her unhappiness to Ann, who was by now the sister she needed. She couldn't do it. What she said was that perhaps she should see a gynecologist. A woman.

"No, darling, you must make an appointment with my gynecologist, Fred Burham. He's good."

160

Perhaps Dr. Burham was a good doctor, but when Christine found herself trapped on a high table in the humiliating supine position, her feet in the stirrups and the lower part of her body exposed to the probing eyes of the specialist in women's reproductive systems –and his interested nurse–she wanted to get off and run. With superhuman effort, she controlled the hysteria threatening to choke her. Laugh. Don't cry. You want a child. You're the female. While you're here and a stranger is poking his gloved finger into your most secret places, the male of the species is walking nonchalantly on the shores of the Mediterranean Sea. That's where Nick's last postcard was sent–by a benign "tourist" in Cairo. She hates him. She hates all men. She wants out of here. Now.

Dr. Burham brought down the white sheet. *Some joke, that sheet. It covers what?* The man held the cloth in front of the naked part of her body. "You can get down now, Christine."

She reported to Ann as soon as she got home. "Dr. B., as you call him, says I'm perfectly healthy and there's no reason I can't get pregnant." It occurred to her as she was saying it, that perhaps the blame rested on Nick. God forbid.

What she didn't tell Ann was the embarrassing conversation the doctor and she had in his office after the consultation. The gynecologist was old enough to have practiced a concerned professional voice that usually served him well. "Tell me, Christine (he could certainly call her by her first name; he'd seen more of her than any man in her life), tell me, child, do you love your husband?"

"Yes, I do. I do."

"Are you attracted to him? Is he handsome?"

"Very handsome."

"How long have you been married?"

He knew, of course. It was on the sheet of paper in front of him. What he didn't know, and she wasn't about to divulge, was that Nick Tarzini was her fourth husband–albeit the third one in her bed. The next question confused her. "Do you like to sleep with Nick?"

"To *sleep* with him?"

The doctor and the nurse burst out laughing. Christine was peeved because she was blushing again.

"Child, I mean do you enjoy intercourse with your husband?"

Now Dr. B. was definitely trespassing. She didn't have to answer the question. She would not answer the question. She whimpered, "I'll learn to relax. I'm trying, honest I am."

Softly the doctor assured her, "You will, Christine. Give yourself time." The doctor voiced concerns to himself only: *Too bad Nick is away so much. I wonder if when he returns, starved for affection, whether he has the patience this desperate young woman deserves.* He stared at her pensively. Who would believe, looking at the gorgeous Mrs. Tarzini, that the girl is so inhibited, she's unable to enjoy her husband. I'd like to meet the man. I hope he has a great sense of humor. He must be the envy of other guys who believe when they hear her easy flirtatious laugh...Well, I wish Nick Tarzini luck.

CHAPTER 61

▼

A FEW MONTHS LATER, THE OBSTETRICIAN was pleased to confirm Christine was pregnant. The birth of the baby was due at the end of January–give or take a week. "With the first child, it is sometimes hard to tell when the woman conceived," Dr. B. explained.

In August, Christine requested, and received, a personal leave of absence in the fall. When in October she told her colleagues she was six months pregnant, they were surprised. She didn't show at all. No doubt she was pregnant, though. No morning sickness. It was in the middle of the afternoon, upon returning from work that she vomited her breakfast and her lunch onto the driveway.

Nick was delirious. He was so happy, it made Christine forget that she loathed being pregnant. She wanted the baby. Yes, she did. As much as Nick did. She despised being pregnant. She hated her protruding belly which sent her off balance when she forgot and moved too quickly. When she went downstairs very fast, the surprised baby jumped up to hide under her ribs. It punched. It hurt. "Move over," she'd whisper, pushing the bony elbow or foot away.

Christine had never liked sewing, knitting or any of the needlework Nicole enjoyed doing. Nevertheless, she bought wool. She made tiny sweaters. Socks. Hats. All white, because it wouldn't do to dress a baby girl in blue or a baby boy in pink.

"What do you want, Christine?" asked Dr. B. one day. "A boy or a girl?"

"A girl. But I'm not sure about my husband."

"Did you ask him?"

"Ask him? No." After a pause, "There's nothing we can do about it. We'll be happy with what God sends us."

"Why do you want a girl, Christine?"

"Because if it's a boy, and he never wants to play football..." She stopped.

"A Tarzini boy must play football?" with a chuckle.

"Yes, of course."

"What if he didn't?"

"His father would be very displeased. My husband and all his friends played football. Nick has loads of trophies. He was the football captain in high school and in college."

"I see."

She could tell Dr. B. took pleasure in teasing her. "And you, Christine, are you athletic?"

"Me. No. One day I told Nick he went to school on his brawn and I went on my brains—quite a difference."

Dr. B. burst out laughing, "What did Nick say?"

"He showed me the one trophy that proclaimed him the athlete-scholar or the scholar-athlete—I forget—of that year."

When Dr. B. stopped bantering and became extremely serious in the last two months of her pregnancy, Christine was fearful. She felt anxious. Something was wrong. Because it was her first pregnancy, she didn't know what to expect. She told Ann the baby hardly moved nowadays. The woman promptly reassured her, "The baby is much bigger. It can't flip around. It's head down, getting ready to come out."

To whittle away the slowly passing days and hours, Christine knitted more baby blankets and more tiny garments. She made double and triple sets of crib sheets, bordered with delicate lace. She made a dozen little camisoles. She sewed a ruffled skirt to the bassinet they'd keep in their bedroom at first. She even made panties to cover the unsightly diapers. Ann teased her, "That Tarzini kid's going to be a picture of French elegance."

Christmas time came and went. Christine was so irritable, her relatives stopped trying to cheer her up. She was uncomfortable. She couldn't sleep even with the pillow Nick tucked under her belly. She bumped into things, not so much because her ridiculous stomach stuck out a foot in front of her (from the back she didn't look pregnant), but because she worried it was all for nothing. She had a growing premonition they were heading for a pit. A black hole. A disaster. She cried at night. She wanted Nicole and Claudette near her. Why were her best friend and her sister so far away from her when she needed them so much?

Nick tried to remain cheerful. When they brought the baby home, Christine would be her sunny self again. She was resilient. Every day she was getting better equipped to deal with her overwhelming memories. In the

U.S.A. she was free from all that had happened to her in the long four years shared with the Nazis. The emotional scars were fading slowly.

Nick knew that Christine had reconstructed her life. She found a great deal of comfort in being in a strange land—one that was no longer foreign to her. Now that her belly was huge, she tried to remain far from Nick in bed, but he would reach for her anyway. When she didn't move, he slid toward her, holding her close so her warm stomach, where the baby lay inside her, pressed into him. He put his hand on her swollen abdomen and brought his lips to her neck, "Don't be afraid, honey, soon the baby will be born. You'll be fine, sweetheart."

Nick's mother's descriptions of her own peculiar moods during her pregnancies were the tonic that strengthened him. But they didn't help Christine. She refused to be cheered. Nothing anyone said could dispel her gloom.

In his heavy heart, the man was catching his wife's melancholy. Anxious for the baby to be born, Nick tried to believe the last remnants of Christine's war wounds would finally be annihilated by her love for their first child. And his own war wounds too.

Two weeks after her due date, Christine insisted Nick take her to the hospital. She was too distressed to realize her husband was very upset—her foreboding contagious. Outwardly, he remained his usual self. Watchful. Solicitous. Tender. Careful not to add to her anxiety.

CHAPTER 62

▼

IT MUST BE LATE AT NIGHT, Christine thought, lying in the hard bed. She focused on the pale-green curtains, the acoustical ceiling tiles–she was in a hospital. It was very dark outside her window. She sensed the presence of other people in the room. Whispers. From time to time, laughter.

She patted her tummy. It was flat. Her baby had been born.

She turned her head on the pillow. There was a second bed in the room. A radiant young woman was sitting up, her back resting on two big pillows. A man held her hand on top of the bedspread. There were other people there.

"She's awake," the man whispered.

The happy new mother said, "She doesn't know yet that her baby's dead."

Christine let out a loud cry; she shrieked on and on.

The young father looked appalled. His wife shrugged.

A nurse entered the room. As she walked toward Christine's bed, she spoke to the stunned visitors, "I knew that one would be trouble. A foreigner. A pampered daddy's little girl."

"Why is this woman in the same room with my wife?" asked the young husband who seemed to have a certain degree of compassion.

"She's not contagious. She's a maternity case. That's why she's here."

Head nurse Powell was shoved aside roughly by the hand of Nick Tarzini, who'd just arrived, "I can't believe they put you in a room with another woman, darling," he bellowed. He picked his wife up and carried her out of the room. He had brought a warm housecoat and a blanket in which he wrapped Christine up. He placed his weeping wife gently in the wheelchair a green-striped aid pushed forward. They went down the hall while the shrewish nurse was shouting, "Stop. You can't do that."

"I can't?" Nick barked. "Who says I can't?"

"What I mean is she has to be discharged. She has pills to take to stop the milk. She..."

The wicked woman was interrupted by Dr. Burham. The man was furious. "I told you to put Mrs. Tarzini in a private room, Mrs. Powell."

"I don't see why. She's a maternity case," the stubborn harridan reiterated. On the sly, she mumbled, "Some of us in this hospital know the great Dr. Burham never delivers a handicapped kid." She was interrupted suddenly. She hollered when Nick Tarzini grabbed her by the arm and threw her forcefully into the nearest room.

CHAPTER 63

▼

WHEN ANN OR AMELIA ARRIVED WITH homemade minestrone or a dish of pasta, Nick thanked them and promptly showed them the door. "She wants to see no one." They knew better than to insist. They went to church to light candles in front of their favorite saints.

Nick was not a man who attended church services regularly. His seven years in the American army —- five of them in war-time in Europe–had not taught him how to pray. Why would God allow such atrocities? And now, why Christine? Why me? Why us? Nick hurt deeply. He wished he could put his grief into words. Why couldn't he communicate his feelings? Why couldn't he ever express all the pent up emotions in his soul? Some ancestral genes. . . In his profession, he was not timid. Within the walls of his own castle, all he could do was ask the woman he married to talk to him.

Right now, Christine was silent. Nick murmured, "Better we didn't have to see this poor little girl grow up. We'll have other children, honey. Healthy children."

"I would've loved her."

"Yes, darling, you would have." He stopped abruptly. He hoped Christine had not heard the accusing words spoken by head nurse Powell. But she had. The spiteful remarks continued to replay themselves in Christine's troubled mind. She whispered, "Nick, was the baby born alive?"

Troubled, the man stammered, "No, darling, she was not." He caught his breath, and added, "The baby was stillborn."

Christine insisted, "Could she have been saved if she'd been born on the due date?"

For days, Nick had mulled over the same disturbing thoughts. "I don't know, sweetheart, honestly, I don't know." His wife's sorrows and his own, overwhelmed him. Slowly, he admitted, "Personally, I feel it's better the baby didn't live. What good does it do to watch a handicapped child suffer through life. That's my selfish way of looking at it." Wistfully, he repeated, "We'll have other kids, honey." He needed to believe it.

CHAPTER 64

▼

DR. BURHAM HAD BEEN INSISTENT, "YOU'RE a clean living man, Nick; this is not your fault. Neither is it Christine's. Unfortunately such things happen. Your wife will bounce back. Not tomorrow certainly, but she will. You know she's a strong woman."

Nick had been attracted by her looks –she was so beautiful–and also by her infectious, quick laughter, her love of everything around her, her courage to let the past lay dormant. She didn't dwell on the hurts of previous years. Given time, once again she would heal. The man admired her inner strength. Twice widowed in her new country of adoption, after all those other deaths in France: mother, brother, grandfather–and now her baby. This last calamity was the last straw.

As the days passed, Christine's depression worsened. She refused food. She did not sleep. For weeks she didn't bother getting dressed. She dragged her feet from here to there. In another world altogether. Flagellation. Despair. An eye for an eye. A tooth for a tooth. The God of her youth had gotten even with her. Did it mean he'd see to it she'd never have any children? It was years ago. Did God hold a grudge that long? Nick didn't sin–he should not be punished. Is that what marriage was about? From now on, both Nick and she would travel hand in hand together. Together they'd suffer, cry, despair, rejoice. *Nick, I love you so much. I need you so much. Please tell me you love me–even now when I let you down. . .*

In other moments, Christine would have spoken to Nick. After a while, he might, just might, find his own words. Right now, though, she was mute, her grief silent, her hurt private. Nick sat by her bed. From time to time he caressed her hair softly. If only he could cuddle her in his loving arms. He didn't dare. She didn't have to tell him to stay away from her. He hoped to God she didn't blame him. Helplessly, he whispered, "Fred Burham says they don't know why those accidents occur. It happens in the best of families."

Christine made a superhuman effort to penetrate the black layers shrouding her mind, she knew the dreaded cloud had descended upon her once more. *I am mad,* she thought. *Again.*

Her dreams haunted her. A flowered dress on a feminine specter who carried a corset box preceded her on the steps of a city bus...A beloved brother was calling her from a mountain top in Sicily...An eerie warrior, yesterday so vital, crushed by a tidal wave of German panzers walked between the crumbling walls of a long-defunct rectory...A tall, white-haired old man who never liked the soldier rode his bicycle under an aerial fight...A drunken maniac held his wife's hair like a wig between fingers that were deadly hooks...A stillborn baby girl was crying in an empty crib...

Everyone had died. She was so guilty...

She never told her mother how much she admired her. She didn't marry André Grassin, the man; she married a dream she had created over a period of eight adolescent years. She followed Brian O'Connell to Boston because she was fleeing from gnawing boredom and brutal death. She made a bargain with Pierce to secure the right to stay in the Promised Land. She could not give the one man she really loved a child. *I am a complete failure,* she told herself over and over again. *A fraud. A shame.*

Chapter 65

▼

As they sat by Nick's wife's bedside, Gina and Ann were chatting about a friend of theirs who believed she needed the services of a shrink. Christine was having a fairly good day. She enjoyed their bantering. Not understanding the American jargon, she asked, "A 'shrink,' what kind of a creature is that?"

"It's some guy who calls himself a doctor. Mary will pay fifty dollars an hour just to be able to talk to him."

"That much money, just to talk?"

"She tells him all her marital problems and she walks out of there a new woman," Ann said, laughter in her voice.

"As a lizard sheds its skin," Gina giggled.

"And Mary has a good husband, two nice kids, a gorgeous house and plenty of money to boot. But she says she is very unhappy," Ann added, more soberly.

Christine murmured absent-mindedly, "Maybe talking with a stranger helps." "But a 'shrink,' you said?" Her sisters-in-law burst out laughing. With feigned indignation, Ann explained, "Not someone who shrinks your brains with some perverted instrument of torture–a psychiatrist, honey."

In her darkest moment of despair, the "shrink" seemed to only way out. Surreptitiously from a pay phone in a nearby drug store, Christine made an appointment with Doctor Jeff Greenberg. In his waiting room, she told herself that if her unbearable pain could be only shrunk and not cured, it still would be worth the money.

Reclining on a Marie Antoinette sofa, she felt so foolish that she wanted desperately to walk out of there on the spot. She mustered her courage and stayed. Dr Greenberg was seated behind her. She couldn't see him. The psychiatrist didn't say ten words to her. But the flood gates suddenly opened and Christine talked and talked and talked. She was interrupted by the man's voice, "Thank you, Christine. On your way out make your next appointment with my secretary, please."

The efficient receptionist had already checked a page of her agenda a week hence. She raised her face and stared at Christine with an astonished look, "Mrs. Tarzini, did you say a *month* from today? You mean a week from today, don't you?"

"No, Dr. Greenberg said a month."

"I see."

On her way home, feeling much better, Christine decided she would cancel the appointment and use the money to buy a pair of high-heeled sandals––the ones in the pastel shades would go well with several of her spring outfits. *It will be a much better use of the fifty dollars,* she thought, laughing. The half-hour of uninterrupted monologue in Dr. Greenberg's office was the medicine she had needed. It cured her.

She was so relieved she talked aloud to herself in the car. *Oh, yes, I'm healthy again. I simply had to unravel my guilt feelings. I needed to recline on Marie Antoinette's sofa. Much, much better than a session on my knees in a confessional.*

Driving through the Virginian meandering country roads, she recited in a loud voice: *"Agnus Dei, qui tollis peccata mundi..." The Lamb of God had erased her sins; her soul was purified.*

CHAPTER 66

▼

FROM THAT DAY ON, CHRISTINE WILLED herself to get better. To clear her befuddled brain, she showered three or four times a day. She made herself eat. She took her husband by the arm and they went out in the beautiful Virginia hills in search of the wild flowers she put in colorful handmade pottery. They discovered lichens which bloomed with abandon near the clear water of their brook. "I don't care if they're not really flowers," she said, "I like their vivid colors."

They felt twenty or thirty years younger. Two kids bent over a worm, a snail, an ant hill. They studied the crevices in the bark of a tree very seriously. They listened in awe to the caroling of the robins. The numb, gray mood melted in the warm April sun. Christine's carefree laugh cured Nick's sick heart. They went home to make love in the afternoon. In a magic moment, their bodies met in an intimacy which transcended the threshold of language.

Christine waited five months before she finally made an appointment with Fred Burham. He didn't have the heart to scold her. He put a jar of calcium pills in her hand, "Take them. You can't drink milk, but you must make strong bones for the baby. And save your beautiful teeth," he teased.

Somewhere in the eighth month, Christine had reached the end of her brave act. She couldn't go on any longer. Nick was away. She got dressed at two o'clock in the morning. It was a warm night. She slid, with great difficulty, behind the wheel of the car. She's took herself to the hospital to have this baby right then.

A frantic nurse on duty rang Dr. Burham at home. She stuttered on the phone. She–like all other nurses–was afraid of him, his temper, and his knowledge. Nothing escaped him. To her surprise he said, "Don't do anything. Let Mrs. Tarzini sit in the waiting room. I'll be right over."

Silently Dr. Burham walked cautiously into the dark lounge. On the way he had rehearsed, "Hi, sweetheart. Bad night?"

"I've been good for eight months. I can't wait any longer. I want this baby out of me."

"Let's talk this over, shall we?" He smiled from ear to ear, braced with professional understanding.

"Don't tell me the baby's fine. You don't know. You're not God. I've got labor pains."

"You don't have labor pains, honey. You just imagine you do. Go back home, sweetheart. In the next four weeks, the baby will gain a couple of pounds. A seven pound baby is a lot easier to raise than a five pounder, believe me."

A resigned Christine went home.

On Good Friday, a healthy baby girl was born: seven pounds, eight ounces. They name her Désirée. Desi for short.

That same day in the hospital, the hated Mrs. Powell decided to take a week off. The nurses were having a great time. The woman had finally met her equal. She was afraid of Nick Tarzini. Gentle Nick, who brought something to "the girls" every day: French chocolates, Italian *torrone*, American peanut brittle. "That's my daughter," he joked, "fifty percent French, fifty percent Italian, one hundred percent American."

The "girls" loved him. He was so handsome. Nice too. A charmer. And he was in love with his cute French wife. The nicest couple. And now they were a family as he whistled down the hall..."And baby makes three."

Another nurse was not so enthused–the morning one. "Christine does not want to be awakened at six o'clock in the morning to be told to brush her teeth and to have her temperature taken," her husband told Fred Burham. "A new mother needs her sleep. Don't go see her before eight. And make sure the first cup of coffee you bring her is hot, not lukewarm." With glee, Dr. B. decreed Nick Tarzini's orders must be followed. It was an outrage.

CHAPTER 67

▼

ANN CHASED HER HUSBAND AWAY. HER two hands on his back, she pushed him, "Go home, Pete. You're not needed anymore."

"Bye, girls." He winked at his mother-in-law as he left. He had come to move furniture. The nursery was ready for Desiree. The small couch and the old desk there last year reclaimed their rightful place in Nick and Christine's huge bedroom. The last time, Ann and Amelia cried themselves sick as they frantically removed the crib, the bureau, the dressing table. Now the furniture was brought down from the attic once again. Last time, no baby. Today, a beautiful little girl.

They placed the bassinet in the parents' room, next to Christine's side of the bed. "Not a good idea," says Amelia. "Christine will have to get used to the baby sleeping in her own room. Newborns make all kinds of frightful noises. Our Christine is high strung; she'll worry about every sniffle."

"Look who's talking," Gina jibed. "The mother who held the hands of her toddlers through the bars of the crib until they were three years old." Gina couldn't wait to see Nick's daughter. She came from New Jersey to visit Christine and the baby in the hospital.

"A mother is a mother," Amelia declared profoundly.

"You're a good grandmother, also, Nona. We all love you."

"A new baby in the family makes everybody sentimental. I'm weepy. We close ranks around the little ones, don't we?"

"It's your seventh grandchild, Mom." With a big grin, Gina admitted, "But it's Nick's first-born. That makes Desi special."

"But she's special to me, also," Christine asserted a week later, "and I should've had something to say about the christening."

"I'm sorry," retorted the sheepish father. "My mother planned everything for Desi as she did for her other grandchildren. I should've told her you wanted to take care of things. I guess I give in to her too easily. For the sake of peace," he finished lamely.

175

Christine found the admission disarmingly frank and somewhat unexpected.

"Ann and Gina don't object," she caught herself just in time. *Better not say 'she's their mother, not mine'. Besides, I like Nick's mother. She's my mother, also, and she keeps telling me how happy she is Nick married me.* Mollified, she acquiesced. Let them have their way now. She told herself she didn't care if the baby was baptized in the Catholic church or in any other Christian church. Later on she'd have *her* way. No use fussing today. Nick had obviously agreed to everything. The man was impervious to hints–she'd be wasting her time.

Christine had better things to do than fret over some decisions she wasn't asked to make. She had a precious baby to cuddle. She was in awe of her beloved *fructus ventris* (she had not quite forgotten her Latin). Hers. Sure, Desi was Nick's child, also. But hers many times over. She devoted her every breath to the little girl. She carried the infant on her left shoulder while she cooked dinner or pushed the vacuum cleaner with the right hand. A small rag doll. The little body warm. The unique odor of newly-made baby skin. Mixed with scents of talcum powder, formula, burps, soiled diapers. Promptly changed. Desi was a sweet smelling baby at all times.

Mother and daughter bonded as Christine had not been allowed to bond with her own mother thirty years before. When she was but a few weeks old, Desi recognized her mother's voice. Usually it meant she cried to get her attention and to tickle her worrybone. If Nick wasn't home, Christine would run to Nona. She was glad the woman never made fun of her. She understood new mother's anxiety. She remembered. "A little colic. No reason to call the doctor."

Nona placed the baby on her stomach across her lap. She rubbed the little girl's back. A man-size belch came out. The two women laughed. The baby was already sound asleep.

CHAPTER 68

▼

WHEN NICK WAS HOME, HE SWUNG the infant way up near the high ceiling, flying her like an airplane. Christine was frantic. When she was way up there, the baby was so little in the man's big hands. Desi loved it. She shrieked with a mixture of terror and delight. Secured already in Daddy's hands. Daddy.

Her first word: Daddy.

Christine pretended to be upset. Pretended? Nick said casually—too casually—"The sound of D is easier than M." Christine wasn't convinced. She'd reproach Desi. "Young woman, you're only five months old. Already you turn to mush when you hear that man's voice. That's not the way I'm bringing you up."

Nick bellowed, "Christine, are you jealous?"

Christine saved her resentment for the right time. On the pillow. Dear "Daddy" would have to beg a little tonight.

The baby was what everybody called a very good baby (is there ever a bad baby)? On Mother's Day, when she was but three weeks old, she slept from the last bottle at ten until five in the morning. It seemed natural to Christine. She would learn with the next children what was natural, or not, Nona would warn. Not every infant sleeps through the night. Some switch night with day. The new mother walks the floor while everyone else knows it's dark: time to sleep. Not for her.

Christine was unable to hold a grudge—especially one that was illegal, so to speak. After all, Nick hadn't done anything except make his daughter fall in love with him, with those strong arms and that wonderful deep, male voice—just as he had made her mother do three years ago. Christine didn't push back the hand reaching for her across the king-size bed. She couldn't. She was learning to respond to Nick's caresses with some of her own. She ran her fingers along his broad shoulders, his stalwart chest, his sturdy muscles. It was Nick's turn to hold his breath, lest he make the wrong move.

At breakfast the next morning, Nick took his wife's hand and squeezed her small fingers playfully. The happiness in his brilliant, loving eyes closed the door forever on her past ambivalence. He had the look of a tom-cat satiated with cream, she told herself. She giggled. From now on, she would be one hundred percent cream.

Midmorning the cleaning lady stopped mopping the kitchen floor to listen to Christine, who was talking to the baby. Not that it made any sense to the puzzled woman. Young Mrs. Tarzini said, "You see, Desi, I should have known I am not skimmed milk. After all, I grew up in Normandy where the culinary ingredient *par excellence* is cream. The richer, the better. No skimping ever. *La crème de la crème,* from now on that's me. Just let him wait and see."

She was walking back and forth with the baby in her arms. They stopped in front of the huge mirror in the hall. It was a game they played. "See Dee," the mother would say, pointing at the smiling little girl. *See me,* Christine thought, surprised by her own reflection. *See me. I'm glowing.*

She hardly recognized the flushed elated woman in front of her. Her strawberry blond hair had taken a vitality all its own, her eyes sparkled, her skin was radiant. Love surely made her beautiful. *Oh, Nick, my crème de la crème. I love you so much.* She was pensive several long minutes, she yearned for the words she longed to hear. *Now, Nick, my love, if you could share your thoughts and your feelings with me...if you could only talk to me...*

At five months, Desi loved the "tot wheels," as it was advertised. The padded chair on eight wheels under a circular base was the greatest American invention, as far as Christine was concerned. Desi was mobile. She sure was. She was always under foot. Her mother and the housekeeper were constantly whacked in the legs by the soft round bumper. When Desi had to stop, she stood up on her sturdy legs, obviously delighted to be a human creature who would not wait long to walk like other humans. Nick laughed when the overly-educated mother boasted, "I can tell Desi is bright. She won't ever crawl with Rousseau's 'noble savage'; she'll stand up proudly with our Voltaire."

Amelia Tarzini was constantly on the lookout for innovations in the nursery. The day she bought the 'tot wheels,' she also bought Desi a new high chair–a contraption that didn't even exist when Ann and Gina had their babies. It was a square table with the seat in the middle. "Another great invention," Christine declared. When the little girl was tired of standing up, or when she had to be removed from the kitchen for her own safety, she sat like a queen in her play table. The suction cups under the toys anchored them in front of her. The ones which couldn't be anchored were attached to strings. When Desi dropped them, expecting her mother to run and pick them up,

Christine didn't budge. She teased, "Sorry, kiddo, you dropped it. You fish it back."

It didn't take long for the little girl to learn that inside that table, she was on her own. She played happily for hours, babbling with her dolls, her cats, dogs, cows. She loved the pictures in the books. To Christine's dismay, she liked to tear the pages off. One book could keep her busy forever while she made the pieces of paper smaller and smaller. Until she tasted them. End of game. Her mother laughed, "There are better ways to ingest the printing words, Desi. I can't wait for you to be able to read."

CHAPTER 69

▼

WHEN CHRISTINE WAS SURE SHE WAS pregnant again, she told Nick she wanted to take her daughter to France to introduce her to her grandfather, her great-grandmother, her Aunt Nicole, and her cousins.

Both Nicole and Claudette had daughters, also. They were eagerly awaiting Christine and Desiree. All during the years of separation, the three French women had compared notes in lengthy, detailed letters. They called one another on the very expensive long distance phone. It couldn't compare with a real visit, naturally, when they would have hours of conversation face to face. They'd become reacquainted. No longer young and single, they were wives and mothers now. They were also called housewives. The word itself amused them. They were not married to a dull, uninteresting, tedious job twelve hours a day. They had plenty of help with menial tasks. They were satisfied women who made a happy home for their husbands and children. They were fulfilled. If only they could have lived much closer to one another, their lives would have been perfect.

Amelia Tarzini was not pleased. "She wants to take *her* daughter to France. That's *your* daughter, also, Nick. If you don't want them to go without you, they'll have to wait until you can go with them."

"Mom. Relax. Christine's visiting her sister and her father. France is not exactly a backward country. My girls will be fine."

"I never wanted to return to Italy."

"Mom, you're you. Christine is Christine."

"How long does she plan on staying there?"

"A month, that's all."

Ann ventured, "I suppose that since you're leaving again for parts unknown, brother, you can't very well forbid your wife to go visit her family."

Nick took his wife and daughter to New York City to sail on the *Ile de France*. Without telling Christine, he had changed their previous accommodations from tourist class to first class. He wanted them to be well-taken care of during the winter crossing, which could be choppy.

Christine was touched by her husband's thoughtfulness. "A far cry from the *Seattle*," she joked mindlessly. Instantly, she wished she could take her witless remark back. Nick had made it clear, once and for all, she was never to mention her previous husband. One husband–singular. She had told Nick that Pierce drowned on the beach in Martinique. She also told him that Dr. Pierce Hundley was the American officer she met in Normandy in nineteen forty-four–was engaged to and married upon arriving in America. Nick never questioned her after that. He himself never talked about his own past. Christine was satisfied life had begun on the day she met the enigmatic man who took his sweet time to admit he was interested in a relationship.

Since she had become Mrs. Dominick Tarzini, to their new friends in Virginia, Christine's story was that Major Tarzini had met his French war-bride in Normandy where they were married in nineteen forty-four. It seemed they were willing to accept, without inquiring any further, the romantic love affair of a dashing American officer rescuing a pretty damsel in distress. Only once did a woman ask with malicious undertones, "Where did Nick keep you hidden until he brought you here to Mama?"

The inventive Mrs. Tarzini didn't bat an eyelash. "Oh," she murmured, "we lived near New York City while I got my master's at Columbia." It satisfied the nosy woman, who obviously didn't know Nick and Christine had been married but a couple of years–in a very intimate ceremony with only Nick's close relatives at hand.

The first time Nick heard the version of his discovering an educated, beautiful, willing French virgin of his own, if he was astonished, he didn't let on. From the look of approval in his merry eyes, and the upward twitch of his luscious lips, Christine could see he liked the new fable. From now on, she stuck to this revision. A big improvement, she thought.

Her husband did not comment on it one way or another.

On his way back to Virginia–from where Special Agent Tarzini would soon take off for some troubled part of the world–Nick reproached himself his inability to deny Christine anything she wanted. He should've made her wait to return to France until he could go with her and the baby. He was amazed he had never realized until now how homesick she had been. Seeing her so elated and exuberant left him with traces of anxiety he wanted to ignore, but deep down he knew she would return to him. After almost seven years in the United States., the woman would not turn her back on the life she had created for herself. Her innate honesty wouldn't permit her to steal Nick's children from him. She loved him. She loved the U.S.. She loved their home. She had no intention of remaining in France.

So it was his turn to wave good-bye…suddenly he appreciated Christine's unflagging steadfastness—until today, she was the one who had to watch him go four or five times a year for periods of undisclosed lengths. He could do no less than reciprocate once. In the spacious cabin that was their home for eight days, he had hugged his wife in a long, silent embrace, he kissed the sweet baby on her blond curls. "Have fun, girls," was all he could trust himself to say without getting emotional.

CHAPTER 70

▼

THE TRIP FROM NEW YORK TO Le Havre closed the chapter on Christine's pioneer years in America. Seven years prior, a petrified twenty-two-year old French girl was on a troop-transport ship going west, to be reunited with an American husband she nowadays barely remembered. Going east to France that week, the mother of a beautiful baby girl (and soon of a son, she hoped), a happily married mature woman, she counted her blessings. She looked around. She compared the former skimpy cabin, with four primitive bunks and no floor space, to the luxurious one here today: twin beds, a chest of drawers, an armoire, a private bathroom. In her mind, she visualized the two medium-sized suitcases of war-time clothing. Last week, Nick had sent three huge trunks to be placed in the hold.

The heartsick, hesitant, speculative young girl of 1945 was now a well-to-do Virginian, surrounded by a loving circle of relatives and friends, a daughter, and a perfect husband (well almost–he had forgotten a famous quote by Dickens, "Never close your lips to those to whom you have opened your heart"). Although his spouse was too proud to beg for one "I love you" from him, the reticent husband might–just might–say those three little words one day.

Christine refused to dwell on three little words missing from Nick's vocabulary. Deep in her heart, she was certain he loved her. She read his love in his tender gestures and his happy eyes several times each day. That was enough for her.

The voyage in mid-January could have been described as rough. The weather was wicked, but for Christine and Desi, it was eight glorious days. Every time Christine rang a bell to announce she was leaving her cabin, a sailor came promptly to carry the baby. Desi was delighted because the man sang *Il était un petit navire* all the way to the well-appointed nursery where, in addition to the ship employee, two nuns returning from their missionary years in South America played with the little girl all day long. Never very far from her child, the mother read or catnapped on a lounge-chair in the enclosed deck from where she heard the delighted laugh of the baby doing patty-cake in French with Sister Marie-Paule.

Sister talked to the baby expecting an answer. The nine-month old didn't let her down. Was it because Christine spoke to her in French when they were home alone that Desi understood Sister Marie-Paule? "How does the boat go, sweetheart?" (*'Comment il fait le bateau?'*), the happy little girl replied with glee, "*Ci-ça...ci-ça,*" shaking her head and her shoulders left and right. The travelers laughed. Smart American kid who understood French. *Who's to say how a child's brain learns a language?* Christine asked herself.

CHAPTER 71

▼

IN LE HAVRE, PHILIPPE TOURNEAU NEEDED the help of a willing longshoreman to put one cumbersome cardboard box in the trunk of the car. The other trunks Christine had brought were placed on top of the car. The brand new Peugeot, long and rather narrow (*Probably because French streets are so narrow*, she thought, when comparing it with wide American cars on wide American roads), was brought low by the heavy load. For one brief, painful moment, Christine recalled another Peugeot in a convoy of refugees fleeing the inexorable advance of Hitler's army. The woman next to her father this morning had been married to Philippe more than eight years already. The first wife—Christine's mother —forgotten.

"Pray, Christine, tell me what's in the big box? Gold ingots?" Philippe inquired with a grunt, looking at his daughter over the mirror, as he used to do when she was young.

"Baby food."

"Baby food? What on earth is 'baby food'?" still amused, but obviously puzzled.

"I'll show you when we stop for lunch, Dad."

At noon, in the parking lot of the restaurant, Christine asked her father to open the box in the trunk. She took out three small glass jars she carried inside. When they were seated—Desi happily in a high chair—Christine asked the waitress to warm up her daughter's lunch. "A jar of puréed chicken and one of mashed sweet potatoes. Just open the third one; don't make it hot. It's dessert; it's tapioca pudding—Desi's favorite."

The waitress was speechless, as were Philippe and Odette.

"Wait until they see that in the kitchen," the woman said. "Americans are so clever."

"I'll be darned," Philippe said. "You'll see, Odette, there's a whole box of those. Baby food. I'll be..."

Odette patted his hand to soothe him, "Now, now, Philippe, you promised," she murmured enigmatically.

In Le Mans, while they were stacking Gerber's jars on a shelf Odette had cleared up in a kitchen cabinet, Christine explained, "For breakfast, I give the baby cereals into which I add one of the fruit compotes; at lunch, a meat, a vegetable, a dessert and the same at night. Now she can have 'junior' food also."

"Junior food?"

"A bigger jar of soup or macaroni and cheese. Then perhaps a banana."

Odette Tourneau was smart enough to appreciate the fact she wouldn't have to worry about the baby's menu, when the food she'd serve that day was obviously for adults. And also when they dined out; they'd take some of those handy little jars along.

Philippe disagreed, "Did you believe the baby would starve here with us, Christine?"

"No, Father. French children, including me, have grown up without the help of Gerber's foods. But with them, Desi gets a balanced diet and I don't worry about ingredients and vitamins; it's scientific, you see."

Philippe snorted, "While she's in my house, my granddaughter eats the food I eat. She'll like it better than the tasteless spongy pulp you've been feeding her."

While they were at sea, Christine had prepared herself for her father's authoritative ways. Why would the man have changed in the last few years? She didn't bow abjectly, she simply gave in when it wasn't worth arguing. After a couple of days, both father and daughter compromised. Most meals prepared by the housekeeper contained a dish the baby could eat—mashed potatoes, cream spinach, peas. Desi loved to pick them up with her fingers.

Christine expected the grandfather to remark on the baby's atrocious table manners. He said nothing. Odette smiled. Often, the two women fed the baby in the kitchen. Later, she nibbled happily at her French ladyfingers, while she watched the adults around the table. She prattled. She smiled. She conquered.

CHAPTER 72

▼

CLAUDETTE CAME TO VISIT ALMOST EVERY afternoon. Her daughter–Annette–
was five years older than Désirée.

Nicole had moved into their father's house with her three children–
Patrick, Fabienne, and Aline–while Christine was visiting. The sisters did not
want to be separated. Captain Marcet was once again in harm's way in the
rebellious French colony of Indochina. After Christine's departure, Nicole
would return to her apartment in the military base camp near Le Mans.

The first French word Desi learned to use was *donne*. She knew how and
when to use it. She knew it meant "give."

"Donne," Annette said to her, snatching one of her American toys.

"Donne," said Patrick, five years old; Fabienne, four; and Aline, two.

"Donne," Desiree yelled right back, crying. She was at a disadvantage.
She was inside the playpen–the other four kids ran away with the inflatable
dog or cow or car...The animals, the boy or the girl, the car or the engine, once
inflated, balanced themselves on their base. They were anchored by magnets.
They fascinated the French children

Before the end of the month, no doubt envious of those who could run
on their chubby legs, Desiree decided to walk–between falls and tears and
bumps and black and blue spots. "What do you expect?" Nicole said, "She's
only ten months old."

The five kids were playing. The three mothers had reminisced non-stop.
Nicole went to the attic. She came down with a huge box of pictures. "I'll
take them when you leave, Sis," she sighed. "I'll be very depressed when our
marvelous time together is over. With Maurice away, I'll need to keep busy
after your departure. I'll put the family pictures in albums."

Unnoticed, Christine snatched several pictures she intended to destroy.
André Grassin didn't belong. She tore up the snapshots he was in. And also
the ones Captain O'Connell was in.

One picture of the American M.P. was left, and Nicole was holding it in her hand. "Look, Sis," she remarked, "it's uncanny how André looks like Brian who looks like Dominick."

The three women froze.

"Dominick?" Christine stammered, with a touch of hysteria.

"In his pictures. Thank God you do send us lots of snap shots," Nicole countered lamely.

Claudette was relieved. Nicole's faux-pas was not the calamity it could have been. With forced aplomb, she asked, "When do you think your husband might come with you and your children, Christine? Is he always called suddenly and must remain in Virginia, waiting, is that it?"

"I know nothing about Nick's job, really. That's the way he wants it to be. I guess the government wants it that way. All I know from listening to conversations between Nick and his friends is that he is in International Intelligence, whatever that is."

Blanche Tourneau had just arrived to have dinner with her two granddaughters and her four great-grandchildren. It was time for Claudette to leave. She stayed long enough for a small apéritif. Every time she left, she hugged her friend in a bone crushing hug. The five weeks were going so fast, it was almost time for Christine to go back. With false cheerfulness, the women made plans to meet again soon. When would the next time be?

Deep down, Christine was ready. For nothing in the world would she admit the last days dragged. She was anxious to return to Nick–or if he wasn't at home, to her house, to Nona Tarzini, to her in-laws and her friends. To her life in Virginia–where she belonged.

CHAPTER 73

▼

AT FIRST THE VOYAGE FROM LE Havre to New York was pleasant. The passengers were friendly, the staff helpful, the food delicious, the comfort superb. Christine lounged in the nursery with two or three other mothers, content, relaxed. They watched the toddlers play under the trained eye of the employee, who obviously doted on Desi.

Rather wistfully, Christine replayed in her mind every moment of her visit in Normandy. Life would be perfect if France and the U.S.A. were not separated by a big ocean. Her grandmother had aged a lot since grandpa's death. Nevertheless, Blanche Tourneau was still very active. She continued to shower the children of her tenants with handmade sweaters and crib blankets.

Never as good with math as Pascal, Blanche had hired a part-time accountant to keep the books. She didn't mind when Philippe came over to check them. He was a better businessman than she was, she'd admit. Usually it meant he brought Nicole and her children along. Blanche loved to watch her great-grandkids play. She was delighted to hear their boisterous laughter.

The old woman did not weep openly when Christine came to say good-bye, but her granddaughter felt the silent sobs shaking her body. Neither one spoke. Each knew what the other was thinking—would they meet again some day, or was it good-bye forever?

Philippe had promised to come and see the Tarzinis in Virginia. Christine believed it was doubtful because Odette Tourneau had made it clear several times she did not want to leave their house for more than a day or two. She was one of those women who worships her home to the point of blasphemy. Ten times a day, she dusted tables, knickknacks, even the stairs. She adored her new furniture, her new drapes, her new carpets. Her husband was amused and indulgent. Aunt Sophie snickered that obviously Philippe was pleased his lame-brained second spouse had an all-consuming interest in "her" house. Odette was no Madeleine. If crystal and silver kept her happy, who was he to object?

For both Christine and Nicole, the sharp pain of parting was a tiny bit assuaged by the hope there would be many visits back and forth in the years to come. Certainly the two sisters would never again let five or six years go by. Neither one had revealed the initial shock upon seeing each other that first day. Have I aged as much as my sister? Nicole's waist had thickened after giving birth to three children. Christine was in her fourth month of pregnancy and not pencil thin. Their faces were more mature. Their attitude more assured. The "girls" were gone, replaced by women who had inherited from their mother poise and self-confidence. They were women who could stand on their own two feet. Women who made important decisions alone. When their husbands were not at home for long periods of time, life went on.

The return trip from East to West was dragging. After four days with nothing to see but water all around, Christine grew tired of the monotony. Even with the awesome, colorful sunset reflecting in the timeless everlasting waves, it was still waves and more waves forever. Christine couldn't wait to get home. She prayed Nick would be there. Although her husband, when he traveled, occasionally dared to send a postcard with a false return address, Christine had not heard from him since she and Desi had left New York five weeks ago. Not a card. Not a phone call.

The day before, the baby had been fretful. She was unhappy wherever she was. Demanding to be cuddled. She refused to eat. She felt feverish. At midmorning, when the nurse who had come to help took her out of her warm bath, measles were covering her face and her body.

Unaware of the excessive dread of Americans for communicable virus diseases, Christine was at a loss to comprehend why she and her daughter were so promptly moved into the ship's hospital. And all their belongings with them. "I guess one of my sister's kids passed the contagious illness to Desi," she speculated to the ship's doctor. "Maybe my two nieces and my nephew also came down with it. I'll find out later. I didn't expect a common childhood illness would put my daughter and me in the hospital, that's for sure." The physician smiled indulgently. Foreign women had suffered so much during the war. A case of measles seemed like nothing. . .

From that day on, the only two passengers in the hospital were pampered by two nurses and several other staff members. Meals were served on heavy, silver trays. Bed sheets were changed every morning. Truly a great rest for the mother after the scare the doctor gave her, "Christine, are you pregnant?" "Yes, about three months." "Christine, did you ever have the measles?" "Yes, when I was about ten. Why?" "Because a pregnant woman exposed to measles could deliver an unhealthy child."

Not again. Dear God, not again.

CHAPTER 74

▼

THE MORNING THE SHIP DOCKED IN New York, Christine was not certain who'd be there at the pier to pick them up. Perhaps Nick had not yet returned to the United States. She was very happy and relieved to see the tall man arrive unannounced right into their room where he had been escorted by the police. The police? Christine's face lit up with the unmentionable question. The police? With his index finger on his wife's tempting lips, Nick Tarzini pecked her cheek. "Don't say a word, darling." She understood. The father reached into the crib to pick up Desi who, obviously, had not forgotten him. She cooed happily, "Daddy. Daddy."

"Just follow us," Nick whispered to his perplexed spouse.

It was not until they were safely in the car with no witnesses to hear their conversation that Nick Tarzini burst out laughing, "Thank God, honey, the ship doctor, Charles Contini, had met me before. He called headquarters. That's why you and Desi came out on the pier before the sick baby who caught a French illness could have contaminated the whole crew and all the passengers."

Still chuckling, Nick tried to explain to Christine the phobia American authorities have about foreign germs of all kinds. His French wife remembered the observations made by her Uncle Jacques on her eighteenth birthday. Nick was not really surprised when she jeered, "I guess that's their Anglo-Saxon genes. The Germans also disapproved of our Latin laissez-faire."

In her car seat, Desi giggled. "Precious child of mine," Nick chortled with glee.

Although he had been overseas for most of the past month, Agent Tarzini had counted the days until his family returned to him. His job prevented him from contacting Christine either by phone or by mail. He had missed her and the child very much. Now that they were reunited, he knew he was the happiest man on earth. When he had returned home three days before his spouse, the house had seemed so empty and forlorn he realized his life would have never been fulfilled without Christine. It would be desolate and unbearable. He knew he had been right when, after dealing back and forth with his conscience for months, he had granted himself complete absolution for his deceitful, unconfessed sin of omission.

In answer to her questions about his mother and sisters, Nick became almost talkative. He actually chatted about daily happenings. Christine was only half-way listening. She was ecstatically happy. She was back home with her husband.

Nick didn't tell her how close his "two girls" had come to being quarantined.

CHAPTER 75

▼

DANIEL TARZINI WAS BORN IN AUGUST. It was a sticky, steaming Washington, DC, summer day when a woman wished she had no hair clinging to her itchy neck, and no sweaty, damp bed sheets under her.

"Dr. Burham himself called your husband to tell him he has a son," a wide-eyed young nurse reported to Christine, as she entered with a couple of pills in her hand and a cupful of water.

"When our daughter was born, he let an assistant call my husband," a surprised Christine murmured. "Someday we, the women, will make ourselves heard. When will the men stop believing that males are superior beings? Why do I have to take these pills?"

"To stop the milk. It says on your chart that you will not nurse the baby."

"I couldn't nurse our daughter either," she said sadly. She perked up immediately, "Desi's very healthy, though—our son won't miss his mother's milk either. No doubt he will cost us a fortune in formula and Gerber's baby food."

The hospital aide in the white and green stripes who deposited the baby into Christine's eager arms smiled, "Here's your big bruiser, Mrs. Tarzini."

The beaming father had just entered the room with a basket of flowers. Bemused, Nick watched the new mother in tears. Clumsily, he deposited the arrangement on the night table. He bent down to touch the baby's cheek softly and with the tip of his fingers. He kissed Christine on the forehead. "What's the matter, honey? Are you hurting?"

She hiccupped. "No, it's the baby. Look at him."

"I'm looking, sweetheart. He's beautiful. Eight pounds, four ounces. A big bruiser."

That did it. The new mother wailed. "Why is he black and blue?" she moaned, caressing the face of the infant. "Look at the spots on his cheeks."

Nick Tarzini howled with mirth. "Oh, honey, those are the marks of the forceps. They'll be gone in no time. The baby is a 'big bruiser'; that's a compliment, sweetheart. It means our boy is strong and healthy."

Christine sighed happily. Will she ever someday conquer the pitfalls of the English language?

CHAPTER 76

▼

CHRISTINE WAS SOMEWHAT PEEVED WHEN IT was obvious Nick had entertained his family with the incident of the 'big bruiser'. As time went on, she learned to turn such occurrences into funny anecdotes. That way, she was the one who amused others when she encountered an English hurdle.

One early spring evening, Gina and Christine were driving back home from a shopping spree. They slowed down on the meandering country road where a sign said, "night crawlers–fifty cents." Next to it, another sign said, "entrance tickets–three dollars." A cross-country car race was in progress in the fields. Perplexed, Christine inquired, "Some people who don't want to pay three dollars to see the race are allowed to crawl under the fence and it costs only fifty cents?"

Gina affirmed much too convincingly, "Yes, they are."

"Liar. What's a 'night crawler'?"

"A big earthworm."

"What does a bag of squirming worms have to do with a car race?"

"Nothing. The sign is in a good place to find customers; our husbands fish with night crawlers."

The American cookbooks were the most treacherous. Christine was confused by the archaic measures: a quart, a pint, a cupful, a spoonful. "Why don't Americans adopt the clever metric system?" she asked Nick. Deadpan he replied, "What would happen if during a football game, the quarterback ran fifty 'meters' with the ball?"

One afternoon Christine was intrepid. She was baking for Nick–who had a sweet tooth–his favorite upside-down pineapple cake. Like a hardworking student who will have a good grade because she follows directions to the letter, Christine very carefully measured flour, sugar, butter, eggs. Although she knew she wasn't about to turn into a baker, she was proud of herself because the batter in the bowl looked smooth. She dipped her forefinger in it and tasted it. Fine. All she had to add was the spoonful of soda. Puzzled, she did what she always did in such a case, she telephoned her sister-in-law, "Ann, I'm baking a cake for your brother–the pineapple one he likes. It says to add a spoonful of soda." She didn't finish her sentence, because at the other end of the line, Ann had burst out laughing, "Nick always has coke in the house, that should do."

"Ann, you're pulling my leg."

"No. No. Try a spoonful of Coca-Cola. You don't like our sodas. You don't have any others." Ann's voice had not yet returned to normal. It was still full of mischief. Christine laughed, "Okay, what 'soda' do they mean?"

"Baking soda, honey. If you don't have any, I'll be right over with mine," stated the woman, repenting.

Later on, it was unanimous: if Christine had made a Coca-Cola cake, she might have won a blue ribbon at the next Fauquier County Fair.

"Why do the guys insist on calling us 'girls' when we are thirty-five or forty years old with three or four kids in tow?" Christine asked her sisters-in law.

"Since they're going to be 'boys' until they're nonagenarians" (she had just placed the word in a Sunday crossword puzzle), Ann chuckled. "It stands to reason we must remain 'girls' forever."

Nick Tarzini, a "big" boy who was well over six feet and weighed close to two hundred pounds of muscles and sinews, had three hobbies: a weekly one–poker; a seasonal one–golf; a yearly one–cars.

CHAPTER 77

▼

ALMOST EVERY YEAR, NICK BOUGHT THE newest model out of Detroit. "Give me credit for buying American," he'd retort when his friends teased him about one more addition to his impressive collection.

He never put an old car to pasture; he couldn't part with it. It joined the others on the field in the back of the racing stables. They were not an eyesore. They were not seen by visitors. In a park-like setting, with more than three hundred and fifty acres of land, there were eight stall barns with wash stalls, tack rooms, paddocks and run-in sheds. All enclosed within miles of four-board fencing. From time to time, Nick would clean his discarded cars. Wash them. Wax them. Even take them for a little trip up and down the hilly fields.

If a tenant needed to borrow a car, Nick would say, for instance, "Take 'Betsy.' It has a full tank of gas." Or perhaps, "Take one of the pickup trucks. 'Joe' still runs very well." Every one of Nick Tarzini's cars had been endowed with a name—a never-forgotten name. The car keys hung together in one of the barns. No one worried that someone would steal one of Nick Tarzini's old cars. The cops in Warrenton would spot the vehicle in no time. Their plates all ended in TZN.

The year their third child was born—a girl, Dominique, after her father—Domi for short—Nick bought a car for his wife: a Chevrolet Bel Air. Christine fell in love at first sight. The vehicle was gorgeous. She was awed by its beauty: from the classic front grille to the stylish tail fins and the ribbed brushed aluminum panels on the back sides, every detail was exquisite. The manual in the glove compartment stated that the body was "dusk pearl" and the roof "India ivory." Far from Christine to argue the car was light brown with a beige roof. Far from her, also, to admit she didn't share Nick's excitement when he looked under the hood with every male who envied her the gift from her husband. "It's got a two hundred and eighty-three cubic inch V-8 engine with fuel injection," the big boy would gush with admiration.

One day, Christine herself informed a friend her beautiful car had "a two hundred and eighty-three cubic inch V-8 engine with fuel injection." The woman was amused, "You heard it from Nick so often, you regurgitate it effortlessly."

"Oh well, boys will be boys. Nick loves his cars."

"Amen," the friend rejoined. "And thank God our husbands have stable financial positions."

"And substantial investments to fatten our monthly incomes."

"Our men can afford their expensive toys," the woman rejoiced. "That's the American way of life."

She was unaware that Christine finished silently, *For some lucky women like us.*

CHAPTER 78

▼

THE THREE CHILDREN WERE GROWING UP. Their mother was with them every minute of the day, or at least she was never gone from them more than a couple of hours or half a day. At such times, their grandmother usually came to stay with them and the housekeeper. The kids adored their "Nona" who always arrived with candy and with freshly baked cookies.

With an amused smile, Christine would reprimand the woman. "Too much sugar is not good for them."

Amelia Tarzini would reply, "Why do you think God created grandmothers, if not to spoil their grandkids?"

Nick envied his wife her ability to live in the present moment. She didn't mind the daily routine. Someone once said that the same faces across the breakfast table, the lunch table, the dinner table put the "lock" in wedlock. Unconsciously, Nick also came to cherish the rituals. Because it was difficult for him to communicate his love verbally, he learned that the familiar habits helped them recover their equilibrium when it was disturbed by some minor or major chaos.

When the man came home from the world of cloak-and-dagger, he was always distracted. The body was back, but the mind was still within the tense ambiguities of the cold war. He watched his wife's assured ways. He heard her ready laugh. He was home in their own private isolated paradise. A place radiating happiness and gaiety.

Christine always had a funny story or two to tell her returning warrior. They concerned the children, whom they both adored. She knew their father missed them terribly while he was away from them.

"I'm warning you, Nick. I'm known as a mother who whacks her children."

"Impossible. Can't be."

"Last Sunday morning, Domi refused to go to nursery school. She wanted to stay in church with me. She promised to be good. Midway through the service, naturally, she had to go to the bathroom. I was angry. I told her to go alone. She went downstairs. Five minutes later, she was back. She said very loud, "It's a boy down there by the door of the girls' room. I can't ask him to pull my snow pants down. A boy! Please, Mom."

"I picked her up and walked down the aisle carrying her. She patted my face. She kissed me. All the while, she was saying, 'Don't spank me now, Mommy. Wait till we're home. Don't hit my behind now, Mommy.' Needless to say, the whole congregation was in stitches."

Christine continued to stir the béchamel and to relate past events, "And then a sad thing happened while you were gone. Suzanne Cortney's husband died."

"Jacob Cortney died? Was it a car accident?"

"His clothes caught on fire when he poured gas on a log in the fireplace. He was badly burned. He died on the way to the hospital."

"Stupid thing to do."

"I told the children I had to go to the wake. Your mother was coming over. I gave them their bath. I put them in their pajamas. I explained I wouldn't be gone long and they had to be good for Nona. Dan asked, 'What's a wake'? I said, 'Suzanne is my friend. Her husband died. I must go and tell her how sorry I am.'"

"And?"

"Dan asked very seriously, 'Did you kill him, Mommy?'"

"Logical enough for a five-year old. You said you were sorry. We ask the clumsy boy to say he's sorry if he hurts one of his sisters while they're playing."

As sad as the story was, the two adults laughed.

Invariably the father felt he had some catching up to do. Nick loved his job in intelligence, but while he was away from his children, he missed them. Back at home now, he needed to know everything his wife and kids did or said while he was overseas. He inquired, "Any more of those conversations?"

"Maybe one I overheard between Dan and Domi. Our son had asked me what a woman meant in nursery school when she said Domi was a spitting image of me. I didn't have time to respond. Domi piped up, 'When you asked Mommy what hole we come out of when we come out of her fat tummy, I know: she "spitted" us out of her mouth.' Dan accepted his sister's answer as gospel truth."

That same night, Nick himself added to Christine's collection of children's *bons mots*.

"Dan, now that you're in kindergarten, what's the name of your new girlfriend? Last year in preschool, you liked Caroline. Good taste, my son. Caroline's a very pretty girl."

"I don't have a girlfriend this year, Dad."

"Why not?"

"Because I'd have to kiss her. I don't kiss girls now. I'm too big for that."

"Well," Nick Tarzini whispered, "move over, girl. I want to kiss you. I'm not yet too big for that."

"Don't you ever..." she giggled, sliding promptly to his side of the bed.

"Ann tells me my mother's doing our laundry. I don't get it. What does Betty do on Monday?"

"What she does on Tuesday, on Thursday, on Friday, and on Saturday."

"Can you be more specific?"

"All right, on Wednesday and on Sunday, the girl is off. The rest of the time, she cleans house. She watches the children if I ask her. She helps me and Marie in the kitchen. On Monday—you probably didn't realize—I used to do the laundry myself."

"Hire another girl if you need to."

"That's not the point. I still do the wash. I want to do it. By the way, I've been looking in the stores for a more modern clothes washer. I'll get one soon. What happened was I got tired of your mother rehanging my wash after I'd already done it, Nick. It will stop, because I'm going to buy a dryer, also. We won't have to hang clothes anymore."

She looked at her husband. The fact that her non-explanation touched off a glint of displeasure in his darkened eyes forced her to go on, "It's simple," she sighed, "your mother didn't like the way I hung *your* clothes on the line. *Your* shirts shouldn't have the marks of the clothespins on the shoulders, *your* socks shouldn't hang from the tops—it will stretch them out of shape, *your* underwear..."

"I get the picture," the man interrupted dryly to put a stop to the litanies.

"So I bring the basket of freshly washed clothes to her. She hangs them on the line her way. And because I'm not such a great one with the iron, she irons them before she sends them back. That's the story."

Nick shrugged, "If it makes my mother happy, why not?" Perhaps Ann was slightly jealous of the loving relationship between her mother and her sister-in-law. He dropped the subject. He was in the mood for love. His long arm covered Christine's stomach. His strong hand brought her closer to him. He turned toward her, "Never mind the laundry, sweetheart. I didn't get the kisses this big boy deserves."

She laughed softly, "*Deserve,* did you say? Prove it."

CHAPTER 79

▼

WHEN SHE THOUGHT ABOUT HER OWN mother, Christine wondered what it would have been like for them to grow older together. Would Madeleine have mellowed when she became a grandmother? Would the daughter still have reacted in anger as she used to do at sixteen? It made her sad to think Madeleine and she never got to really understand each other. They were both at fault. Neither one made the first step toward the other.

Christine gave the unused filial devotion to Amelia Tarzini, who was easy to love. The two of them shared laughs as well as recipes. Gina and Ann either already knew how to make the Italian dishes or they were not interested in learning. During the depression, although Luigi had kept on putting money in the coffers because the government subsidized his business (building highways was beneficial to the men out of work), meat was scarce and they had spaghetti every night–so much that nowadays, the Tarzinis ate it only when they visited their mother.

Christine was a good pupil. She learned to cook the delicious food of Northern Italy. Compared to that of Southern Italy, the so-called spaghetti "sauce" contained little tomato paste. It was more brown than red, less spicy, more meaty. It was really close to French cooking. Except for the pasta, practically unknown in Normandy when she was growing up, Christine concocted meals very similar to the ones Amelia prepared. Both liked to cook fresh vegetables in season.

With the help of her mother-in-law, who had a green thumb, Christine cultivated a substantial herb garden. Their caretaker also grew all the flowers both women liked to place in vases around their homes: mums, carnations, lilacs, tulips, zinnias, sweet-smelling roses of all colors, many others.

Amelia was addicted to the cowboy pictures on her TV screen. She'd recite the plot from A to Z to a bemused Christine who couldn't keep up and mixed everyone up: Hopalong Cassidy, Tom Mix, Gene Autry, Roy Rogers. .

.Dale Evans. . . Somewhere in there was an Indian named "Tonto." Christine surmised that someday, such a name would not be politically correct. Would a white man have accepted being called "stupid" by all the kids who watched the weekly show? But a black man named Sugar Ray Robinson had become a world champion, so white men were getting competition. Ever so slowly.

It astonished Christine that in her country of adoption, racial prejudice existed to such an extent. She had eavesdropped one evening on a conversation between Nick and several friends. She heard her normally cool husband spit an explosive oath, "I don't give a damn. I suppose I should be satisfied the guy didn't call me a guinea or a wop. I might've bashed his ugly pale face. Who can tell us...we Mediterraneans...who our first ancestors were: Christians? Jews? Muslims? Our olive color skin can't even testify that no blue blood is running in our veins with all those vessels docking and unloading sailors onto the shores of Italy."

His contagious guffaw lightened the mood. When Nick saw his wife enter the room, he stopped abruptly. Christine almost groaned inwardly: So, even Special Agent Tarzini, who spoke several languages fluently, was well acquainted with discrimination. There was a long, rocky road ahead if her beloved new country was to become a great melting pot, free of racial and ethnic prejudices.

CHAPTER 80

▼

CHRISTINE BELIEVED AMELIA TARZINI WAS ONE of God's special people. She died peacefully one early evening while she was watching a western on the small screen. The housekeeper said that the old woman called softly twice: "Nick. Nick," and sighed a long, deep, sorrowful breath. She "passed on," in her seventy-fourth year. Christine missed her terribly.

It was not unusual that several years would pass by the young Tarzinis of the East Coast without a word from their cousins on the West Coast. When he was barely out of his teens, Charles Tarzini–the first-born son, Nick's older brother–had had a memorable fight with his father. Luigi kicked the rebellious boy out. Right then and there he cut him out of his will. He forbade his wife to get in touch with the son who opposed his authority. The boy who dared to resist him openly. Defiantly. The name of Charles Tarzini, the insurgent, was never to be mentioned in Luigi's presence.

One evening near her seventieth birthday, Amelia had confessed to Christine that she–a Northern Italian girl–had married a Sicilian boy–Luigi Tarzini. After the intransigent head of the family was deceased, her eldest son called her once or twice a year.

So, it was no surprise to Nick and his sisters when Charles showed up at their mother's wake. Being civilized and warm-hearted, the Virginians welcomed their long lost brother and uncle back into the fold. Understandably, Charles refused to attend the reading of Nona's will. As he was about to enter the airport limousine taking him back to Idlewild near New York City, Charles jibed, "Enjoy Luigi's money, brother. And you, too, my dear sisters. I don't need a handout from the old buzzard. I've got more than..." They didn't hear the end of the sentence because the chauffeur had shut the door of the long vehicle behind their visitor. The prodigal son was returning to Mountridge in California. But perhaps from now on, the Eastern family would hear from him and his wife and children once in a while.

Luigi Tarzini had left his immense fortune in four equal parts to Amelia, Nick, Ann, and Gina. After their mother's death, what was left to argue over was the "big house" and the land. It was estimated at six million dollars. Nick's sisters had no interest in the old mansion. For one thing, the place needed too much work. Then, it was too big. And they had their own modern houses.

Christine loved the house, and she knew Nick did too. It didn't take much work on her part to convince him their children should grow up in a place framed by American history. The inheritance was easy to settle. Nick paid his sisters: Gina got two million from him. Ann also got two million. Their brother kept the property, which was named *Portorosso* from a tiny hamlet north of Genoa from which Amelia came at the very beginning of the twentieth century.

Christine had lots of time on her hands now that the three children were in school. Domi in kindergarten, Dan in second grade, Desi in third grade. There was not enough for her to do. She had been thinking about teaching. Nick had no objections, but he felt she should first renovate the house.

That was a great idea. Christine devoted every minute to the job. She researched the history of the place. It was used as a Union hospital during the Civil War. She explained to her children: "For America, this is an old house. In France, it wouldn't be."

Desi said, "But Mom, you told us it's at least one hundred and eighty years old."

"Darling, my grandparents' farm in Avreville in Normandy is more than six hundred years old."

The numbers did not make sense to a girl who was eight, so Christine said to Desi, "Next year when we're in France, you'll see what we mean over there by an old house."

When they were told that when their father was granted a leave the five of them would go to France and Italy together, the children were not exactly thrilled. The prospect of soaking up European cultures did not interest them. They did not want to upset their perfect life one iota. They were very happy where they were, in the pastoral green fields, riding their horses along with friends and a watchful groom. They fished in the six-acre pond. They played hide and seek around the gate house, the carriage house, the barns, the sheds, the woodshops, dad's old cars, the smokehouse and the historic graveyard. They quarreled over expected sibling rivalries–whose turn it was to have the tennis court, when they could invite their own friends for a swimming party, who had taken their library book and misplaced it...

Christine was supreme court judge. No appeal. Either Dad was not home or he'd send them back to their mother, "What did Mom say?" They'd shrug, "All right." They were never angry for long. Temper tantrums were not allowed. There were plenty of activities to choose from. Plenty of children their age to play with. In the three tenants' houses on the property, there were ready-made friends. Frequently their own cousins came to ride horses, to swim in the pool, to ride farm tractors around the fields. The perfect pastoral life: peaceful, simple, natural, well regulated.

The kids knew there was no point arguing with their mother over the daily schedule. They had breakfast together before going off to school. They had dinner together. The took turns saying grace. They ate what was placed on the table or they went to bed hungry. They did their homework—perhaps they could watch a half-hour of TV, then bath time, prayers, goodnight kisses all around.

Meanwhile, Christine was busy. She had no qualms about spending Luigi's money. Glad the old man's pockets had been very deep. Nick was highly supportive of her extravagance. He gave her carte blanche. After he had offered the services of an interior decorator—which his wife refused—he trusted her to do the job right and to her liking. It was her house; what made the woman happy was always all right with him.

Christine respected the architectural design. She loved the cavernous entrance hall, the three-story winding staircase, the twelve-foot ceilings with the original moldings, the carved mantels of the seven fireplaces.

She hired people to clean the seasoned oak woodwork and the heart-pine floors. In the five bathrooms she kept the claw-footed old bathtubs. She bought old-fashioned cast iron stoves and had the kitchen completely redone. A local Italian cabinet-maker made all the doors and drawers by hand. Behind them and the bought patina of a century, were all the modern gadgets.

Christine loved the thud of hammers and the whir of drills.

Even if it took almost a full year to complete the job to her satisfaction, nobody objected. The house was so huge, the workers were never underfoot. Their mother made a game of telling the kids why they had to stay out of a certain place. "You saw the picture of what your bedroom and sitting room are going to look like when it's done; you chose the furniture, the drapes, the colors you want, darling, simply be patient."

A couple of times, Christine tore down a wall to have spacious open interiors. She kept the stair brackets and the balustrades to echo the details of the late Eighteenth Century house. Nick greatly appreciated the classic southern architecture. They both loved the full-length covered porch. One of the many side porches was made into a delightful, huge, airy sunroom with tropical plants in abundance. Christine took her book there during a rare winter storm. All her senses were pampered. Her soul knew no boundaries.

Her mind surfed freely over the printed words, making them part of herself. She was in heaven.

When she realized that Nick enjoyed accompanying her, Christine dragged him to auctions. They went to Fredericksburg, Leesburg, Middleburg and as far as Shenandoah County. With a sketch of the room to be furnished, they bought antique pieces of furniture she recognized as the right ones: an Eighteen-Twenty Deerfield walnut sideboard. Comb-back Windsor chairs. A cherry four-poster bed accented with acorn finials. Her flair was natural talent backed up by the French magazine she studied in great detail–the collection of the Musée des Arts Décoratifs in Paris.

Returning from a pleasant shopping weekend–anxious to hug the kids who were nowhere to be seen–Nick turned to his wife with a strange look on his face, "Do you smell smoke, darling?"

Wicked amusement sparkled in her green eyes, "It is not the first time the ghosts made a fire." Not the first time she'd caught a whiff of smoke from one of the huge chimneys when certainly no fire had recently died in it. She stated, as a matter of fact, "Our American ghosts may not be six hundred years old as mine were in Avreville when I was growing up, but they're just as real."

Nick added mischievously, "They'll be here for the next six hundred years because you and I started a dynasty of French-Italian Tarzinis who'll take good care of their phantoms."

The day of the housewarming for the completely renovated mansion, two hundred guests declared *Portorosso* the most beautiful house in horse country. In this part of Virginia, the Tarzinis had certainly been entertained in more opulent residences, but they were pleased with their own home: a great place, indeed, to raise happy American children.

CHAPTER 81

▼

WHEN NICK WAS HOME, THE BEST moment of a normal day was between the children's dinner and bedtime. Since Christine navigated blithely between the customs of the new world and French traditions, supper for the very young children was at six o'clock and the kids went to bed at seven-thirty. Rightfully, the evening hours belonged to the adults—with children out of the way. "In France, young children eat dinner early and they never come out of their rooms. Their parents have a right to a peaceful, adult meal-time much later in the evening," she explained. She believed it.

Just before seven-thirty, Christine clapped her hands. "Go brush your teeth." It was useless to argue. "Go," she added, very forcefully. It was then that Father had his own half hour. When the kids were bathed and in their pajamas, lying on his back, Nick balanced one child on his feet, another on his knees and thighs, the baby in his hands...Cries of terror...Squeals of happiness...Lots of laughs ..."My turn, my turn." The voices of the man and his three children mingled in a quartet so sweet to Christine's ears, she'd turn around to wipe away a tear.

Definitely, the happiest moments of her life, she'd affirm years later. Yes, there had been many good times when the children were growing up, but the memory of her four "kids," there on the living room rug always stood out as the uppermost.

If someone had told her between 1939 and 1950 that some day she would have such a perfect family life, would she have believed it? Did she perhaps earn those marvelous years at *Portorosso* during an endless decade: five years of adolescence torn by war and death, five more years of a painful search for maturity; a tortuous trail in pursuit of elusive love. Was it Pope who said, "Fond hopes to all, and all with hopes deceives?" So many "bridal days," so many tears.

One day, out of the blue it seemed, it occurred to Christine that none of her three previous husbands had botched her life irremediably. Every time she had managed to salvage it. God knows she had achieved more than many women her age. She didn't go to bed alone at night, with no one to give her hugs. Big loving hugs from Desi, Dan and Domi. And that gleam in Nick's eyes on the morning after. She was truly blessed.

For himself, Nick recalled moments when he felt left out because Christine ran their home with an iron hand inside a kid glove. Their children accepted her rules and boundaries. Yet, she was a passionate woman who believed in speaking up. Frustrations. Tears. Anger. An occasional screaming session for good measure. No sooner erupted, it was over. Good thing, too, because Nick hated the shouts. As far as he was concerned, there was no excuse for such swift outbursts. He knew Christine was chagrined and remorseful after losing control. She never wanted to imitate her own mother. She would advise Dan or Domi, "Don't stay near me when you see I'm losing it. Just go away." The kids learned to obey *that* order promptly. Whenever they returned a few minutes later, the storm would be past.

Early on, Christine had made it clear that because their father was the unusual Italian who never uttered a cross word, it didn't mean she could be as laid-back as he was. She'd explain to the children there was nothing wrong with a show of emotion. Men as well as women were allowed to express their feelings. "Yes, Dan, a boy *can* cry when he gets hurt, and a grown man also."

Once when they were in Paris, Dan was about eight or nine when he witnessed his French grandfather in a three-piece suit greeting a tall French officer who was his Uncle Maurice in uniform, his *képi* firmly planted on his head, his chest covered with military medals. The boy was impressed. At first, the two men shook hands. Then they threw their arms around each other in a tight embrace. Tears rolled down their cheeks.

His eyes as big as saucers, the American boy looked from his father to his mother. Nick's face remained blank, but Christine smiled, "It's not a sign of weakness, darling. Your grandfather and your uncle have not seen each other in four years. Your uncle was in the war in Indochina and he could've been killed. It's the American men who believe they have to be macho all the time."

She didn't finish because Nick snickered, "Watch out, son, your mother has joined the ranks of the feminists." He grinned. "Macho," he repeated, "I'll be darned."

Christine was amused. "Don't worry, Nick Tarzini. To Maurice's offspring and to your own three kids, their fathers are their Rock of Gibraltar. They count on you. You've never let them down." *And I will forever love you, too, darling. Even if, God forbid, you were to shed tears with me some day. And perhaps even to whisper 'I love you.' Nick Tarzini, my Rock of Gibraltar, just three little words from your virile mouth, 'I love you...'"*

One evening, after the departure of some dinner guests (the children had gone to bed hours ago), Christine had remained so very quiet for so long, lost in her nostalgic reminiscing, it took the arrival of her husband into the room to bring her back to reality.

Nick was leaning on the door to the bar. As far as she was concerned, he was the only husband she had ever had. The others had long ago vanished from her memory unless she willfully recalled them—a very rare occurrence.

As he stood watching her, the man had a speculative look on his chiseled face. He teased, "A penny for your thoughts."

"Hah! A penny won't buy much these days. Maybe in nineteen forty-four, but with inflation..."

Nick held up his hands defensively, "Stay where you are. Don't move. I can still see the black and blue marks on my shoulders the morning you discovered the dollar bill on the night table," his voice shook with hilarity as he remembered the incident. He had promised to give her his winnings at the poker game before he could. . .

"You deserved them. You *paid* me one dollar for waking me up at four o' clock in the morning so you. . ."

"What a fireball you were, honey," he said, laughing.

"And nowadays I'm just a feisty middle-aged woman, right?"

"Feisty, yes. Middle-aged? Never."

"I hope we'll get old together, darling. Too late for divorce now," she teased, not believing for a minute it could happen.

A subtle disturbance stirred inside Nick where he usually managed to maintain peace. Lately at times he felt dizzy and weak. Nothing to worry about. He smiled, "You'll never change, sweetheart. You will always move faster than the rest of us. And I will always be with you," he taunted.

I couldn't go on living if I didn't have you right by my side, he said to himself. *Oh, Christine, my woman, how blessed I am. You are my whole life. Our three children are God's way of agreeing with me. I am fulfilled and so very happy because you are—dear Christine Tourneau of France—not only my bedmate but my soul mate.*

CHAPTER 82

▼

SEVERAL TIMES IN THE DECADE FOLLOWING the establishment of *Portorosso*, the five members of the Tarzini household traveled to Europe together. They were all multilingual. The trips abroad helped them perfect their fluency in German, Spanish, Italian, and most of all, French.

Their first voyage together was the most memorable.

The new liner *France* was the epitome of comfort. Their two large cabins were adjacent—each with a shower and a powder room. A comfortable lounge completed the unit. The children were old enough to wander from playrooms to libraries to the pool, to the gym, not counting the many snack bars and the numerous machines with popular games.

Father had explained at breakfast, "You're free to go to the places we've mentioned but we expect you to follow our rules, no ifs or buts. On land you would not go into unknown parts of town where you would not recognize anybody around you. On this ship, the three of you stay together all the time. If you wish to go for a swim, your mother or I will go with you. If one of you wishes to go someplace alone, come and get us. We want you to have a good time and be safe."

Domi shook her head to acquiesce, but her siblings realized they had to watch her every minute. She was a wanderer. If Dan or Desi did not anchor her, holding her hand or staying right by her, the girl might just move on to the next place and she'd be lost.

It was the first time Christine had crossed in good weather. The Atlantic Ocean was as calm as a lake. She had to pinch herself and think—indeed they were on an ocean liner, traversing the Atlantic on the way to Le Havre. When they watched a movie in the theater, she completely forgot she was not on land.

They dressed up for dinner. The food was superb. Nick and Christine were gratified when the stewards repeatedly told them how well-behaved their kids were. It irked them to detect that–as far as the French staffs were concerned–many American children were unruly brats.

When the Tarzinis went to dinner together on land, the procedure was that the kids could choose their hors d'oeuvres. Their mother decided on meat, fish or pasta. At the end of the meal, they were allowed to select a dessert.

On the ship, between the appetizers and the sweets, Desi and Dan rehashed the events of the day, but Domi went to sleep in the comfortable armchair–her elbow on the table and her chin in her hand. She was lulled by the soft pitching of the bow and stern rising and falling. When the dessert carts rolled into the dining room, the four conspirators would whisper. It would be great fun if the girl didn't wake up so they could share her dessert. They never pulled it off. "I swear, she smells the cakes in her sleep," Dan complained.

One late afternoon, when they were supposed to be getting ready for dinner, Domi was missing. Dan and Desi searched for her frantically. They were not afraid of being reprimanded as much as they worried about their younger sister. Where could she have gone? When they didn't find her, they went to the deck where their father was engrossed in a Mickey Spillane novel–the tough cop Mike Hammer was no longer shooting gangsters with his "45" but taking on the "commies." Their mother put down *Peyton Place*, which she was comparing with her own restricted life in northern Virginia. Indeed she was acquainted with some of Grace Medalious's characters.

Nick and Christine were alarmed but they remained calm. Certainly the child was not very far. Indeed, they soon found Domi. Or rather, she came toward them, escorted by a gentleman who introduced himself, "I'm Robert Goulet. Domi's a delight. I'm afraid that while we played the machines, we forgot the time." He winked at the little girl.

Neither Nick nor Christine were name-droppers. At the pre-dinner cocktail hour, they were at ease with whoever was chatting with them–the famous and not-so-famous people. Special Agent Dominick Tarzini also met the infamous ones in the course of his professional life.

Nick was fully aware that while it was a time of great turmoil all over the world, his country was blessed with peace and ignorance. Ignorance of lurking dangers: the threat of a third world war. Powerful socialist and communist governments. Countries that hated the prosperous U.S.A. The Berlin Wall. Atomic power. Fidel Castro. Some Arab countries were making biological and chemical weapons of mass destruction on the sly. Great numbers of black people were starting to rebel against their white autocratic leaders. A puzzling illness which seemed to be sexually transmitted was spreading like brush fire on the African continent. A treacherous cauldron was simmering. Any moment it could boil over.

At *Portorosso*, life was so uneventful, it seemed that a magic wand of peace dispersed the disturbances and confusion Special Agent Tarzini had left behind and surrounded him instead with a delightful, modern earthly paradise.

On TV, the kids watched "Leave it to Beaver" and "The Nelsons." The shows embodied the virtues of the all-American family. Naturally, Nick's choice for his children was "Father Knows Best." "If not for the show itself, for its title," Christine quipped. Nick retaliated by teasing her for her Monday evening addiction to "I Love Lucy." "I'm not the only one," she retorted with indignation. "Do you know Marshall Field's closes all their stores on Monday evening so their employees can go home and watch Lucy?" Nick's reaction was the deep roaring guff of laughter that always filled his wife with instant joy.

"Tell me," he asked, "I read in *The Post* that forty-four million people watched the birth of the Arnez boy while twenty-two million watched the inauguration of President Eisenhower. What does that say about the American people?"

"Maybe that on TV, images are more important than substance?"

"Maybe that we're becoming indoctrinated and we're too stupid to see what's going on."

That last remark, Christine realized, had little to do with the antics of Lucy on the screen. The day before, they'd watched "Rebel Without a Cause," and although the ambiguous title should've pacified Nick, he was still seething. James Dean played the alienated young man who blames all injustice on his parents and their generation. "Movies like that one and books like *The Glass Menagerie* endanger the well-being of adolescents," Special Agent Tarzini declared.

Meanwhile, most Americans their age were unconcerned. Life was good. Their children were growing up well-adjusted and happy.

On land, there was a wide choice of adult entertainment. The Tarzinis went to hear the celestial soprano of Maria Callas in *La Traviata*. They were guests of the French Military Attaché in Washington who was a college friend of Philippe Tourneau. They were invited to the United Nations in New York. Closer to home, they dined with well-known journalists and writers, with state senators and movie moguls.

While at sea, they enjoyed the gracious social life. Every evening was a special event. The children had no complaints. A teenage girl baby-sat them. The daughter of a French diplomat returning to Paris, she played endless games with Desi, Dan and Domi. Everyone slept late the next morning. They loved to have breakfast brought to their cabin with the push of a button on the wall, whenever their mother allowed it.

CHAPTER 83

▼

THE *FRANCE* DOCKED IN LE HAVRE less than five days after leaving New York. "Only four nights now instead of ten after the war," Christine mused. Philippe and Odette Tourneau were waiting at the pier. They had never seen Christine's family, other than Desiree when she was ten months old. Another couple near them waved, also. "My sister's here. And her husband. I've never met your Uncle Maurice," Christine explained to the three kids.

It took a while to secure the luggage on top of both cars. The men worked as fast as they could. They all wanted out of the hubbub of the harbor. It was not the place for conversations. Dan and Desi were brave. They rode with their new-found uncle and aunt. Domi stayed with her parents in her grandfather's car. His wife had given her place to Nick in the front seat. Domi sat between Odette Tourneau and her mother who conversed in French over her head. Right then and there the girl decided that someday she also would speak French.

They had been on the road less than ten minutes when Philippe started questioning his daughter, "They don't have orthodontists in America?"

"They do. If you mean our son has a space between his front teeth, he's too young to wear braces, Dad. We'll wait until he's about eleven."

"You're too skinny Christine. You look emaciated like you did during the war. Are you sick?"

"I've always weighed one hundred and five pounds, more or less. Last time I was here with Desi, I was pregnant, so I guess I was fatter."

"You husband smokes too much."

"That I do," admitted Nick with a sheepish grin.

Philippe was taken aback, "Nick understands French. I'm glad."

Nick also understood right then and there that his very competent wife was still, and would always be, her father's little girl. He winked at her. They choked back their amusement.

A worried Dominique asked, "Is Grandpa scolding Mama?"

214

"No, darling," her father reassured her, "your Grandfather talks to your mother the way we talk to you. And guess what, you'll always be my little girl, too, no matter how old you get. And I will scold you also when you're forty years old, you'd better believe it."

The four French cousins and the three American cousins were soon inseparable. The Marcets and the Tarzinis had rented a large beach house on the Atlantic at *Soulac–sur–Mer* south of Bordeaux for the month of August. There was no language barrier between the children. In front of a toy store, Pascal–Nicole's youngest–and Domi exchanged their opinions. "The green car is prettier." "*Non, la rouge est la plus belle.*" "I don't like the red one." "*Et moi je n'aime pas la verte.*"

Occasionally, it was the adults who ran into semantics. "*As-tu du feu?*" asked Maurice to his American brother-in-law while they sat on a beach blanket. Nick raised his eyebrows in Christine's direction. She smiled, "Darling, he's not asking you whether you're hot stuff or not in bed. All he wants is a match to light his cigarette."

To Christine's dismay, her father displayed a preference for his youngest grandchild, Dominique. She told her husband she dreaded the inevitable confrontations between the smug old Frenchman and the spirited little American girl they called among themselves "*l'enfant terrible.*" Not because she was a problem child, but because she was prompt to make disconcerting remarks.

One morning at the breakfast table, Philippe asked, "Tell me, Dominique, what were you doing walking from room to room at two o'clock in the morning?" He had told Odette his own children wouldn't have dared go into their parents' bedroom at any time. "Why did you go into your parents' room?" Christine translated her father's questions and Domi's answers.

Domi answered fearfully, "I needed to talk to Daddy."

"What on earth for?"

"There was a mosquito in my room."

"A mosquito?"

"It buzzed around my head. I wanted Daddy to kill it."

Philippe turned to Christine, "There are no mosquitoes in America?"

"No. I mean yes. I mean no," she stammered, ready to pounce on Nick who was laughing. He teased her about the fact she got riled up by her old man. Slowly, deliberately, she enunciated. "What I mean is we don't have mosquitoes inside the house."

"You stand at the door and inform them they're not to enter?"

"We have screens on the doors and the windows."

"Screens?"

Dan piped up, "Like the net on the front of the old-fashioned icebox in your cellar, Grandpa."

"Clever idea," Grandpa admitted.

The second crisis also concerned Domi's behavior. Frequently, the Tarzinis were invited to an apéritif at a friend's house. Naturally, the children were tempted by the goodies on the coffee table. Their mother warned them they'd be expected to eat dinner at Grandpa's house later on and not to stuff themselves on cheese and crackers.

At nine o'clock at night, Domi would have much preferred to be allowed to go to bed. Seated next to her formidable grandfather, she was desperately trying to stay awake at the table.

The maid waited at the door of the dining room. She could not remove the soup plates because Domi had not yet eaten her soup. Philippe became aware of her dilemma. "Take my granddaughter's plate to the kitchen, Marie," he instructed. He turned to the baffled little girl, "Go to the kitchen, Domi. Go and eat your soup there."

The child left her place silently. Walking as if in a trance, she did not look at anyone. Her glazed eyes fixed on the woman's back, she followed her and her plate of soup out of the dining room.

Nobody said another word. The clicking of forks and knives resumed with the arrival of the main dish. So did the conversations, as if nothing had happened.

Desi glanced at her mother. A look that clearly said she was sorry her sister would be deprived of her favorite dessert, called a "floating island." It was a delicious vanilla cream with soft meringues. Poor little Sis.

An hour later, Domi had a radiant look on her face when she followed the maid and the dessert. "Grandpa, may I return now?" The old man knew better than ask what happened to the soup. He had read the furious reproach Odette sent him from the far-away end of the dining room table.

In their room later, Christine whispered to her husband, "I wonder what my father said to Marraine when she admitted she threw the darn soup down the drain."

Nick smiled, "She didn't. She ate it herself."

"How do you know?"

"Domi told me."

The grandchildren called Odette "Marraine" (godmother) because she was not really their grandmother and she was the godmother of Philippe's oldest grandson.

"Domi told you what exactly?"

"That Marraine ate the soup so Domi wouldn't lie when her grandfather asked if it was still in her plate."

"He didn't ask. I was afraid he might."

"He had had time to remind himself the child is a visitor who'll be going home soon. She is not you. She is not his daughter. She is his American granddaughter."

Nick was certain the three months of summer vacation were always an excellent education for their children. They soaked up an ambiance different from their own. They learned what is and what is not acceptable within boundaries of foreign cultures. Fewer mistakes would have been made in his field, he felt, if all the agents had received this kind of enlightenment in college. Hopefully, his children would never be tagged as ugly Americans.

Nick was well aware that many educated Frenchmen were a bit humbled by the dazzling display of American technology, which left their proud country years behind the U.S.A.

Christine lamented, "It's not their fault if they can't keep up. Lack of space. Lack of resources, be it manpower or funds."

"Tenacious clinging to traditions. Lack of imagination. The old world will always lag ten or fifteen years behind us," the secret agent concluded, a little too smugly.

Seeing his wife's brows meet over her shiny pupils, Nick knew she disapproved. Nevertheless, he added, convinced, "Your father and his friends have a great deal of envy and jealousy well hidden behind their arrogant attitude."

Christine knew her husband was right. Sadly, she moaned, "It would be great if we could have the best of each world."

Nick teased her, "Since you cannot have a foot in France and the other in the U.S.A., darling, what will you choose? The civilized slow-moving European tortoise or the impetuous, aggressive American hare?"

Christine rewarded the man with the jubilant laugh that never failed to make Nick's heart soar. "Darling, you forget I don't have to decide. At *Portorosso*, in the beautiful Virginia horse country, I have the best of both worlds."

And so have I, Agent Tarzini whispered to himself. *My lovely wife, the French import I adore, and my American children in our beloved Virginian paradise.*

CHAPTER 84

▼

AFTER ALMOST TEN YEARS AT HOME, one day Christine decided she was ready to return to work. Just as she was about to send feelers out, she received a call from Dr. Steven Barley, school superintendent in Langley. Nick said he'd met the man several times. They had talked about the need for American students to become fluent in foreign languages. Christine was precisely the kind of teacher Steven Barley wanted in the schools of Langley. She eagerly accepted to start in the fall.

Special Agent Tarzini no longer traveled on long assignments. He joked he was semi-retired. He rarely went out of the country. His office hours were flexible. He didn't leave the house before eight thirty or nine o'clock. Most days he was home around four. He spent more and more time with his children. Both their mother and he believed in a strict discipline with well-defined boundaries. Desi, Dan and Domi were somewhat coddled and spoiled, but they also recognized they were expected to behave like civilized people.

During a normal school day, the family was together for breakfast. The kids reminded their parents of special school activities: baseball games, football, music lessons, dancing, and the myriad of things which were part of the life of an adolescent.

In turn Christine jotted down the many appointments. A haircut. A dentist. A checkup with the family doctor. Overdue books in the library. The needed paraphernalia for a certain homework assignment and much more.

As a high school teacher, Christine was home with her children during each vacation period. She always knew where they were, who they were with. The Tarzinis wanted their offspring's social life to be happy and aboveboard. They met other parents at sports events, at PTA meetings, in church. Often not only the kids but also their parents socialized. They exchanged dinner invitations, church suppers, sporting events, and family picnics–in addition to holidays, birthday parties, weddings, baptisms, and showers. . .adults and children all had a busy social life.

Many a time, Nick reflected how lucky he was to be able to remain at *Portorosso* nowadays. He was called away occasionally, but it was for short periods of time. If it stretched to a week, ten days, the man was anxious to return to his home and his growing children. Most of all, he would miss their dinner together at the end of a busy day: It was a moment everyone brought their concerns and also their joie de vivre to other members of the family. A time of great conversation about books, friends, sports, religion, politics.

The father accepted that the adolescents kept their personal problems for a private conversation with their mother when she was able to wheedle their confidence. Since he could not easily express his own feelings, he was glad the three teenagers were at ease with Christine most of the time.

At night in bed, Christine would tell Nick what the perplexing or difficult situation was. Because the man remained calm, whereas his wife was as emotional and confused as her son or daughter, he was better able to suggest a possible solution. At that point, it wasn't rare for their mother to admit she had consulted their wise father. Usually the boy or the girl was willing then to listen to Nick. Years later Dan would say, "Dad didn't want me to go to the college I had chosen simply because it gave me a football scholarship. He wanted me there with no strings attached. I could play football if I wanted to but not because it was demanded. I'm glad my old man insisted. I certainly paid more attention to my studies."

One day at a Christmas reunion in *Portorosso*, Nick heard his older daughter's confession, "I didn't want Dad to know I had quit college a few weeks before graduation because my heart was broken. My boyfriend had announced he was moving to the East Coast; our love affair was over."

How well did the father remember. He too was heartbroken when Christine explained why Desi was suddenly at home in February of her senior year. The three of them talked for hours about love, first love, other loves later on, better loves—until the young woman decided she should go back to get her diploma. She did.

The years went by so pleasantly that after Domi had also graduated from high school, Christine asked herself how she could possibly deal with the empty nest syndrome. She was fed up with conjugating regular and irregular verbs in Spanish, German or French. She was not tired of high school kids; she loved to teach. She was, nevertheless, ready for a new challenge.

She approached Nick. "I want to get a doctorate. If they'll have me, I'll go to Middlebury University in Vermont." It amazed her that her husband looked crestfallen. He had done *his* thing all his life. She had waited on the kids and on him hand and foot for twenty some years.

The man quickly saw it would do no good to try and dissuade her. He promptly recovered, or at least he covered up his alarm with questions, "And when does that happen? How long will you be away?"

"I might be able to do it all during several summer sessions. I hope they'll grant me the credits in English because of my Phi Beta Kappa at Columbia, and I shouldn't have to fulfill the requirement that graduate students spend a year in Paris. After all, I speak French rather fluently, wouldn't you say?"

"Have you applied yet?"

She didn't have to answer, because Nick laughed, "I bet your bags are packed. Do you have a full tank of gas? Do you need a map of the Eastern states? Do you want an extra Visa card? Will you promise to call me every night?"

On the day Dominique graduated from the University of Pennsylvania, Summa Cum Laude, Christine received her Doctorate in Modern Languages.

With her degree in business and management, Desiree was the vice-president of a chain of upscale women's clothes. Happily married, the mother of two adorable children–Amber, three, and Anthony, five–she lived in the suburbs of Philadelphia where her husband practiced corporate law.

Daniel was teaching foreign languages at a pastoral, aristocratic college in Ohio. His live-in girlfriend and he would be married any day now–before the old-fashioned trustees discovered one of their favorite young men was living in sin.

Dominique was a psychologist for children who suffered from emotional instability. Their impulsive behavior and their inability to learn from experience left her quite exhausted at the end of a harrowing day. She claimed she was in no hurry to get married. "She's only twenty-three. She'll change her mind the day the right man comes along," Christine told Nick. The inner voice added, *I don't wish for her to try matrimony three times before her knight in shining armor finally appears.*

Nick had retired. Christine had a part-time teaching position. She was an adjunct professor in a nearby community college. They had plenty of time to enjoy each other's company. Because Nick had logged so many hours in planes and on foreign assignments, he was reluctant to leave his lovely home to go on cruises with their friends. Over the years his impetuous French spouse had finally learned to relax. He heard her explain to a colleague, "We won't go with you on the safari to Africa in June because we love to be at *Portorosso* to enjoy the blessed Virginia weather."

The woman was persistent, "Honey, you're too young to take to the rocking chair. You used to go a mile a minute."

Christine cut her off with a chuckle, "Believe me, both Nick and I have reached a point in our lives when we appreciate the slow motion of the passing days. Yes, if someone had told me twenty years ago I'd be satisfied to sit on our front porch for hours, I would have protested."

With a touch of his personal sagacity, Nick commented, "Perhaps it's because we've each seen more than our share of affliction, sorrow and tribulation. Nowadays we're looking forward to long moments of contemplation and serenity."

That afternoon, Nick raised his head from the novel he was reading and stared at nothing. *The Godfather*, from Mario Puzo, triggered some deeply-buried scraps of conversation an eight-year old boy heard while he was hiding under the kitchen table and the old men drank their Chianti. How funny the bottle looked, with its straw skirt and the long neck of a giraffe. Quite unexpectedly, the reader said aloud, "I'm ready now. You and I didn't want to go there on our previous trips, but I do want to go this year."

Taken by surprise, Christine asked, "Go where, darling?"

"To Normandy. To the landing beaches."

CHAPTER 85

▼

IT MEANT THEY'D FLY ON TWA or Air France–their favorite airlines. A rented car with a chauffeur would be waiting for them at Charles de Gaulle Airport. Nick didn't relish driving on the roads of France nowadays. If there was a legal speed limit on the French highways, one wouldn't know. Cars were going by at better than one hundred miles an hour. One hundred and ten. One hundred and twenty-miles, not kilometers. The gruesome joke was that the helicopters of the efficient rescue squads never transported injured people to the hospital; they carried bodies to the morgue.

Philippe Tourneau had died three years before. Christine had chosen not to fly over for the religious memorial ceremony for her father. Nick pointed out that she was still carrying a grudge against the Catholic church because her mother had been denied blessings by a priest. She didn't attempt to deny it. What she said was since her father had given his organs to scientific research, there would be no body and no coffin in the little church where Philippe and Odette had been married almost four decades prior. Well aware that the Catholic Requiem would make her resentful, the daughter whispered softly, "Requiescat in pace, Father, I love you."

In Warrenton, Christine did ask the minister of her Protestant church to conduct a service in the miniature historic chapel at *Portorosso* where she frequently prayed with her children and grandchildren. Nick understood the old wound was still an open sore which refused to heal.

Taking the advice of the Marcets, the Tarzinis decided to arrive a full week before the date they had planned initially. From the landing beaches they would travel to Le Mans to pay a call to Claudette and to Odette Tourneau.

Philippe's widow was in her seventies. She lived alone in a modern apartment comforted by the fact that her son and his wife lived nearby. She valued her independence which she referred to as her autonomy. She did exactly as she pleased. She had sold most of the furniture from the big house. She had kept the streamlined pieces she liked. There was a perfect spot in her modern apartment for carefully-selected gadgets and knickknacks. Her friends and relatives suspected she got up early every morning to dust the furniture and to make certain everything was in order.

As usual when Dominique and Christine Tarzini visited, Odette entertained "the Americans" in one of the best restaurants in town. It was a lovely dinner party. She invited Claudette's family and all Christine's cousins. Christine missed her gruff father but treasured the chance to be surrounded by other loved ones.

CHAPTER 86

▼

MAURICE AND NICOLE MARCET HAD EASILY convinced their guests they should revisit Omaha Beach before June sixth. The fortieth anniversary of D-Day was sure to bring crowds from all over, especially from America. Their pilgrimage would be desecrated by the hordes of tourists. The Tarzinis agreed to go straight from Paris to the landing beaches.

Christine and Nick walked silently hand in hand. (Frequently they walked hand in hand.) They stared–still numb after all those years–at the remnants of German bunkers and the cliffs of Pointe du Hoc. They stood at the entrance of the American cemetery. The rows upon rows of white crosses brought sobs from Christine's constricted throat. Nick put his arm around her shaking shoulders. They remained darkly entranced, lost in their private memories of hell.

On June sixth, the four "veterans" of World War II sat in the Marcets' living room in Montpellier, reminiscing. The television was on, but they were not really watching. The military music and the speeches droned on and on.

The phone rang.

Somewhere in the recess of Christine's mind–another time, another world–another phone was ringing. Her sister had also answered it that day.

As before, Nicole got up to answer the phone. She listened. She caught her breath, " Yes. Yes. Thank you."

She hung up.

The men were engrossed in their own arguments pro or con–DeGaulle... Eisenhower...Churchill...

Christine looked at her sister, who did not look at her.

The phone rang again. Nicole answered it. "Yes. No. Yes. Thank you."

Belatedly Maurice asked, "Same person? Wrong number?"

"Yes," said Nicole, who was lying. She went to the kitchen.

Christine followed her. "Tell me," she begged, the taste of bile in her throat. "Tell me, Sis. I want to know."

Nicole remained mute. A vacant expression on her face. She trembled. Not looking at her sister, she mumbled through the hoarse noise in her throat, "André Grassin is right this moment making a speech in Caen."

Sensing something was very wrong, Dominick had followed the women. He caught his unconscious wife before she hit the hard floor. He deposited her on a kitchen chair where he held her with a strong hand. Nicole wet a cloth with cold water and handed it to her brother-in-law, "Wash her face with it. That used to bring her back," she said, watching him do it.

As the woman reopened her eyes, she heard her husband ask, "And who is André Grassin?"

"My first husband," Christine mumbled in a shaky voice.

The man dropped the wet cloth. With his two big hands under her armpits, he lifted his wife and sat her straight up in the chair. It gave him time to get his numb brain into gear. He bent down. His face close to hers, he stared into her unfocused, unseeing eyes. He stammered, "D-d-did you say first husband?"

Defiant, she articulated clearly, "I did say André Grassin was my first husband."

"Did I hear you tell your sister the guy died forty years ago?"

"And she answered, 'Apparently not.' You heard her."

Maurice and Nicole were standing by—mute, in a trance.

That's when Special Agent Dominick Tarzini straightened to his full six feet two and threw his head back to bellow into the air, "No such word, woman. No such word."

On and on, Nick Tarzini laughed. He laughed when the phone rang. He laughed when no one was saying anything. All day long, he kept making little choking noises that told Christine he found the situation extremely funny. He kept on repeating, "No such word. No such word."

"What does he mean by that?" asked Maurice, who'd been brought up-to-date. I know it means *'ce mot-là n'existe pas'*, but why does Nick keep on saying 'that word doesn't exist'? Do you know what word he's talking about?"

"No, I don't. And when I reflect on Nick's past behavior, I'm afraid we'll never find out," Christine decreed. She did not wish to disclose that when Nick seemed to withdraw from an obstacle—no doubt to tackle it alone with no interference from her—his face was suddenly as cold and blank as a wall. He became completely inscrutable. Long ago, she gave up trying to make him talk when he didn't want to.

Still, today the man had a good reason to be vexed—which is why his on-going hilarity was so puzzling. I most certainly would be furious, Christine told herself if out of the blue one of Nick's previous wives suddenly materialized.

A wife he had forgotten to mention. A first husband Christine had been very careful never ever to mention. What if Nick found out there had been one more husband somewhere in the very distant past–a time so remote Christine could not recall what either André or Brian or Pierce looked like. . . On the day Special Agent Tarzini and Christine Tourneau had exchanged vows in front of a Justice of the Peace, she had hold her groom she had only been married once, to an American officer named Pierce Hundley. She moaned softly. Why couldn't André Grassin have remained dead?

Two strong Pernods before dinner, a bottle of Beaujolais with the meal, and a couple of Armagnacs to help their digestion–no wonder both Maurice and Nick decided to call it a day around midnight. Maurice bent down to peck first his wife, then his sister-in-law on the cheek, but Nick walked out without saying good night.

Nicole and Christine sat next to each other on the couch in companionable silence.

"So long ago," Christine murmured, her expression pensive and far away.

"Maurice wants to know where the guy went from the forest of Maneval the day the panzers destroyed the camp...and *where he was* that very day."

"Please, Nicole, let bygones be bygones. What good will it do at this time in my life?"

"That's what I said. It was all so long ago. I wouldn't worry, Sis. I believe Maurice himself would prefer not to reopen an old war wound. Remember when Mother kept on saying the Grassin family was more German than French and that they had changed their real name which was *Grasseins* to fool us?"

She stopped abruptly, realizing it wouldn't help if she repeated what her husband had said several times, "The guy your sister married in the maquis was a traitor..."

A few minutes went by. Nicole stretched her arm to reach Christine's knee. She squeezed it, "I've got my own confession to make."

"The long-buried husband returns from the dead and my beloved sister confesses a well-hidden crime," Christine stammered with a pinch of mischief. *I'm getting hysterical,* she thought. Turning to Nicole, she said, "I'm all ears."

"When I left the apartment that day in Englewood, the second man in the car was Nick. You refused to accompany me to the ship. You were crying so hard you never noticed him. And he didn't want you to see him, I could tell."

In a far, far away fog, Christine heard the now-familiar male voice, "You know an attorney, do you?. You'll get your five hundred dollars back."

She said nothing.

"That's not all," continued Nicole, who'd made up her mind her sister should be told the rest of the story. "One day about one year later, Nick came to see me. He said he was passing by. I didn't believe him. I was certain he was in love with you and he was checking if you told him the truth about Brian and Pierce."

"I never told him about Brian. I told him Pierce was the American officer I married in Le Mans in 1945."

"Sis!!!"

"Brian O'Connell was dead." After a few sighs, "Too late, is it?"

"Nick knew about Brian."

"He did?"

"I told him."

Nicole didn't in the least feel compelled to deny her role in the script of Christine's turbulent love life. For forty years, a wide ocean had failed to truly separate the two sisters. They were born of the same womb. They had lived from the cradle to adulthood in a close-knit environment where they had always understood each other wordlessly and still did.

Nicole grinned, "Yes, Sis, one day in Dijon I told Nick you had gone to Boston married to Captain O'Connell of the American Military Police."

The mischievous smile on Nicole's face soon reflected on Christine's mobile features. At the same time, they turned toward each other. They burst out in a fit of uncontrolled laughter. At the same time, one speaking in French, the other in English, they both said, "The cat's out of the bag."

It was Christine who added, "Let's see what Special Agent Dominick Luigi Tarzini is going to do with the cat."

CHAPTER 87

▼

TWO WHOLE YEARS WENT BY BEFORE Christine realized her predictions to her sister had materialized: Nick never mentioned André Grassin.

It had been a very busy year: Dan got married. Domi was engaged to Paul Skidmore. A happy year. A time to sit on the "morning" deck with a second cup of coffee. A time to linger with dear friends upon returning from a concert or a play. A time to play with grandchildren–Desiree's two lovely toddlers–and to really enjoy them, because tomorrow their parents would claim them, and the house would be very quiet again.

There also was an 'evening' deck where Christine and Dominick always sat very close to each other. Silent, Nick smoked his pipe. His left hand covered his wife's right hand. They had no need for words. Within herself, Christine referred to those blessed moments as her Angelus: the incarnation of perfect love between a man and a woman.

On Thanksgiving day, Desiree asked her father what her mother and he had planned for their next wedding anniversary. "If you want, Dan, Domi and I will help you celebrate, wherever you wish. Just tell us; we're all looking forward to it."

Nick Tarzini stood up. He walked back and forth in the large living room, apparently lost in thought. They all waited. For no reason, Christine was on edge. Why didn't he answer his daughter?

Everyone in the room was taken aback when the big man stopped in front of his wife and smiled at her, "I've planned a real surprise for your mother this year," he chuckled. "A real surprise. Just for the two of us. We'll celebrate with kids and grandkids a bit later. Our anniversary will be just for your mother and me and few of our old friends."

Their father had never been very clever when it came to surprises for their mother. She usually guessed what her mother's day gift or her birthday present was. "Because your dad makes a definite point of asking me if I like this fur

228

coat in the window or that gold bracelet in the jewelry store," she'd giggle
with the kids. "Don't worry. I'll act very surprised."

She was a good actress, the children admitted. And Daddy had good
taste.

Nevertheless, they were all going to be on pins and needles until the day
of their parents' wedding anniversary. What kind of surprise did their father
have in mind?

What Desi, Dan and Domi couldn't possibly fathom was their mother's
intermittent anxiety every time she wondered what her enigmatic husband
was doing with the cat in the bag.

Nick, too, was having his anxious moments about the anniversary plans
Should he have done what he did? It was too late now. It was done. He
wouldn't change his mind.

Would one of the other players in this game throw a real monkey wrench
into the delicate works?

Would his beloved wife be disturbed? Angry. . .extremely angry?

They had always been able at certain times to read each other's mind. The
woman taunted, "Still don't want to talk? You'll never change."

CHAPTER 88

▼

HOLDING THE PRIORITY MAIL PACKAGE IN his left hand, the tall white-haired man stood still. He was in no hurry to open the mysterious dispatch. He started to turn the thick envelope around and around slowly. Deep down he wasn't even certain he wanted to open it.

He had been burning a stack of old documents, bank checks, tax returns and whatnot he had found in their attic. Maybe the overnight envelope from the U.S.A. would quickly turn to ashes and the Frenchman could tell himself he had never seen it.

Unable to make it fit through the narrow opening of their mailbox, the mailman had left it on the ground, at an angle in front of the door. The man was glad no one had come by since the delivery at eleven o'clock. He wouldn't have welcomed the curious inquiries about it.

Rather absent-mindedly, he now studied the red, white and blue "International Express" logo. He mumbled to himself, "That's another thing we have in common with the Americans." He grinned. "Although naturally the Americans got it backwards." That jolly thought cheered him up. It dispelled the initial feeling of mistrust—at least momentarily.

Suddenly he wanted to know the content of the missive. He became unable to resist the puzzling, enigmatic return address: an APO number—the name of the sender, that of the guy he'd met that night and until today he had been unable to remember.

He tore up the sticky strip of gummed label. In his haste to pull out the handwritten page, he let go of another piece of paper which fluttered in the entrance hall. Ignoring the short letter in his right hand, he stared at an official-looking round-trip plane ticket he was holding in his other hand.

Paris to Washington, DC.

Washington, DC, to Paris

On the Concorde.

He went back to his office to get his reading glasses. He deciphered the scribbled handwriting with more and more astonishment. "A limousine will be at your disposal upon your arrival at Dulles Airport. A chauffeur in uniform will stand by holding the sign 'Executive A to Z limousine, and in green ink at the bottom the two words, *'Bienvenue Ami.'*"

The reader guffawed, "What the hell's going on?"

He remembered seeing another paper. He looked around for it. Where did it go? There it was, caught between the wall and the grandfather clock. He put his glasses back on. He was holding a cashier's check made out to him in the amount of three thousand dollars.

He said aloud, "Three thousand dollars and a trip on the Concorde."

He sat down on the next to the last step of the staircase—his feet firmly planted on the floor, his glasses in one hand, the letter, the plane tickets and the check in the other—reminiscing.

The only time he'd met the friendly American tourist was at the terrace of the Café de la République a year ago. Since it was his habit to go for his apéritif there every day at seven, it was not the first time a stranger started a conversation. American men of his generation frequently enough traveled alone in Europe. They were, for the most part, sociable and anxious to meet the natives.

After a couple of Pernods they both diluted with flat water and no ice cubes, it was but one short step to a shared dinner. A bottle of Burgundy and a Rémi Martin brandy later, the evening was declared a pleasant one. The tourist had insisted on paying not only for his own meal but also for the wine and after-dinner liquors. The friendly American had mentioned where he lived in the United Sates and told the Frenchman he should come and visit some day. Just a casual dinner conversation after a few drinks.

And today a reality.

The man looked at the dates on the plane tickets: four days from today—this coming weekend. A widower, he was at loose ends—rather bored. Why shouldn't he accept the offer? What could keep him from going? Certainly no one would miss him. He could disappear for a few days and nobody would know where he went.

His daughter Jacqueline never called, never visited. Since their disagreement at her mother's grave last year, she was too busy being the socialist "Doctor of the Workmen" to give any sign of life. She advised the factory workers injured on the job: how to sue their employer, how to prolong their medical leave, how to bleed the government.

He told himself he didn't miss her. They had never been close. Her mother had seen to it he was excluded from their female world. If Jacqueline had asked, he would've told her he had his own busy life. He didn't need her. She might believe it.

For some unfathomable reason, he had renewed his passport a few weeks after the American had dinner with him. He went to the attic to get his bag.

* * *

Before reading the message on his fax machine, the lawyer searched for the signature of the sender. He cursed when he saw the name.

Unaware he was passing his fingers over and over again through the longish white hair touching his shirt collar, he read the cryptic five lines. He froze, his stomach roiling at the thought that the guy wasn't done with him yet. What did he want now? After so many years. He had not been in touch with him for so long, it required an effort to recall the exact date of the last meeting.

Certainly they had concluded their business to their mutual satisfaction. When was that? He was loath to search his memory for a precise year. The whole situation had been enough to send him around the bend. Apprehension and dread were burdens he had no wish to carry. He always closed a door solidly at the end of an unpleasant chapter. This new and totally unexpected happening was puzzling, to say the least. What did the guy expect of him at this point in their lives?

Sparks of curiosity burst out in his brain waives, trained from a life as an attorney to consider every angle—there was no way the past could be brought back to haunt him. Or could it? Had those agents kept track of him? Was there somewhere a personal file full of incriminating evidence?

With the newfangled ability of the so-called Internet to dig up some deeply buried facts in people's private lives, everything was now possible. If he didn't find out what that damned command performance was about, he would never again enjoy a night of undisturbed sleep. He would wonder what he missed, what he should know. A door would be left ajar. That wouldn't do.

He looked at the date again. This coming Saturday. The guy didn't believe in giving a body time to make up his mind. Recalling their previous encounters years back, it was obvious the rascal hadn't changed much. Likely he still was the same arrogant, contemptuous bastard.

For the third time, but with a much cooler head, the man read the printed directions. A night in an opulent Washington Inn. Ten brand-new one hundred dollar bills. And most of all, the meeting? He had to go. He decided to drive the Ferrari convertible. On Friday night he'd sleep at the Harvard Club in New York, half way.

He was not going to let his kids know he was passing through, or they'd tell their mother. Jane herself wouldn't ask him his destination; she knew better than to pose questions that wouldn't be answered. He went his way and she went hers.

The "puppeteer" orchestrating this affair expects me at the Four Seasons in DC on Saturday, he thought; *I'll be there.* The "puppeteer": the name was given to the fearless operative who didn't hesitate to cross oceans to find him—given to him by the men in the group because he pulled the strings that made them do his bidding. *He could make me jump,* he reflected, feeling the sting of old resentments.

Well, nowadays, he was a free man. He could refuse. Or he could go.

But it had been ages since he got so intrigued by anything or anyone. So he was going.

* * *

In a comfortable townhouse in a suburb of Washington, DC, two good friends enjoyed their well-organized, pleasant lives. The younger man repeated the question he had just asked,

"Pierce, would you like me to read you this latest fax?"

The older man tilted his head so his good ear could catch his friend's sweet voice. The new Beltone gadget had cost him a fortune, but it didn't do him much good after all. He'd have to go back for another test soon. Useless probably. It was not that he didn't like living in a silent void; he hated to be constantly reminded he was deaf. He wanted to be able to hear when he was in the mood to listen.

Seeing the frustration on his friend's aristocratic face, John just tore off the message. He placed it under the Tiffany lamp on the desk. Then he quietly moved away to let his companion read it.

Instantly John saw his companion tremble. He could have sworn he himself felt a slight whisper of air—a ghost from the past had entered the room.

When abruptly John heard the delightful infectious laugh, he was relieved; it couldn't be news of a calamity if tears of mirth were rolling down Pierce's furrowed cheeks.

All the younger man had to do was wait. The esoteric communication would soon be explained.

It didn't take long. Pierce stopped giggling long enough to stutter, "John, when you have a moment, please pack my overnight bag."

"For this evening?"

"No. No. Saturday night. A good suit. The best of everything. I trust your flair, dear—the best tie, best shirt, best shoes."

John's expressive face displayed his disappointment even more than his curiosity. His friend reassured him promptly, "Pack your bag, also. You're coming along, naturally."

"Where to, dear?"

"A very short trip. But one I wouldn't miss for the world."

"Where to, dear?"

"Washington."

"Washington?"

"You don't mind a night in DC, Johnny. You remember the excellent entertainment at the Four Seasons, I'm sure." In a soothing voice he added, "I'll join you there before midnight. It won't be a long meeting."

"A meeting?" John felt he sounded slow-witted, but he was bewildered by the instant acceptance of an invitation that brought such merriment.

With his usual perspicacity, the elder man tittered, "Stop imagining an old rival, Johnny. It was eons ago and she barely existed."

"*She?*" with a cry of utter amazement.

"I'm sure the evening will be highly entertaining..."

While he was packing his mentor's best suit, John muttered snappishly, "Highly entertaining? Speak for yourself."

CHAPTER 89

▼

NICK TARZINI TOLD HIMSELF OVER AND over again that the first five minutes would be the most critical. At first he had invited only the three ghosts of his wife's past. Then he had decided it would be prudent to include a few old friends from Quantico. They knew about the plot and were delighted to have a part in it. The parties at *Portorosso* were always delightful, but this one would undoubtedly be memorable.

Nick really believed that Christine's former husbands would be pleasant. After all, each one was coming on his own accord, expecting to be entertained—or enlightened or exonerated? —all expenses fully covered by the generous host.

With the trained mind of a sleuthhound, Special Agent Tarzini had baptized them in the order of their appearance in Christine's life–Number One may have had knowledge of Number Two through the grapevine. He might think his spur-of-the-moment dinner companion was Number Two.

Number Two had definitely known about the fleeting existence of Number One. What would O'Connell care to find out about his successor if anything? About the time the Irish Mafioso had "died" in the U.S., he was so engrossed in establishing his new identity in a different country, he could not possibly have connected an investigating American Agent with the woman who had walked out on him.

Naturally Number Three was well aware of the existence of Number Two. However, he had never fathomed the possibility of a Number One or he would have been only too happy to tell. It had been obvious from the start that Hundley was not a man who could ever keep a nasty secret when it was so much fun to unravel it all.

In his mind's eye, Tarzini imagined that at first the three men would be incredulous. He expected them to recover quickly. With their favorite, potent drinks in hand, they would capitulate and be ready to enjoy the next few hours. They were, all of them, highly intelligent, shrewd, devious, cosmopolitan characters. They would share carefully selected anecdotes from their resourceful, prolific lives. Indeed it promised to be an unforgettable evening...for three strangers in the midst of well-known guests and unsuspecting neighbors.

As far as the hostess was concerned, Nick admitted he had, for that wedding anniversary, added a wild card. Christine might faint. She would have to be revived on the spot with a cold, damp cloth. Unfortunately, any one of the guests might make a quiet exit during those minutes.

Perhaps she would scream at the top of her lungs. Although, she didn't yell much these days (no reason, no kids around), her vocal chords were still well practiced—as recently as yesterday when she bumped her toe on an end table.

Or she might beat on Dominick with both fists—to the enjoyment of their guests.

If she runs to lock herself in her office, what then? he asked himself. The party would go on, but Nick would not enjoy it. Christine must be by his side. Without her presence, the moment would be meaningless; more, it would be sacrilegious. The whole charade was not meant as a requiem. In Nick's heart, it was a *Te Deum Laudamus* to the life of the woman he adored. He hoped this would finally overcome his handicap...his inability to form the three little words "I love you" out loud to Christine (yet he could say them over and over again to his children and grandchildren). After today, his precious wife would know how much he loved her from the first moment he set eyes on her.

CHAPTER 90

▼

BY EIGHT O'CLOCK, SEVERAL GUESTS HAD already arrived at *Portorosso* mansion. Unexpected guests were no surprise to Christine. On their frequent Saturday night get-togethers, there were always some people she herself didn't know. It didn't faze Christine. Dominick was used to inviting friends, acquaintances, and even strangers on the spur of the moment. "Come on over! We're having a few friends Saturday night. Drop by. We'll be glad to have you."

Christine heard her husband's special mystery guests as they were greeted by him in the entrance hall. Getting a glimpse of them over a balcony, the sharp pang in her heart was so painful, she gasped. With great effort, she caught her breath.

The bastards...the four bastards. She is going to give them the show of a lifetime! She grabs her glass, forcing her hand to be still. She will be the usual self-assured hostess she always is.

Acting as she would in a normal Saturday get-together, Christine decided to ignore a bunch of reminiscing veterans in one corner of the formal living room. With a glass of Dubonnet in a firm hand, she passed by on her way to another room–daring Dominick Tarzini to stop her. Five or six pairs of brilliant male eyes were on her. One man, a neighbor, chuckled, "Hi there, Christine, you're gorgeous as always. Our French hostess with the mostest."

She went to her own lounge where she pretended to be interested in a female conversation with a couple of good friends. When they left early because they had to be in church at the crack of dawn the next day, she remained alone in the room.

She figured she wasn't expected to shake hands with their departing guests. She sank down into a deep armchair by the fireplace. She stretched her legs on the matching footstool, closing her eyes. She was exhausted and exhilarated. More than fifty years of her life had been unreeled. Actually that's how fast half a century seems to roll on –- a whole lifetime encapsulated in a few fleeting seconds.

She heard Dominick enter the room quietly.

237

Chapter 91

▼

CHRISTINE REMAINED IN HER BIG ARMCHAIR in front of the fireplace, unable to move. She didn't make a sound. She didn't touch the drink Nick had placed on the table near her. Her hands were folded on her hap. She stared at the void space in the familiar room. As he retold decades of personal events, Special Agent Dominick Tarzini's beloved male voice sounded strange. It seemed to come from an alien, and it caused flutters of exciting wonders deep in her soul. *My God,* she thought, *The man is trying to convince himself he did the right thing by resurrecting ghosts from my past...*

Without seeming to, Nick studied her face with sharp eyes, noting every detail. His attention was firmly focused on her. Even as she didn't look at him, she was all ears.

"It all started the day your sister was caught in the nets of Immigration," Nick Tarzini began. For two hours, the reticent man talked non-stop. Who'd have thought he had it in him.

"I happened to have dropped by the diner in Montville for a quick cup of coffee before I went to my sister's house for dinner. It wasn't the first time the owners lost their illegal kitchen staff. They were not the only restaurants caught that day. In the bunch of greasy-looking sailors-turned-cooks on land, I saw a pretty young woman who stood by herself, crying. I was told she was French, her name Nicole. The proprietors were adamant. In her case, they weren't guilty. She had a social security card. How were they to know she wasn't supposed to be working? Her sister was a high school teacher. They lived together in Englewood, a town five minutes away. I was amazed. I didn't know your sister had been visiting you for almost a year.

"I called you. The judge in Newark permitted Nicole to stay for six more months and she was allowed to work.

"Those were very busy years for me. Yugoslavia. Italy. Germany. France. To bring the proliferation of communism to a halt, the Marshall Plan was finally put into action. Between long overseas assignments, I would sneak visits to The Clinton Inn under the pretext that I was paying a call to my nieces and nephews. At first, I made certain you didn't see me. I told myself I did not want to get involved. I just wanted to look at you.

"I contacted a friend in Immigration. I went to the ship to make certain Nicole had nice accommodations. I knew you received your five hundred dollars back. I asked Gina to invite you for Thanksgiving dinner. Then I left abruptly the same day for my longest stay abroad. During those long months, your delicious laugh and your sexy voice haunted my nights. I couldn't wait to get back to Tenafly.

"When I returned in March of forty-eight, well-meaning friends were eager to inform me you were seen here and there with a Columbia professor. I told myself I had no claim on you and it was all for the best. I was thirty years old. Until then, no woman had tempted me to give up my freedom. The job was my whole life."

He hesitated to continue. He forced himself to go on.

"By now, I suspect Nicole has told you I went to see her a year after she left you. She told me about Brian O'Connell." He groaned. He stopped walking back and forth and stood by a window. He sighed.

"Nicole told me that O'Connell had died in a brawl in Boston and that he was buried in Ireland. I returned home determined to learn all I could about a captain in the Military Police named Brian O'Connell. Educated. A lawyer. Living on the edge with a perfect cover. Often suspected. Never caught."

He got up to pour himself a stiff Scotch on ice. He sat down, far from his wife. A few silent minutes went by before the man decided to carry on.

"To get myself assigned to the still open case of the mysterious shooting at Connolly's Bar was a cinch. I went to Ireland and met a cocky bastard named Brian O'Connell — he didn't bother changing his name. His tale was that the not-quite-dead corpse had been resuscitated upon its arrival in the green land of Ulster."

Christine did not move. She didn't make a sound. But she turned her eyes toward the narrator. The mocking mischievous look sent a familiar quake down Nick's stomach.

"Yes," he admitted. "Yes. I was in law enforcement. Honest. Staunch. Unflinching. Unwavering. Until I lost myself in your hazel eyes: green one minute, blue the next. And oh, so gray when the woman is mad at me. And the voice, hoarse, husky, bewitching.

"Oh, I took my time. I dueled with the voice of my conscience. Just in case the day would come when I had to give you my name so our kids would be Tarzinis, I went back.

"I went back to Ireland.

"O'Connell promised to stay dead in Ireland.

"By then I had brought you home to Mother...," he laughed. "I was still trying to make up my mind, yet deep down I knew I wanted to marry you even if your husband was very much alive. Since you believed him dead, and you could present his death certificate, I told myself you wouldn't be a bigamist. I'd be the only one who'd know the truth."

Suddenly he stopped talking...He stood up. He resumed his walking back and forth, back and forth, across the room. He seemed unable to go on.

Depositing his empty glass on the mantle, he bent down to add a huge log to the crumbling ones in the fireplace. He turned around. He walked toward Christine. He gazed down in her still dark amber eyes. He ruffled her silky blond hair. He kissed her forehead. He cleared his throat to mumble in contrite tones, "I loved you so very much. I couldn't go on without you. Yet, I said nothing. I'm not very good at voicing my personal feelings."

That's the understatement of the day, the woman said to herself. The return of the amused look in her eyes made the man unwind.

"Do you remember the day I asked you where you kept your birth certificate, your diplomas, your husband's death certificate? I had planned that moment for days. Telling myself you would have to finally admit you were legally Christine O'Connell. Then we would proceed from there. I intended to let the guy remain dead. I'd marry his widow. You see, I had by then made my peace with our American laws: the Bostonian was not a problem since you could present his death certificate.

"Then you dropped a bomb. I was used to double dealings and stabs in the back, but I had never been hit so hard. You had married Hundley. I was dumbfounded. And petrified. What now?"

The man resumed his laborious trekking in the room.

"I tried to put you out of my mind. I asked for dangerous assignments. I worked very hard to forget you, but I always came back to you.

"I dug up all the facts about Pierce Hundley, pretending to myself it was strictly professional interest. My bosses felt his drowning was a fishy story. A former student of his reported the death. They were supposed to have been lovers. Jack Smith had embezzled funds from the admissions office at Columbia. I volunteered to do the investigation.

"Not only was Hundley very much alive, but he gladly filled me in on his wife's status in the U.S.A. They had gotten married, he said, because it gave him the cover he needed and an added edge at Columbia—he didn't want to lose his teaching position—and because Christine wanted to become an American citizen. She did.

"For days I walked around in a complete fog. I refused to admit you had married twice and each dead husband was enjoying life in a chosen paradise. And you did not know.

"After a period of seesawing between belief and disbelief, reality and dreams, I woke up one morning convinced that since you were my woman—mine forever—we might as well make our union legal."

And that, the relentless, inner voice murmured in Christine, *is the man who had honesty and integrity stamped on his face.*

"Our children would have my name," Nick continued. "The week before Christmas when you said the only ring you wanted from me was a wedding one, I said to myself it was what I also wanted and what a fool I was for having hesitated. And, darling, I've never regretted it.

"I flew back to Martinique to make Hundley promise to stay dead. He signed the divorce papers that made it legal for us to marry if one didn't look too closely. No one did that day, if you recall.

"Five years ago I learned that both guys were in the States. Why not, I thought. There's no better place on earth than the United States of America.

"I had mellowed, you see. Thirty years of married life with a trigamist does that to a man."

Christine had a sweet, wistful smile on her beautiful face.

She ages so well, he thought.

He still is the most handsome of all, she thought. *The sweetest and the smartest.* But Nick's sage was not finished.

And now comes the long-forgotten Frenchman, Christine said to herself, sheepishly.

"On June sixth, nineteen eighty-four, I checked the Webster's dictionary. There is a word for polygamy. That's not your style, darling," he chuckled. "There is a word "bigamy," a word "trigamy." To account for the existence of the Frenchman, there's no word. No such word."

No such word, Christine mumbled. *Not for André Grassin. For Dominick Tarzini.*

Nick and Christine stood up at the same time. She ran into his open arms, "I love you," the man said, loud, firmly. He repeated, "I love you. Oh, I do love you, darling."

"I love you, too," she whispered, tears running down her cheeks.

"That's what you always said, sweetheart, right after we made love."

"I said 'I love you, too' because first, I pretended you had said 'I love you'. You never did, but in my heart I heard it. So I answered 'I love you, too.'"

"What a fool I was."

"Not a fool, darling. Never a fool. Your heart knew how to love. Oh yes, it did. Your mouth didn't know how to form the three little words, 'I love you', that's all."

"Until five minutes ago," he said, with deep regret.

"Better late than never," she sighed happily.

ABOUT THE AUTHOR

Paulette B. Maggiolo came to the U.S.A. as a French war bride married to an American officer right after World War II. She holds degrees from the University of Caen in France; The Sorbonne, Paris; and from Columbia University in New York (from which she has a Phi Beta Kappa key). Dr. Maggiolo received her Doctorate in Modern Languages from the University of Middlebury, Vermont. Her thesis, "The Myth of the Earth in Colette's Novels," was published by the university.

Currently a Virginia resident, she has taught forty years in American public schools as well as several more years in private schools, including a military academy. She often travels outside of the United States. Recently retired from the high school classroom, she continues to teach French privately, do translation work in French and Spanish, and write novels that incorporate many of her own life experiences in the classroom, in a military academy, and in international intrigue.

While *No Such Word* is a work of fiction, the author was able to weave in many autobiographical experiences from her teenage years living in occupied France and her mixed feelings of emancipation and fear adjusting to life in a new country as a war bride, so far away from all she had known and loved. These will ring true as you read the remarkable story of Christine Tourneau. The Clinton Inn, where the novel's characters, Christine and Nick, first meet, was an actual and very popular inn in Tenafly, New Jersey, during the 1940s. Rebuilt in 1908 from an original 1800s structure called Clinton Hall and Hotel, it was eventually demolished in 1977. The current property is called The Clinton Inn Hotel (http://www.clinton-inn.com/).

No Such Word is Paulette's third novel, including *The Guilty Teacher* and *The Terrorist Trap*. Others are on the way.

Made in the USA
San Bernardino, CA
15 October 2016